PRAISE FOR *THE DAVES NEXT DOOR*

'Stirring. Ambitious. Irreverent. Compassionate. Completely devoid of giveable fucks' Dominic Nolan

'Will Carver is a thought-provoking and masterful writer of gut-punching fiction ... a powerhouse of a novel. Think Ira Levin at his best' Michael Wood

'Move the hell over Brett Easton Ellis and Chuck Palahniuk ... Will Carver is the new lit prince of twenty-first-century disenfranchised, pop darkness' Stephen J. Golds

'Provocative, twisted and mind-bendingly original' Sarah Sultoon

'Impossibly original, stylish, sinister, heartfelt. *The Daves Next Door* is so wildly fresh and unmatched, and once again proves that Will Carver has talent and creativity to burn' Chris Whitaker

'So clever, so dark – and utterly original. Where does Will Carver get his ideas?!' Victoria Selman

'Once again, Will bends and twists the genre with a novel that is astonishing, profound and hard-hitting' Dave Jackson

'I honestly don't know how Will Carver does it. Every character has you fully invested, and he has this uncanny knack of delving into your soul and revealing all the things you really think but are too scared to voice. Absolute GENIUS' Lisa Hall

'Fantastic as ever. Nobody writes like this except Will Carver' Liz Loves Books

'Returning with another sharp, wild and thrilling novel, Will brushes aside the bullshit of humanity, leaving souls laid bare and our views less rose-tinted than they were when we first voyaged into the pages of this original read ... of course it's the right level of shock, darkness and twistiness ... you really MUST add it to your TBR this summer!' Danielle Louis

'Expertly treading a line between the metaphorical and the literal, it examines humanity as only the most outstanding books can. *The Daves Next Door* is an exceptional novel; this is risk-taking, provocative fiction at its absolute finest. An unmissable read' Hair Past a Freckle

'I have been left completely speechless. Every book Carver writes just gets better and better. This is completely unpredictable and definitely unputdownable ... written in a way that pulls you in and consumes you ... worthy of all the stars' Little Miss Book Lover 87

'The gritty realism of Christopher Brookmyre, the fantasy of Neil Gaiman, touches of the humanity of Terry Pratchett and mixing it together to yield a delightful palate-cleanser of a book' Adrian Scottow

PRAISE FOR WILL CARVER

LONGLISTED for Theakston's Old Peculier Crime Novel of the Year Award

SHORTLISTED for Best Independent Voice at the Amazon Publishing Readers Awards

LONGLISTED for the *Guardian's* Not the Booker Prize

LONGLISTED for Goldsboro Books Glass Bell Award

'Incredibly dark and very funny' Harriet Tyce

'I fell in love with Carver's murderous Maeve. This is an Eleanor Oliphant for crime fans. Carver truly at his best' Sarah Pinborough

'A darkly delicious page-turner' S J Watson

'Will Carver's most exciting, original, hilarious and freaky outing yet' Helen FitzGerald

'Vivid and engaging and completely unexpected' Lia Middleton

'Dark in the way only Will Carver can be … oozes malevolence from every page' Victoria Selman

'Equally enthralling and appalling … unlike anything I've read in a very long while' James Oswald

'Creepy and brilliant' Khurrum Rahman

'Possibly the most interesting and original writer in the crime-fiction genre, and I've loved his books for years … dark, slick, gripping, and impossible to put down. You'll be sucked in from the first page' Luca Veste

'One of the most compelling and original voices in crime fiction' Alex North

'A twisted, devious thriller' Nick Quantrill

'One of the most exciting authors in Britain. After this, he'll have his own cult following' *Daily Express*

'Unlike anything you'll read this year' *Heat*

ABOUT THE AUTHOR

Will Carver is the international bestselling author of the January David series and the critically acclaimed, mind-blowingly original Detective Pace series that includes *Good Samaritans* (2018), *Nothing Important Happened Today* (2019) and *Hinton Hollow Death Trip* (2020), all of which were ebook bestsellers and selected as books of the year in the mainstream international press. *Nothing Important Happened Today* was longlisted for both the Goldsboro Books Glass Bell Award 2020 and the Theakston's Old Peculier Crime Novel of the Year Award. *Hinton Hollow Death Trip* was longlisted for the *Guardian*'s Not the Booker Prize, and was followed by two standalone literary thrillers, *The Beresford* and *Psychopaths Anonymous*.

Will spent his early years in Germany, but returned to the UK at age eleven, when his sporting career took off. He turned down a professional rugby contract to study theatre and television at King Alfred's, Winchester, where he set up a successful theatre company. He currently runs his own fitness and nutrition company, and lives in Reading with his children.

Follow Will on Twitter @will_carver.

Also by Will Carver and available from Orenda Books:
Good Samaritans
Nothing Important Happened Today
Hinton Hollow Death Trip
The Beresford
Psychopaths Anonymous

THE DAVES NEXT DOOR

WILL CARVER

ORENDA
BOOKS

Orenda Books
16 Carson Road
West Dulwich
London SE21 8HU
www.orendabooks.co.uk

First published by Orenda Books, 2022
Copyright © Will Carver, 2022

A catalogue record for this book is available from the British Library.

ISBN 978-1-914585-18-0
eISBN 978-1-914585-19-7

Typeset in Garamond by typesetter.org.uk

Printed and bound by CPI Group (UK) Ltd, Croydon CR0 4YY

For sales and distribution, please contact info@orendabooks.co.uk

For God's sake

❖

'God moves in a mysterious way.'
—William Cowper

'Hell is other people.'
—Jean-Paul Sartre

'In an infinite multiverse,
there is no such thing as fiction.'
—Scott Adsit

AUTHOR'S NOTE

This is not a book about terrorism. Nor is it about terrorists. However, through researching many real-life attacks, reading media coverage, eye-witness accounts and survivor testimonies, there are certain threads and consistencies that have been used for authenticity. The attack mentioned is purely fictitious and so absurd in its scale and intricacy as to separate it from any real-life event. Care and sensitivity have been taken but, in places, likenesses have been unavoidable and serve only the quest for realism.

The terrorism, or threat of terror, forms only the crime element of the story. It is a small aspect of what happens. This is a story about cause and effect. It is about the interconnectivity of everything and everyone on this planet. It is about compassion, understanding, listening, and asking the right questions.

The events of this book are as real as I can make them, but none of them actually happened. Though, as the book explores, perhaps, somewhere, across the universe, everything I have written as fiction, scarily, has the possibility to be fact.

INTELLIGENCE AND SECURITY COMMITTEE
35 Great Smith Street, London SW1P 3BQ

14th February 2023

Could this have been prevented?

The ISC has, today, begun an investigation to review the intelligence concerning the London attacks on 21st July 2022. The initial report into the fourteen bombings and four vehicle collisions has been set aside. Though useful for documenting the events, the scope of the report only offers a broad understanding of how the incidents unfolded on that day.

The prime minister has asked how so many of the perpetrators of this crime were unknown to British intelligence and whether prior knowledge of several of the bombers should have meant that they could have been stopped.

The Intelligence and Security Committee intends to deal only in the facts. Public opinion has been swayed by conjecture and conspiracy theories that will not be entertained by this investigation. (A separate investigation will be conducted regarding the allegations of an eighth underground bomber who did not detonate and walked away.)

Information will be derived from police logs and transcripts as well as photographic and video evidence. Those people involved will be questioned and re-questioned. False articles and inaccurate reporting have resulted in needless distress for the families of those affected and the people who survived the ordeal.

In order to achieve the accuracy required, the ISC intends to examine the most minute of details over a minimum period of twelve months. The final report will be lengthy and without summary, so as not to misrepresent the facts.

The prime minister's questions, as well as the concerns of constituents, deserve to be investigated and answered, and the ISC's duty is to present only the facts of what actually happened on the morning of 21st July and the days leading up to it.

PROLOGUE?

There's a bigger story here.

Of course there is.

There always is.

There has to be something greater than we are. God, or the universe. And there is always somebody worse off than us, too. But these larger events are the result of something smaller that occurred before. And then something even smaller than that. Something that seemed insignificant at the time, unrelated.

Then there is a knock-on effect.

An event, seemingly meaningless or trivial, sparks something more revealing, until it eventually implodes into chaos or poignant catastrophe.

When a psychopath is captured after going on a serial-killing spree, the bigger story is that of his victims and their families and the atrocities that occurred. There's a smaller tale where a young boy whose frontal lobe did not develop the way that most do – due to bad genetics – leaves him with an incapacity to empathise or feel true remorse. As a child, he innocently dresses up one time in one of his mother's gowns, complete with stilettos and jewellery, and her reaction is to curse and beat him for doing so. She locks him in the cupboard beneath the stairs for a couple of hours.

There's another, smaller story which might explain the reason she reacted this way.

And, of course, something smaller before that.

In some other universe, she laughs at his playfulness, hugs him and kisses the top of his head.

When a glacier melts or the earth quakes or a tsunami hits, the bigger story is concerned with the devastation and the loss of life.

Then there are the smaller flutters that form a chain linking to the main event. Tales of greed and lies and drilling and the invention of the combustion engine and money and farming, and they don't seem to correlate, they don't appear to be related in any way. But they are. It all is.

Everything is.

Everybody is.

And when a carefully orchestrated attack on a capital city occurs, when seven train carriages explode, followed by four buses and the foyers of three high-rise buildings, and unmarked vans indiscriminately plough through pedestrians on four of the bridges that cross the Thames river, this is the effect of all the indiscretions and secrets and decisions made before it happened.

All the wrongdoings of government, all of the policies passed to preserve the self-interest of the few, all the political rhetoric and religious contradictions and arguments so old that nobody can remember where it all began or why they are supposed to hate each other.

All the Mental Health Weeks that seemed more like a marketing strategy than a true address of a growing problem. All the hashtags that diminish the size of the responsibility we have towards one another as human beings, seeking an identity, striving for recognition or equality.

All of these things. They are related. And they build and mutate until the only outcome is a killing spree. A volcanic eruption.

An explosion.

One café and two office blocks in the financial district.

The Central Line.

Bakerloo Line.

Hammersmith and City.

Jubilee.

Northern.

Piccadilly.

And the Circle Line.

A flash of white light, followed by chaos and terror.

Then the buses. And the bridges. And Earth feels more like Hell.

Look backwards for the causes and forward for the effects. The broader picture tells the larger story, but, to understand how every choice, every micro-decision impacts more than just ourselves, to see how linked we are, not just locally or globally, but universally, we must continue to think big while looking at the small.

One incident.

One train carriage. Edgware Road. The Circle Line. 08:51.

Thirty-two passengers.

Infinite possible outcomes.

And one bomb.

There were many vantage points on that train car. Everybody saw what happened, how it unfolded. Some saw a brainwashed kid, others saw horror. They saw a terrorist. And one may have even seen God.

All of their stories are different.

All of them happened.

And all are true.

Not one thought or prayer can make the slightest difference.

THOUGHTS (AND PRAYERS)

Our prayers are with the families of the seventeen schoolchildren gunned down by a former student at some American high school you've never heard of.

The prayers of our entire nation are with the people of a state or island or coastal town caught in the path of Hurricane *Whoever*.

Thoughts and prayers go out to all those who were fortunate enough to have known this celebrity and national treasure, who passed away last night after a long struggle with a disease that normal people die from every day.

People do this. People say this. People have the ability to affect gun regulations. People can change laws. People can run drug trials and cure illnesses.

But people pray.

They pray for guidance and forgiveness. They pray for themselves and they pray for you. Then they pray for others they have never met but are going through a hardship they are lucky enough to never experience themselves.

And maybe they think it's enough. Maybe they think it helps.

It doesn't mean they are stupid because they put their faith in a God. Hell, it doesn't even mean that there is no God.

He's just stopped listening. He's busy. He's given up on His experiment because the free will thing blew up in His face.

All day, every day, people are talking *at* Him. They want help or they're sorry. Mostly, it's because they don't understand what's happening, how things got so bad. They have questions. A million questions for one God every minute.

He can't keep up. He can't answer them all. He has no assistant, no secretary. No idea when things got so out of hand.

What He does have are questions of His own. Surely.

Who does God pray to?

PART ONE

THE **DARK**

1 THE DAVES (AND THE NEIGHBOUR)

One of the Daves says that his tongue exploded. That he had an allergic reaction to something. It swelled up in his mouth so much that it just ... popped. And he ended up in hospital. That's when they found it. The tumour on his brain.

Then he says, 'They reckon I've got a twenty-five percent chance. Of living.'

Not a seventy-five percent chance of dying.

He sounds mistakenly optimistic.

But the fact that he sounds like anything other than a drunken muffle leads his neighbour to conclude that this Dave is probably lying.

This Dave stinks of white wine and piss. And surely the inside of his mouth should look like strips of week-old deli meat if something detonated in there recently.

'Shit, Dave, that's ... What, they can't treat it?'

What else can you say?

Sorry to hear that.

Still a chance, eh?

Show me your tongue, you damn liar.

The damn liar insists that he's on some medication that can shrink the thing. That he has to keep going to the hospital for check-ups.

'That's probably why you haven't seen too much of me over the last three or four weeks.'

It's true. He's been cooped up inside his flat, trying to drink himself to death. He rents. The tongueless idiot has changed the locks on the front door so the landlord can't get in. He hasn't paid his rent for months. Blames it on the tumour. And the tongue thing. That's why he hasn't been at work or whatever.

'Yeah, I might have to stay in hospital for a bit while they do some tests. See if the thing is getting any smaller. You know?'

His mouth is disgusting. Teeth like a burnt fence. Thick, white globules of saliva forming in the corners, stretching as he spits out another of his made-up tales. The neighbour can't stop looking at it, though. Trying to catch a glimpse of the allegedly blown-up flesh inside.

This Dave is on edge. He doesn't like being outside the flat in case the landlord shows up. But he also has a compulsion to check his letterbox on the ground floor five times a day. No one knows what he is expecting but it must be important. Perhaps a letter from his fictitious doctor about the imaginary tumour.

'Oh, right. You'd have to stay in there long?' The neighbour regrets the question immediately. He just wants to leave. Now it's a conversation.

'I don't know. It needs monitoring.' The Dave stutters. Caught off-guard, he hasn't prepared this part of the story and has to improvise. Now neither of them wants to be here.

The neighbour nods, politely.

This Dave stares at him for a few seconds then says, 'Anyway, I just wanted to check the mail. I'm expecting a cheque.'

Damn. The neighbour is intrigued but bites his tongue. His plump, present, intact tongue.

'Well, I'll let you get on.' He wonders whether he should mention the illness, say sorry or something, show some sympathy.

'Yeah. I'm sure I'll see you around.' This Dave smiles, but not an open-mouth smile that would reveal anything mangled behind his decaying incisors.

The neighbour is not sure when he'll catch another glimpse of this Dave. Maybe he does have a brain tumour. Maybe it will pop like his tongue. The only thing he knows for certain is that the Daves' door will slam at six-thirty in the morning when he next runs downstairs to check his empty mailbox again.

2 THE OLD MAN (AND THE ANGELS)

'Am I dead?' the old man asks, the tingling in his right shoulder reverberating down to his fingertips, stabbing at his skin from the inside as it descends. He smiles through the pain, hoping he got it right this time.

The couple look at him then at each other, their gaze planted somewhere between welcoming and apathy.

Their necks creak back in unison towards the enquiring pensioner.

But say nothing.

At ninety-one, the old man is, indeed, old. Elderly. Aged. Senescent. Yet, beneath that crepe-paper skin and drooping brow is a man of sound mind, of memories. His birth, sandwiched between two wars, has left him resilient and unforgiving. But the old lady's death two years ago to this very day has kept him anchored on all sides by his grief.

All he has are the memories. Snapshot recollections that no longer resemble her.

And he doesn't want them any more.

'Am I dead?' the old man asks before folding over and retching his solitary heartache towards the kitchen floor, trying with all his might to keep the pills inside, so that they may do their worst to him; so that they may punish in order to end his punishment.

The couple look down on him and the dribble of bile that hangs from his thin lips, then turn to one another, their mood perched somewhere between uncertainty and true mercy.

But say nothing.

They appear like angels before him, not bathed in light but swathed in blur. The old man feels they are here to take him away, to end his substantial time in this realm. He does not mind if there is a Heaven and he is to be rejected from it as a result of his actions. He is not worried about eternal nothingness because it is the presence of somethingness that brought him to this juncture.

His chest fills with cold, and he welcomes the possibility of Hell. It would be a relief.

'Angels. My angels.'

Then he falls.

The old man's legs give way beneath him as his motor skills evaporate en masse, the effects of those small white capsules – and cheap Scotch – betraying his brain. He is losing control.

His face crashes into the hard laminate, cutting below his right eye and grazing his cheek with a friction burn as his delicate skin sticks to the faux wood.

The couple do not flinch even as the old man grunts, the air in his lungs expelled unintentionally as his ribcage smacks the ground beneath, their emotions standing somewhere between anticipation and composure.

But they say nothing.

They remain in silent contemplation, looking down on the pitiful scene beneath them, the old man shaking, writhing in agony as he loses his battle to contain nausea. The woman wants to look away but cannot force herself to do so. She wishes she could offer her hand or a comforting word but something inside of her is preventing empathy.

The old man claws at her feet, desperately trying to pull himself to his knees. Their eyes meet, his show empty yearning, hers glaze with a thin saline film. Her partner watches over the old man's appeal but does not have the inclination to reach out.

'Am I dead?' the old man asks one final time, his hands now clutching at the ankles of the pretty girl whose face remains pixelated, only darting into focus for short bursts.

The couple stare on, unblinking, concentrating. The old man's breath now laboured with the occasional stab of a dry tear, and he asks them the question again. This time without moving his lips. This time his thoughts are conveyed in a look. His query is said in his head.

But they hear.

And this time they answer.

Am I dead?

'Yes,' says the woman, finally reaching out a cold, smooth hand to his bloodied cheek. 'Yes. You are dead,' she reiterates, sliding her hand away from him and releasing his weight to the floor.

She should not have done that.

They should have said nothing.

The old man is not dead, yet.

3   THE NURSE (AND THE SPORTSMAN)

Nothing she sees is a shock any more.

Vashti checks in on the young man whose sporting career looks to have been cut short. His ankle is broken in two places along with four other fractures further up the shin; two in his tibia and two in his fibula. He wasn't even hit or kicked, he just tried to turn around, change direction on a muddy pitch. Every other part of him obliged, but his foot remained in the position it had started in.

When the young man arrived at the hospital, he had passed out through the pain, the toes on his left foot pointing north, to Heaven, those on his right foot pointing to Hell in the south, below the floor. Now, family and friends are visiting, and he will have no recollection due to the industrial strength co-codamol and morphine cocktail in his system.

He's nineteen and he'll awaken to think that his life is ending.

That he has no prospects.

In the twelve years of nursing at this hospital, Vashti can almost dismiss this reaction as commonplace.

In the same way that she disregards the shock of the old woman coming in with a bruise on her ribs, caused by a fall, who suddenly develops pneumonia. Her family write it off as another in a long-line of sufferings, but she'll be dead in two days.

Something arbitrary and trivial descending into solemnity.

She wonders whether it gets easier for the doctors to deliver this kind of news.

The way murder is supposed to become easier after your first kill.

Then she sees something different.

Something unusual.

Nothing.

She sees nothing at all.

The bed is empty; the covers untouched. The pure-white cotton sheet is folded over the paling blue blanket, which is wrapped so tightly around the mattress you could bounce a penny on it.

There's disquiet.

It feels wrong. To Vashti, at least.

Like the things that she is seeing should not be.

Vashti pulls the half-closed curtain to the side, the rings scraping against the curved bar like the excrement raking against the pile-ridden colon of the old lady on her last whimsical visit to Accident & Emergency. She told them she was shitting razorblades. That she was crapping jagged granite.

Her family left her to deal with that alone too.

Because she is a burden on their otherwise unchallenging, fulfilled lives.

She doesn't have any money to leave, they think, so why bother?

Vashti should have felt saddened to see such apathy towards another human being, but that is not how she feels at all; she witnesses it far too often and their lack of caring is contagious.

She can't even remember who was in the bed before it was vacated.

Did they die?

Everybody dies.

But this time, this bed, this pristine cot, leaves her with a sense of unease. Of the unnatural. Of fate being tampered with.

It should contain a man in his eighties, recently pumped full of soapy water to evacuate any remaining pills from his pathetic failed suicide attempt. It should house the old man with his crepe-paper skin and his *am I deads?* and his face cut from falling and his deep-set depression.

The unfillable hole in his heart.

And the unmakeable hole in his memory.

He is somewhere he should not be. Somewhere unnatural. Somewhere else.

Kneeling in front of two angels. As they prepare to drag him through Hell.

4 GOD? TERRORIST? NARRATOR?

Do they see me?

Does anybody notice me riding around on the same circular line, never getting off at a designated stop? Am I merely, like all those on this carriage, simply unaware of my station in life? Can I sit here forever?

Do the people who perch next to me, opposite me, standing in front of me holding on to the overhead bar for balance, ever contemplate the wires that line the underground tunnels? Do they know what each one does? Can they say how long each cable is? Where do they start? Would they stretch to the moon and back?

If I had a bomb strapped to my chest underneath my jacket, would anyone spot it? Where would be the best place to detonate? Should I wait for a tunnel? Would it be more effective to have the train caved in? Would they feel the vibrations in the street above? Or should I wait until it stops at a platform?

Are the women more intimidated by my presence or is it the male population that I frighten most? Are they even scared? Have they even managed to pull themselves from their own solipsism to realise I pose a threat?

Do I even pose a threat? Is my risk physical or metaphysical?

Isn't there always that question of reality and faith and belief?

What if I am not even on the tube? Have I ever been to London? Do I know the stations that are dotted along the Circle Line? It's the yellow one, right?

Could it possibly be that I am not asking these questions and that a third party is forcing these words onto a page? That I am a narrator? I have no face? I have no distinguishing features? My appearance is not described in detail because I am the one who puts forth the characterisations from my invisible room in the reader's mind?

Is that what they called *omnipotence?*

What, then, is omniscience?

I would know that if I was the narrator, right? Isn't one of them to do with God? Is that correct? Is it God?

Am I God?

Are they my angels presiding over the old man? Did I send them to that maisonette to watch over a suicide attempt, allowing an elderly male the opportunity to repent, to save himself? I'd know if I was God, wouldn't I?

You would know?

People would know?

Or is it a bit like that Joan Osborne song? What if God was one of us? What if I am one of you? Are you singing that song in your head now? Do you sometimes hear her name and think of John Osborne the 'kitchen sink' dramatist?

What if I *am* just a slob? What if I am simply here on a scam where I watch the population travel to and from work each day, spotting tourists and visitors, blending into the background so that I can pick a pocket or steal a camera or lift a mobile phone before heading home to sell my stolen goods and deceive my wife into thinking that I have been at the office?

Are there too many questions unanswered?

Should I stay on the train and wait for the old man?

Does he know the answers?

Does he have a question?

5   THE DAVES (AND THE NEIGHBOUR)

There's nothing in the letterbox. There rarely is. The cheque is another lie. But this Dave has gone looking for it so many times, he's forgotten that he made it up. He doesn't know who it is supposed to be from. He has no idea how much it is for. There's no reason he should be receiving it.

There are only six flats in the building. The ground floor is for the elderlies, it seems. Flat one is a pleasant but forgetful old man, who sits ten inches from his television screen for most of the day. He's a year away from receiving a telegram from the queen. Opposite, in number two, are two South African women in their fifties. They're sisters. They live together. They're not particularly friendly.

The middle floor: flat three, above the old man, this place is always changing. One month it was six people, three generations, from Bangladesh. Eternally optimistic and friendly. The opposite of the four men who moved into that two-bedroom apartment after. Now it seems there are two couples in there. It's difficult to know which two people go together. They seem interchangeable.

Opposite, in flat four, is the recluse. The seldom-seen woman in her late thirties. Everything she needs is delivered. She never leaves the building. There's a sports car in her parking space that is gathering moss.

And on the top floor, the Daves are in flat five, and opposite, listening to every argument the two men have, is the neighbour.

Dave talks to himself as he goes upstairs. He says something about a stink in the corridor. That 'fucking stink' is him. He mumbles under his breath about the neighbour he was so congenial to moments before. It's the other Dave who is muttering.

At his front door, he remembers that he doesn't like being outside the flat for too long, in case the landlord makes a surprise visit and asks for the four months of rent she is owed. He fumbles with the keys, looking back over his shoulder. With a click, the door is open. He slinks through the gap, shuts the door behind him and puts the chain on the inside. He locks the door with two keys and turns another latch, which he installed himself, before jamming a screwdriver into the doorframe.

Then he shouts 'Why don't you fuck off?' into the lounge.

If you were there, you'd see that he opened his mouth wide enough on the curse word to reveal his tongue. The one that exploded.

This is another of his habits. The neighbour hears it all the time. Dave creeps downstairs, unlocks his post box to reveal nothing, drags his feet back to the top floor, complains about his own stench, opens his front door, fastens a thousand locks on the other side, then shouts obscenities.

'Who's he talking to?' the neighbour's girlfriend asked on one of the occasions she was watching through the peephole, mesmerised by Dave's eccentricities.

'Nobody. He's mad. He lives alone,' the neighbour confirmed. He didn't like how inquisitive she was being. 'Come away from there.'

'Maybe there's two of them,' she joked. 'Maybe they're twins. Like, old twins. You don't really see old twins, do you? Old twins are creepy.'

'Will you stop saying "old twins", please, and get away from the door.'

The next time she came over, she asked, with a smile, 'So ... how are the Daves?' And it stuck. Mad, old Dave next door became The Daves Next Door.

And the ritual continues for Dave as he turns up the television to a volume that will drown out his voice. He takes a piss and doesn't flush the toilet. He doesn't wash his hands. He goes into the kitchen and flicks on the kettle and puts his pissy fingertips on a slice of bread that he drops into the toaster and he gets butter from the fridge and he stares at a half-bottle of Chardonnay before walking back into the lounge, where he looks straight at the spot where a single-seat recliner used to sit but which is now occupied by a single mattress. And he says, 'Well, what the fuck are you looking at?'

6   THE OLD MAN (AND THE ANGELS)

The stupid old man wakes up in his own bed.

And he thinks he has died.

His vision is compromised. The effects of the pills, probably. He tells himself that it is a result of the trip, travelling to another realm. This is what happens when you cross over to the other side. This is what Heaven looks like.

Blurred at the peripheries.

The world through a fish-eye lens.

Our thoughts and prayers go out to those who see only in black and white.

He is not alone. Death is not solitude. It is not perpetual darkness, nor is it endless light. In the naive, hopeful, expectant, damaged mind of the sick-with-grief old man, death is the flat in which he existed in life. It is the top floor of a maisonette in East London. E3. And he has company.

His two angels are in the room with him. His guides. The girl sits at his feet, her delicate weight barely making an impression in the thin mattress. He tries to lift his head and feels the blood rush to the cut in his cheek.

'Ow,' he exclaims. 'I can still feel pain.'

The other person in the room looks at him, unflinching. His eyes bore into the old man's, and he speaks in something between his true voice and a whisper. A hush louder than a voice, yet softer.

'This is the first stage of your death, Saul.'

He calls him Saul. The old man has a name. He thought it would be lost.

'The first stage,' the man on the chair, who Saul believes to be one half of his team of guides, repeats, hoping he sounds more ethereal than usual. Aspiring to a higher level of poignancy. Of believability.

Then the old man, Saul, starts to cry.

The girl and her partner stare on in silent, unnoticeable trepidation. And say nothing.

Time passes. Haemophilic seconds bleeding furiously into minutes that feel like weeks, as it dawns on the old man that he still has the ability to reminisce. This is the curse he expected would lift with the ingestion of those pills.

All those pills.

For her.

Ada was born in 1927, two years before Saul. The old man. She had lived on Wheatstone Road in West London with her quiet mother, hardworking father and six siblings in a house only large enough for a family without any children. Or pets. Or furniture.

Or food.

They were poor and thin but not unhealthy. And the kids were generally close and not as miserable as the adults. Saul lived close by, on Wornington Road, in similar conditions.

Ada was mischievous all her life. She would lift the corner of her blind to see the planes in the air, the German bombs that rained hell over London. That had destroyed homes and buildings close by. That had fallen on St Thomas's Church. She loved the spectacle, almost admiring their majesty of the skies. The sound had even stopped bothering her. She saw no use in feeling fear.

Even when they told her she only had months to live.

Even when she knew those months would only be weeks.

She was at her best when times were at their toughest. Many people of that time were. And she never lied. Not after the incident with the soup.

Ada had been hungry, her insides hollow at the thought of another bland, stodgy meal made from scraps and leftovers – not that anything was ever left over – and foods that should not be on the same plate but were there to make another equally beige ingredient stretch a little further. This was one of her mother's *talents*.

Ada saw the sign for the soup while playing in the street by herself.

It was outside a local hall or community centre or church – this part of the story was never clear because it was not important to her, only the soup was.

And the bread.

'Real bread,' she would say with a smile that seemed to stretch across her face as far as her mother could stretch a cabbage and some bacon. 'I couldn't remember the last time I had bread like that,' she would ponder dreamily, affectionately.

They were giving away soup, not even the greatest soup in the land, but it was soup, nonetheless, with a crusty roll, at the hall or community centre or church. It doesn't matter which. Children were being fed. Free donated food to help families where the man of the house, the father, the husband, was unable to work or was incapacitated in some way.

Ada went in and told them the lie. That her father was at home. He had no job.

And she ate that soup.

She dipped her bread into the liquid. When that had gone, she poured the liquid from the bowl into her mouth. When that had gone, she used a dirty forefinger to wipe up what was left.

What flavour was the soup?

'I can't remember,' she would answer, still with that ridiculous grin. 'Maybe chicken.'

Later that night, feeling full and healthy and tired, a knock came at the front door. Her mother answered. There were two men on the doorstep, sent from a local office to speak with Ada's father about his lack of employment.

'He swung me around the kitchen that night by my hair. He hit me with a belt and shouted at me for lying,' she would tell Saul or anyone who would listen, never losing that smile or the look up to the left, as though it was being played out for her in an invisible thought bubble.

Then she'd laugh.

'Totally worth it, though.'

On her last day she'd told her husband, Saul, that she could still taste that soup.

The old man sits on the bed, very much alive, passing time he thinks no longer exists, and recalls his wife and her favourite stories.

'I still remember her. My memories are intact.' His voice is much higher in pitch as he weeps with abandon. In death there is no need to restrain tears. He gazes over his paunch into his lap.

'Where is my nothing?' he asks solemnly, his eyes closed, still facing downwards. His heart still wrenching as it did while he was alive, he thinks. 'Where is the dark?'

'It will come,' says the girl at the end of his bed, placing a gentle hand onto his blanket-covered foot in quasi-commiseration.

She repeats the sentence to inject drama.

'But now you should lie down. This is not the hardest part. Death does not always mean rest.' The male voice hits the old man's face from the side as the fake angels form a pincer attack.

But he remains seated, weighted with the sorrow he believed death would erase, and he wonders why that impish, impulsive, fearless woman ever walked down his road, why she spoke to him, loved him, lived with him, died with him. Wasn't she better than that? What did she see in him? He'd never once lifted his curtain to see the Germans fly over London. He never tasted the soup.

7   THE NURSE (AND THE SPORTSMAN)

Vashti's unease at the empty hospital bed sits with her throughout her coffee break. It jumps on her shoulders as she takes a long draw of nicotine in a bus shelter a safe distance from the hospital. The label on the packet says: *Smoking is highly addictive, don't start.*

Why does she not remember the last occupant?

Has she really stopped caring?

Desensitised to trauma.

There are no buses at this time of night. There are no people around. Yet, still, Vashti is forced to trudge across the staff parking bays – of which there are too few – and out of the hospital grounds, past the cemetery, on to the Mile End Road so that she can smoke in peace, without fear of castigation from other colleagues and the invisible threat of a health-and-safety inspector.

A smoking nurse.

A cancer-baiting health professional.

Your doctor or your pharmacist can help you stop smoking.

This is the night shift. It's full of insomnia and screaming in pain and patients pressing their little red button because they need to go to the toilet but their doctor has not provided them with crutches yet despite the full leg cast. This is the part where Vashti takes a pan to the sportsman. Where she offers her help and expertise. Where he declines because he's embarrassed at his current state, he believes his career is over and the last thing he wants is for a woman to witness him shitting in a disposable container.

This is the point where a physically fit, confident athlete gets stage fright. He is desperate to evacuate his bowel but is lying on his back. He feels like a child. A useless infant who has not yet learned to walk. He psyches himself out. It's strange, Vashti thinks. People tend to just go. The sense of self-decency should be left at the automatic emergency doors along with privacy and vanity. Everybody shits in the pan eventually.

But everything tonight is peculiar. It is not as it should be. It is unnatural. The old man named Saul should be in the empty hospital bed being cared for by an intrinsically concerned Vashti.

Or he should be dead.

Somewhere in the universe, both of these things are happening.

Yet, at this moment, Saul is crying in his own bed for his deceased wife, and the nurse, the troubled and trapped health worker, laughs to herself for a moment at the inadequacy and stubbornness of the sportsman who refuses to defecate into biodegradable Tupperware.

Obstinacy may reduce blood flow and cause impotence.

Vashti is still awake on the ward at 7am. The remainder of her shift has been peculiarly quiet. Nobody has died or called out since the sportsman refused the bed pan. He has not slept either. His crutches are not due to be delivered for another three and a half hours.

That is the equivalent to twenty-four and a half days in Hell.

Or Heaven.

It is the same as three and half hours in Saul's bedroom.

Or ninety-five stops on the Circle Line. Nearly four times round the track.

'Good morning,' Vashti whispers to the sportsman, the rest of the patients on the ward still snoozing through their broken limbs and inflamed joints and tumour-clad vital organs. Some in natural, oblivious slumber, others in drug-induced temporary comas.

'Oh, God. Is it? Is it morning? Is it good?' His response is sardonic. He raises his voice and forces the self-loathing in his nurse's direction. 'I told you, I can't go in one of those things.'

'Listen. I need you to be quiet.' She produces a pair of crutches and within moments he is sitting up, his legs have swivelled around to the side of his bed and his arms are outstretched. This is the first time that he has remembered the pain in his leg. It shoots down from his hip to his heel; his toes are blue and without feeling. The sportsman bites his teeth together, tightening the tendons in his face and squaring off his jaw even further.

'Shh...' She hands over crutches. She clicks them to their maximum length after reading his height from the chart. He towers over her. 'Do not wake anybody up. And please act surprised when the doctor comes in a few hours to deliver your real crutches. He will also demonstrate how to use them.'

Before she finishes the sentence, they have been snatched from her grasp and he is rattling his way across the linoleum into the vacant bathroom. He locks the door and hobbles to the toilet. Vashti waits. She hears a groan as he sits down, cracking his heel clumsily against the hard floor, then once more in pleasure as he releases the tension he has held overnight.

She smiles again. But karma is proportional. This is not enough.

Smoke contains benzene, nitrosamines, formaldehyde and hydrogen cyanide.

Smoking when pregnant harms your baby.

Smokers die young.

Vashti, the nurse, is more dead than the old man, Saul. But she has a choice. A decision, still. Life. Or death. Every moment a decision. Every question has two answers.

So many questions.

8   GOD? TERRORIST? NARRATOR?

If I'm not really on this train then how do I know about the Chinese woman who is so preoccupied with the application on her mobile phone that she is clueless concerning the unbuckled satchel on her back that contains her purse with identification and £73.26 in cash? How will she get into her work building without the keycard she keeps in there? When will she realise she has been robbed? Will she feel violated and dirty? Is it better to know that you are being mugged? Does it feel less invasive, though still equally terrifying, that way?

Where was God when she fell victim?

Where was I?

Is this what free will looks like?

Are the other passengers in this carriage aware of my own bag? Would they be more fearful if my skin were lighter or darker in colour? How did you picture me? Am I male? In my twenties? What about my skin? Am I dark? Do you think I am Asian? Or Indian? Is there a difference in your mind? Am I white? With a cross around my neck? What does that say about you? Is life more straightforward if you adhere to stereotypes? Is it more comfortable to fall in line with cliché? And aren't they all born from something true anyway? What about horoscopes?

Does everybody remember where they were when that plane hit that tower that time, and has it informed our thoughts since that building fell down in that street trapping that fireman? What about that place where they have no television? What happened at the end of that episode of that show that the guy from Mary Poppins was in that got interrupted by the news? Did he solve that murder?

What would he think about my satchel?

If you believed you were the god of one religion then found out that you were, in fact, the deity of another faith, could you click your

fingers to deal with it psychologically? Would you even have fingers?
If you did, could you use them to stealthily reach inside an open bag
and remove a purse while the owner dragged a shape across her
phone screen with her forefinger? What would be the point? Is it a
lesson? Are they all lessons? Was that plane a lesson? Is this tube
carriage a lesson? If we are supposed to be learning *more* then why
does the word start with *less*?

Did the man sitting opposite me and three places to the left just
look up over his book in my direction? Who does he think he is?
What is he reading? Is it a play? *The Visit* by Friedrich Dürrenmatt?
That has something to do with a train too, right? It's the one where
the rich woman returns to her hometown and the locals think that
she can turn their fortunes around, right? But they don't realise that
it is revenge, do they? That prosperity comes at a terrible cost?

So, if I say that I am Claire Zachanassian, you understand that I
am speaking metaphorically rather than literally? But what if I tell
you I am God? Does that make me delusional or psychotic? What
if I am a thief, a robber, a thug? What if this knapsack is waiting to
be detonated? Do I think myself a martyr?

Are you hoping I am Claire Zachanassian now? Figurative or
actual?

Have you forgotten about the narrator?

If somebody says that 'blind faith is knowing exactly who you are
at any given minute', and you are still on a voyage of self-discovery,
are you faithless or knowledgeless, and should you be given these
minutes to squander so frivolously?

Did the old man ponder this before throwing those drugs into his
mouth? Has the sportsman temporarily lost his identity? Can he find
a new one? Can identity be created and later be discovered to have
been the truth all along? Why has Vashti stopped caring, stopped
believing? Is it time for somebody to turn the tables, to ask whether
anything is wrong with *her*? Should that person be me?

9   THE COMMUTER (OR THE VISITOR)

Thomas Davant looks over his book at nothing. His eyes throw out a glare that passes through anyone in his direct line of vision. He taps a cheap, blue, chewed biro against his teeth then closes his eyes and nods as though finally understanding the sentence he has just read. In the margin, he scrawls a note that says: *Conscience is a key factor.*

And he continues to read his play, unthreatened by the person sitting opposite him and three seats to the left. Unknowing of his intimidating presence. Uncaring about the contents of his satchel. Unjudging of the colour of his skin.

Thomas, the commuter, the man on the train, does not exhibit any of these emotions. He peers over the top of his bright-orange book and repeats the ritual. Gazing into nothing, tapping the split plastic of his pen against his incisors. Inciting paranoia in the figure sitting opposite and three to the left.

His eyes seem fixed on the now-suspicious man with the knapsack and questions and light fingers. But he does not see him.

10   THE NEIGHBOUR (AND THE DAVES)

The neighbour was at work when one of the Daves checked the letterbox at lunchtime.

Still no cheque.

Now, there's talking outside his front door. Two people in the vestibule knocking for the Daves.

'Come on, Dad, we know you're in there.'

His own nosiness unsettles him. He didn't like it when his girlfriend was loitering by the peephole to catch a glimpse of the fool living opposite. It felt cruel. But suddenly he finds his interest piqued. He shuffles about in the hallway. It's an unwelcome feeling.

Why should the neighbour care?

But what if he is in trouble? What if he does have something wrong with his brain? What if his tongue really did explode? Should the neighbour go out there and try to help? His kids seem worried.

Maybe just a look. Don't want to rush things.

The neighbour spreads his legs so that his feet are either side of the door frame, so that he doesn't cast a shadow underneath the door and alert the sick-with-worry children outside. Through the hole he can see Dave's unfortunate offspring.

The woman to the left is in her thirties, overweight, mousy hair. Greasy. There's a stain on her shoulder, suggesting she has a small child of her own. To the right is the son. Tall. Unhealthily thin. The neighbour has passed him a few times on the stairs and squeezed out a hello, the kind that requires neither party to stop and give anything deeper. He's here a lot. This is the first time the daughter has shown her tired face. It must be serious.

She puts her mobile phone to her ear, and the neighbour is close enough to hear her say, 'I'm going to try him one more time. I don't know what else to do.'

On the other side of the door, one of the Daves is terrified. There is a cupboard next to the front door. It runs from floor to ceiling. There are hooks inside for coats. On the floor, there is a pile of shoes. He usually chooses that spot when the landlord comes knocking. She stays calm even though she is raging inside and tends not to raise her voice, so Dave needs to be closer in order to hear.

When it's the kids, or his ex-wife, he closes himself in the bedroom wardrobe and waits. Sometimes he takes a pillow inside, because he's fallen asleep in there twice. Whether or not there is something pushing on a part of his brain, these are not the actions of a well man. He is shaking. When they first knocked, he started to cry. But he never said a word. Not even to the other Dave.

The neighbour feels that he should offer to help or, at the very least, provide comfort of some kind. But he can't just go out there, say that he heard a commotion and wondered whether there was anything he could do. It would embarrass the woman with the oily hair. There can't be a single point in history when a stranger interfered in the affairs of others and anything good came from it.

He could put his shoes on and leave. Pretend he is going out somewhere. But then he'd have to go somewhere. Where would he go? He could buy something from the shop. Yes. Offer his usual hello and then it would be up to them to draw him in.

But he couldn't just go out there empty-handed, it would look too obvious. The bags for life were in the boot of his car.

In the kitchen, the neighbour throws away some food that is still in date, just to make the bin bag look more full than it is. Perfect reason to leave the flat. He puts on one shoe and there's a knock at his door.

A buttery-haired woman in her thirties is standing on his doormat.

'I'm sorry but I don't suppose you've seen my dad today, at all, have you?'

Don't call him the Daves. Don't call him the Daves.

'Dave?'

She nods.

'I spoke to him briefly this morning. He was collecting his mail. Is everything alright?'

'Yeah. He does this sometimes. Very stubborn. Something just switches in him and he hides himself away. He usually snaps out of it.'

She does seem relieved.

Her brother does not.

'He needs to stop doing this,' the son snarls, then turns back to the door with a screwdriver jabbed into the inside.

'Look, if I give you my mobile number, maybe you could let me know if you see him again. Just so I know he's safe.' She intonates as though she is asking a question but is already fishing around inside her handbag for a piece of paper and a pen. She writes her name and mobile number on a folded page from a yellow legal pad.

'Just a text', she adds, handing over her details, 'if you see him.'

'Er, sure. No problem. I'll let you know.' And the neighbour returns to his flat, takes off the one shoe he managed to put on, pulls the food from the rubbish that was never meant to be there, washes it under the tap and puts it back into the fridge.

He hears the daughter.

'Right, dad. We're going. I'll give you a call again in the morning.'

They leave. The light in the communal areas turns off automatically after a minute. The neighbour throws the woman's details in a pile with his unread mail.

This is why you don't look through the peephole.

This is why you don't listen in on things that aren't your business.

This is why you do not ask questions.

11 THE ANGELS (AND THE OLD MAN)

Let's call the angels Nathaniel and Lailah.

For those are their names.

Let us also no longer refer to them as angels.

Nathaniel sees that the old man, Saul, has now descended into slumber. He places a cold, white hand gently on the frail man's shoulder and tugs at the blanket slightly to cover him. Lailah waits patiently for the signal to stand up from the mattress and exit the room.

Nathaniel flits his hazel eyes quickly to the left. Lailah cautiously edges off the single bed and ekes her way out of the door, followed closely by her partner, who tiptoes backwards, trying to preserve the not-really-dead man's peace.

'Tea?' he asks matter-of-factly, pinching at his throat as though parched from their experience.

'I could murder one. Maybe something stronger though. See what the old man has in his cupboards.'

Saul has very little to offer in the way of refreshment. He has been planning his demise for weeks now.

That's twenty-eight years in Hell.

Or Heaven.

Or a fortnight under half a ton of soil or sealed within a plastic urn – or held together as a bag of ash, if you don't believe in that kind of thing.

In the fridge there is a one-pint carton of semi-skimmed milk that expires in two days. A dribble of liquid remains but would only offer a subtle lightening in colour to a single cup of English Breakfast tea. There is one slice of pre-cut, mild, holed cheese, one slice of turkey ham, a tub of not-really-butter spread and a Granny Smith apple.

'Perhaps Saul was planning a simple sandwich as his last supper,' one of the not-real angels says to the other. It doesn't matter which way around they are any more. They are together in this. They are one.

They are smiling.

They joke at the expense of the man in the next room, who now dreams of his wife.

He remembers her more and more.

This is not how it is supposed to be. It's not what he wanted from death.

Saul had planned to eat. He had factored in that final meal. There are two slices of thick white bread in one of the cupboards to support that claim. Maybe if time had not run away from him. Maybe if he had not been so anxious to end it all so abruptly, if he'd not made himself picture Ada one final time before aiming for complete deletion, he would have spread the fake butter on those white slices. He would have laid the slice of meat and the cheese in between them. He may not have experienced the nausea after taking the pills.

He may have held them down.

He could have died for real.

And this could be a sad story of an innocent couple who rented the bottom floor of a maisonette in Bow, East London, from a tired but pleasant aged man who decided to take his life, leaving his innocent lodgers to discover his body days later as they wandered into his flat with a pocketful of cash to pay the archaically cheap rent.

They could be shocked and affected and in desperate need of therapy.

But that is not them. That is not this story. Instead, they are kissing. And, in the absence of champagne, they each take a half of the uneaten sandwich and touch them together as though toasting the old man's pretend death. There is perhaps the hint of a smile. A shrug of the shoulders.

They kiss again.

Then the bad weather comes.

12 VASHTI (AND THE COLOUR)

Back when she still cared, Vashti had used her hospital contacts to speak with a mental-health professional about her brother, Juned.

She was worried about him. He had self-harmed. Nothing too serious. He wasn't trying to die, just cutting himself, scarring his arms. He was sixteen. Trying to release the pressure, he had said. It was like the cuts let out the tension he was feeling inside.

What tension? He was sixteen. There was school work. Their mother made all his meals and did his washing. He went out with his friends all the time. Vashti didn't understand it.

Dr Edelstein had told her that, often, the self-harming is seen by parents and family as a person's cry for help, but this is not always the case and often comes down to an issue of identity. It's not even that the person doesn't like who they are, more that they just don't know who they are. And, while London is one of the most multi-cultural cities in the world, within ethnic minorities, identity is an issue, and religion can play a large part in this, in our increasingly secular society.

This made absolute sense to Vashti. But it didn't explain the change in her brother. He had been studious in his early teens but it had almost all fallen away. He wasn't getting into trouble at school, but he was no longer achieving the grades he had previously worked so hard to attain.

He was withdrawn, more than teenage hormones could explain. He was angrier. Talking to himself. Glued to his mobile phone, messaging God-knows-who, flicking between apps and conversations at lightning speed, yet was unable to talk with his sister face-to-face for more than thirty seconds without veering off topic, asking about something inane. There was a nine-year age gap between the siblings but it felt bigger than that.

'It is a generational thing,' Dr Edelstein had explained, 'something we need to try to understand, and understand quickly, because technology moves so fast now and kids are exposed to more than you or I ever were.'

Mixing ten conversations at once.

Swiping right to hook up with strangers.

Drowning in images of the perfect body and face and hair and teeth.

Misinformation.

Everything thrown at their face is a soundbite that lasts little longer than their diminishing attention span.

An online persona and an at-home persona.

How are they supposed to know who they are? Of course there are issues of identity.

Vashti didn't like the people her brother was hanging around with. The frequency of calls from her mother, worried late at night, was getting too much. When Vashti visited and her brother could be bothered to stay in, he was vacant, apart from the occasional conspiracy theory he had seen online or discussed with friends.

An intervention was out of the question. Vashti's father would not allow such a thing. But Dr Edelstein agreed to put aside some time if Vashti could persuade her brother to come into the hospital for an informal chat.

'You're just like them, Vash.'

'Who are *they*? What are you talking about, Ned?'

Her brother had seen Vashti's act of concern as betrayal. She was now a part of the problem he was apparently struggling against. There was no getting through to him. All she wanted to do was help and she couldn't find a way.

On his eighteenth birthday, Juned set an early alarm, packed a duffle bag with the minimum essentials and left. He walked out of the family home before his parents awoke and he didn't look back. Breaking his mother's heart, shaming his father and wrenching every ounce of concern and compassion from his loving sister.

13   THE SPORTSMAN (AND THE RISK)

One minute to go.

Three points down.

Backed up on their own line.

'I've got to go for an interception.'

'Don't you fucking dare go for an interception.'

'I'm doing it.'

Anyone else would ride it out. Play it safe. You're on your own line, you defend it with everything that you have. The team needs you to be a team player. Dig in. Defend.

To the sportsman, this was ludicrous. It made no sense. Why would you defend a loss?

One minute to go.

If they were the attacking team, there is no way they would be sitting back and trying to run the time out. They want to hammer it home. Make the win more emphatic. The sportsman knew this because he was a winner. He could see that look in their eyes.

'I'm fucking doing it.' He looked to his teammate inside him and smiled like he could see into the future.

His opposite number had lined up a little wider than usual.

They wanted to spin it out quickly, get the score, rub salt in the wound.

The sportsman pretended he hadn't noticed or he didn't care, and got into his usual position.

One minute to go.

'Do me a favour and run at your man as fast as you can. Don't worry about the ball. Just get on him quickly.'

The ball came out.

One pass.

Two.

Three.

So fast.

The sportsman's inside man did as he was asked. He put pressure on his opposite number to pass that ball out before taking a huge hit. And the sportsman didn't even bother going for his own opposite number. He ran for the gap. Slightly inside the player he was supposed to be marking, and he stretched out his arms as far as he could.

The ball hit his hands. He caught it. Tucked it under his arm, and while everyone else on the pitch was heading in the direction of the line he was supposed to be defending, he already had a ten-metre head start. There was nothing else he could see other than the line he had to place that ball over to win the game.

Which he did.

The semi-final was theirs.

His teammate congratulated him. 'You are a bastard.'

'It was the only way.'

They went on to win the semi-final. The sportsman scored three times in that game but it was the game-saving interception that always made its way into his dreams. With his leg set in a heel-to-hip cast, and an excruciating pain in his bowels, it was the dream that presented itself once more, making him smile in his sleep.

The sound of the rain would eventually wake him and wipe that smile away.

14 GOD?

Do you regard yourself as a fearful person? If there was an accurate way to measure fear, if somebody invented the correct apparatus, where would a fear of the dark rank on the continuum in relation to, say, a fear of wasps or buttons? What about the fear of being blown to pieces on an underground train? What if you don't travel on public transport for this very reason? Isn't that merely a fear of living? Is there a word for that? Is there a phobia for everything one can imagine? Can atychiphobia be seen in a positive light? Can you be atychiphobic and British?

Does the greyness of the English sky fill you with a sense of dread and foreboding or is it a welcoming sight that reminds you of home? Is there anything else that can be so dull to the eye yet able to coat your vision in such grand beauty? What if everything was grey or dark or white or simply a shade? Which colour would you miss the most? Would the grass always be greyer on the other side?

Who is making me ask these questions and which ones are relevant? Are all questions relevant? Should we always examine? What about that girl in your lectures at university who always put her hand up when asked if there were *any more questions*? Could she have left her hand at her side or on her pen or resting against her desk just once, maybe twice? Did it serve her well to repeat the lecturer's final sentence, inflecting her voice to rise at the end of the line, transforming statement into enquiry? What is she doing now? Even though you disliked her, do you find her to be a part of your wider social network? Are there other people within this network who you still dislike? Who was the first person to say 'we're taking this global'?

When someone wants to have a meeting and uses the term 'touch base', does your skin immediately goose-pimple, and should you wear a tie to such a touching of bases? Do people look at my tie and assume that I would use such a term? Do they see me as something

I am not? If these people believe that I work in business, that I sell goods or purchase them or trade in some kind of stock, does that mean I am fooling them? Or does that make it true? Am I, then, not a deity nor a narrator of a story nor a confused individual coerced into the glory of martyrdom, but, instead, a commuter like Thomas Davant or that lady over there in the figure-hugging skirt who is desperately avoiding eye contact?

What if I am none of these things?

Are there people who emerge into the light of the world from the escalator at Canary Wharf Station and feel genuinely excited to see the scrolling red lights of a million acronyms and numbers and arrows flit around the corner of a building? Do these people ever consider themselves to be adding something to the world? Is the real satisfaction in taking?

Am I here to take away? Would the loss of my own life along with the others on this train carriage somehow even out, reaching a state of equilibrium, or am I here to give, to add rather than subtract? Is there a mathematical formula for justice?

15 THE MATHS (OR A FORMULA, AT LEAST)

1 day on Earth = 1 week in Hell
1 month in Hell = 1 month in Heaven
7 hours in Purgatory = 1 hour in London
Length of first stage (also known as *transition)* = Unknown
Distance ÷ Speed = Time
Space = Time
Number of universes = ∞

16   THE OLD MAN (AND THE FAKE ANGELS)

And then it is morning, and the rain hits the window so hard that it awakens Saul to the solitude he believes to be death. He exhales the regret from his lungs, his breath making the sound of Ada's name as it is expelled into the room. He sits, and his face drops, his jowls weighted with remorse. He looks dead.

He should be dead.

Like Ada, only laced with a fear that she never knew.

He takes some time to acclimatise to his surroundings; five minutes, or twelve hours in Purgatory. He sees his narrow chest rise and then fall, dropping with the breath that he can blow out through his nose or mouth. He can feel the cold, the temperature underneath the blanket being different to that which surrounds it. The chill reminds him that he is deceased, while respiration argues otherwise.

He opens his mouth to call out but doesn't know what to say.

Angels?

Guides?

Twisted couple I rent a flat to at a very reasonable price.

Who I have always respected.

Who have always been kind to me.

It takes him another twelve years in Heaven to realise that his eyesight has returned, the peripheral blurring has evaporated. He sees his own room stretched out before him. Trousers left inside the trouser press that Ada had insisted he use. He had placed a pair of navy-blue slacks in there despite feeling he would never need another outfit again. A habit formed many years ago.

To his left he spots a glass of water, bubbles of oxygen dotted throughout, undoubtedly warm from resting overnight. He knows he did not pour it himself. His inner monologue informs him that *it must have been the angels.*

He takes the glass and drinks its contents in one pour. The tepidity ensuring it is less harsh against his throat. It tastes like water. So it must be water.

Is this what they drink here?

There is no liquid in Hell.

Next to the closed door in the far corner of the room is his wardrobe, or what is supposed to look like his wardrobe, a copy, perhaps. It even has the dent in the centre where the bedroom door opens into the soft pine of the surface; that shape of the door handle tessellating with its corresponding dent.

It looks exactly like his home, down to the most minute of details, yet everything hangs in a mist, which leaves him uncertain and immobilised.

He coughs but does not yet have the strength in his arms to raise a hand to his mouth, as Ada would have liked. He blinks, and a picture of the sandwich he never gave himself time to prepare slinks its way into his subconscious. His stomach rumbles. His eyes open and he feels less terrified; it is the first time his eyes have been shut and he has not thought of the wife he feels he never deserved.

Outside the door, Lailah has perched herself on the flecked worktop of the kitchen island. The laminate flooring by her feet has been cleared of the old man's vomit and the small puddle of urine he passed after falling unconscious. In the bedroom, Saul pulls the blanket away from his chest and the stench of ammonia wafts upwards from his lap like a piss-dipped vulture rising on a warm-air pocket.

Saul's cupboards are now filled with tins and packets and loaves and cereals and bottles. The refrigerator is packed and set at the lowest temperature. There is chocolate and alcohol and biscuits and crackers for the cheese. All bought with the money that will not be needed for rent this month.

This is the taste of Heaven.

Nathaniel stretches out on the old man's sofa and watches the ceiling as though the yellow-with-age Artex swirls are moving like the clouds and telling him a story. A joke to which only he knows the punchline. He smokes, just as the old man did and adds his own virus and decay to the flat, which is slowly transforming into a living pit of perdition.

He bolts upright, the cigarette hanging coolly from his top lip, his eyes wide and reflected in Lailah's expression, when he hears the old man splutter.

They have to go in.

But Saul can see now. He will know who they are. He will recognise them, even through the haze and afterglow of his apparent death. The fuzz has faded.

'You,' the old man breathes the word out of his body like a mouthful of dust.

'We've been waiting,' Nathaniel states, donning his ethereal tone once more.

'But ... but ... the angels. The pills...'

'Us,' Lailah joins the confusion. 'It was us. We have been here all along.'

'I thought I was—'

'We merely resemble the last people you saw in your life,' Nathaniel interrupts. 'The first stage. Remember?'

There is a beat as Saul rewinds to the last time this phrase was uttered to him.

'We have taken this form to ease you through the first stage.' Nathaniel takes a convincing lead on the discussion. His eyes dart quickly to his right, taking in the cabinet beside the bed, clocking the empty glass, and he knows.

The old man has taken the liquid down. Reality, in Saul's mind, will start to waver shortly and he will believe Nathaniel. He will have no choice but to believe.

The poor old man is such an easy target. His debilitating grief, mixed with a growing dependence on alcohol, topped up with hallucinogens, is more than enough to make him believe he has died. All it takes is to stir things up with an act of apparent kindness and the offer of hope.

Lailah says nothing. The colour of her eyes is now a corona to her expanded pupils.

'We know that you have been thinking about your wife, about Ada.' Saul recoils as the being that looks like his lodger speaks of his lost love. 'You had believed that she would vanish from your thoughts' – Saul nods lightly, almost undetectably – 'and she will. But you must first make it through transition.'

The old man looks up, his eyes full of hope – a desire he found difficult to grasp in what he thought was life.

And the blurring returns.

Whatever was in the water is now making the walls move.

'If you close your eyes now, you will feel sick. This is the time for confrontation.'

Then both angels say, 'This is transition.'

Open your eyes.

Saul does not hear their voices in his ears. They whisper to him in his mind, and he obeys their command. He knows that he must face the decision he made. He must address the loss of his own partner. Something he saw as unfair. A moment when he would have traded himself for her release.

He opens his eyes.

And is once again alone.

17 THE ANGELS (AND THE NOTES)

Dear Nate and Lailah,

I'm sorry that you had to find me like this.

I should have eaten. It's too late now.

I knew it would be you.

Please don't worry about the rent this month.

It's not fair on you, I know that.

Life can be like that sometimes. If I can pass any wisdom on to you at all, it is that.

I have to get her out of my head. I have to get rid of Ada.

Maybe I could hang on. Do it naturally. Maybe there is a Heaven and she is there.

If I just hang on a bit longer, I will meet her again, and it will feel normal.

But I can't. It hurts too much.

So much that I'd rather go where I am going and have the memory of her erased.

And with it, the pain.

I'd rather not know her at all.

Then I won't have to miss her.

Don't let this happen to you.

Go together.

Make sure you go together.

I've taken care of everything. There's a letter for Ash.

This one is a bit last-minute and I've already taken some pills.

The milk in the fridge might be off.

Saul.

The letter left to his son, Ash, the orphan, is more detailed. It gives more insight into his father's state of mind. It covers the two years since his mother died. It would make Ash understand.

Nathaniel holds the corner of his and Lailah's envelope over the flaming hob of the gas stove. The light glows red and eats away at the paper, altering it to black, disintegrating carbon. He throws the letter into the dry, empty sink and allows it to burn into cinders.

Nothing important happened today.

'Now we are clear. There is no trail. We can start again. We can teach him.'

Lailah looks intently at her partner as he speaks these words like an evangelical preacher. She doesn't ask herself what Nathaniel has become, she does not ask herself anything. She is enamoured by his beauty and serenity in this situation. But also believes that she is the one in charge.

She just nods.

Because she believes.

Then she dips the corner of Ash's letter into the same flame.

This small act, this flutter of wings, this flicker of fire, it shouldn't affect anything. It is creating nothing. The letter is no more. But it is destruction. And there is a cost to that. There is an injustice, and injustice is bigger than the shudder of a flame.

With injustice comes pain.

'Come on, baby, do it, make me come,' she warbles, her back pushed against the headboard, her hands pulling his head in tighter, clamping his nose into her thick hair, making it difficult for him to breathe as he continues to lap at her.

'Make me come,' she repeats in a whisper, the second word emanating at a higher pitch than the rest. She tenses her gluteal muscles repeatedly to bounce her clitoris across the texture of his tongue and he drinks her in.

Vashti has not made love for a long time. Her hours don't permit it. Instead, she does this. She arrives home in the morning after a sixteen-hour shift where she has been handing out bed pans and attaching tubes to peoples' hands, hoping that the broad-spectrum antibiotics will clear things up, wheeling beds down corridors for x-rays, squirting a syringe of morphine into the mouth of a future amputee. She doesn't have the time or energy to shower or fuck. What she has is five minutes of crossover time where her boyfriend can either hoist her up against the wall with his strong hands and bury his head between her legs before he gets up for work or she can lie down and let him pound against her, maybe turning her back and letting him enter her that way. So that she can go straight to sleep.

Condoms, if used properly, reduce the risk of pregnancy and many sexually transmitted infections.

And he rolls off the bed and walks to the bathroom naked, his penis bouncing comically as his arousal slowly lessens. And his shower is far too hot for his skin and his hair is too short for that much shampoo. And the suit he pulls over his body and the tie he fastens into a half-Windsor knot is unnecessary for the job he does every day.

Vashti slides down the headboard like a dying cartoon villain, the top half of her body looking like a tired but clothed nurse. The bottom half, indecent and wet and throbbing and without true feeling in her muscular brown thighs. She can smell herself, her post-coital scent, and she knows this moment of euphoria is short-lived.

She pulls the duvet over her legs.

Those scars on her shoulder blades are burning. As they always do when she does something like this. As they do when she stops caring about a patient. As they do when she takes it upon herself to ease their suffering. As they do every time she smokes or thinks about running away again or takes a mouthful of a man that is not her current boyfriend.

No method of indifference guarantees one hundred percent protection.

Vashti breathes heavily and rubs her left shoulder with her right hand; it's the one that hurts the most. The one she prefers. Her reminder to be better. To do better. To think better.

Her boyfriend exits the bathroom. He smells clean but over-fragranced. Vashti keeps her eyes closed, the burning sensation in her shoulders subsiding and the throbbing between her legs has dissipated. He leans over and kisses her on the cheek and bids her farewell. He says he hopes to see her later before she leaves for her next shift. He doesn't expect a response, he just loves her and wants her to know it.

But Vashti doesn't like it, she doesn't want it. She doesn't want him to be nice to her, because she doesn't think she deserves that. In her head, she wishes that he hadn't bothered, she hopes he will leave soon.

He does. And Vashti falls asleep with glowing scars and the burning warmth of her shoulders. And the unsettling thought of that empty hospital bed. And a dream of that sportsman with his broken leg and his mangled dreams.

INTELLIGENCE AND SECURITY COMMITTEE
35 Great Smith Street, London SW1P 3BQ

28th March 2023

<u>Link between separate attacks.</u>

In total, eighteen bombs were detonated on the morning of 21st July 2022 across London. Seven on the Underground network, four on London Transport buses, one in a café, two in the foyer of financial high-rise buildings, and four within the hit-and-run vans used on Thames bridges. All suicides were successful.

Footage of each perpetrator has been gathered and correlated. All four bus bombers travelled together from Leeds on the morning of the attack. The van drivers all hired their vehicles from the same company in Sawbridgeworth, Hertfordshire, two days prior to their involvement. The man who detonated himself inside the café seemingly worked alone. CCTV footage shows that he walked for almost an hour from Bow to Canary Wharf. The two foyer bombers were seen together in Wolverhampton the night before.

Five of the seven bombers from the Underground attacks were picked up on film, travelling from Bradford early on the morning of the 21st. Unlike the men who came from Leeds, who travelled on the same train, separately, this group sat together for the entire journey, only splitting up on their arrival at Kings Cross.

The remaining two tube bombers were already in London, though one had travelled from Bradford, alone, three days before, and footage shows him riding the trains across the capital during that time.

Evidence of a nineteenth potential bomb that was not triggered or a potential link to this group who opted out at the last minute is still under separate investigation.

Though a clear connection between all factions of the attacks is still inconclusive at this time, the cascading nature of the separate incidents points towards a more intricate and organised group, and that several 'cells' were mobilised at the same time, for the same purpose.

Twelve of the suicide bombers were known to the police and intelligence services before the events of 21st July 2022.

19 GOD? TERRORIST? NARRATOR?

What was that film? The one with Jeff Daniels and Joan Allen? Have you ever had that thing where you dislike an actor or an actress and you don't know why? Have you ever avoided films because you have decided that you don't like the look of Sean Penn? Have you then accidentally watched a Sean Penn film, for example, realised that you don't know where this dislike came from and gone back to watch all the films he ever made? Did you do that with Jeff Daniels? What was that film he was in with Joan Allen?

Am I picking the wrong actors? Would it help more if I mentioned Tobey Maguire? Or Reese Witherspoon? What is the word for when one piece of art references another piece of art? Like, when a soap opera talks about a novel or song or a real-world event as though it were, in fact, a real thing itself ... What is the word for that? What is existentialism? Or anachronism? There's a word for everything, isn't there?

It was *Pleasantville*, wasn't it? They had a black-and-white thing going on, right? If I am the narrator, is it possible that I was thinking about that at the same time I was thinking of the poor sportsman? Did I make him up, too? You don't know what's happened to him yet, do you? Has he woken up? Has he opened his eyes?

If I know all of this, why don't I know who that guy is? What is the name of the man opposite me and three seats to my left? Why is he writing on his play? Is it about me? Making notes? Is he studying? Am I paranoid? Does he see me over the top of his pages? Is he suspicious of me like I am of him?

Why is he standing up? Where is he going? Am I the only one that cares? If they can't see him then how do I know they see me? Is it just phone screens now? Is it bubbles containing letters followed by a yellow face smiling or crying with laughter so that the tone of a message cannot be misconstrued? Is 'I love you' just a cartoon with hearts for eyes? Is that how we emote? An aubergine for a cock? A status update for a thought? A bomb as a protest, a message, a ticket into whatever you call Heaven?

What if you found out that your God was just a man on a tube train with a bomb strapped to his chest? Would you still feel grateful that you spent your life with something to believe in? Do the people who say they believe in science, and say there is no God, actually, believe in nothing at all?

Where is he going? Why has he put his script away? Is nobody going to look at him? Is he getting off? At Westminster? What is it that is so interesting about the man with the play? Is he any less apathetic than the phone zombies peppering this carriage?

What if you go through your entire life and nobody ever really sees you? If everything is connected and everything has its place, do the people who make no impact, who are content with existence, still matter? Do they still play a vital part in the world? Seven billion people seems like a lot, doesn't it? Would the death of everyone on this train make a difference? Won't more people be born the instant we cease to exist, anyway?

Is it easier if I think about something else, anything else? Should I ask other questions? Are questions like people? Do the ones that make no impact still matter? Can they seem irrelevant on their own but are important when the picture is taken as a whole?

Does anyone believe their parents or schoolteacher when they say, 'You can be anything you want to be'? Is positivity better than realism? Isn't that just what faith is? Or is that fear? Who came up with 'God-fearing' as a term and thought it was a good idea? Could I become a lawyer or a dancer or a professional football player just because I want to? Is the man with the play doing what he wants to do, being who he wants to be? Does he have more chance to achieve that now that he has exited the carriage and the doors have closed?

Who will take his place?

20   THE COMMUTER (OR THE VISITOR)

Thomas Davant gets off the underground carriage. He steps onto the platform, and four people who were waiting politely step up onto the train. The doors close behind them. Three turn to the right and one turns left.

Davant stops for a moment and taps his trousers pockets with his right hand.

'Wallet. Keys,' he says to himself.

He taps the inside pocket of his jacket.

'Phone. Good.'

For a moment, he looks through the train window and sees somebody staring back at him. Davant doesn't see a madman or a black man or a Muslim or human bomb or a God, it's just another person. A human being. One in six million commuting or sightseeing or heading home for food.

The train pulls out of the platform. Another will arrive in two minutes. Thomas Davant opens his script and takes his train ticket from the last page he was reading. He walks up the stairs, the ticket in his left hand, ready to let him out through the barrier, the book in his right. He manages to read and walk at the same time. His phone and wallet and keys are safe, but he checks once more, out of habit.

He wanted to be a theatre director. His father was the pushy parent urging him away from his dream and towards something steady and secure. His mother didn't really believe that a theatre director was a job but she was supportive. As long as he did his best. It didn't happen. He still wants to write a play. That's what he tells himself, and anybody who will listen. A story where he can decide the ending.

Today is his day off and he is going to the theatre. Alone. Tomorrow, he will head back to the security of managing a wine bar.

He won't write that play. He won't be that difference he wanted to make when he was younger and fitter and more energetic.

Not on the scale he wanted.

But he does have a gift. A knack as a director for bringing out the best in other people. He can help others. One by one, if that's what it takes.

21   LAILAH AND NATE (AND THEIR COLOURS)

It's difficult to keep up with the LOLs and the FMLs and the WTFs. The younger generations, seemingly, have so much to do that they have to shave precious milliseconds from single-syllable words in order to fit in all the ASMR videos they need to watch on YouTube.

If Lailah had a tattoo on her forearm, it would say 'YOLO'. But she would never be so lame.

It is her mantra, though. You only live once. And Lailah was devoted to it. Whether that meant hitchhiking (solo) across Europe in her gap year or deciding not to go to college after that gap year had finished. Whether it was taking a low-paid job at a music studio just to be around talent or sleeping with the father of the child she was au pair to, Lailah did the thing she wanted and then she moved on to the next town.

If she had a tattoo of a whirlwind on her shoulder, it would be more accurate. But she would never be so hollow.

And if she met a man she liked, she did not dip her toe into the relationship, she jumped in. Both feet. Giving everything she had. If it went wrong, so be it, there were other towns. There exists a definite trail of heartbreak and carnage where Lailah has been. She is the type of woman rockstars write songs about. But the world is a large place when you are just one person and she has a gift for disappearing at the right time.

She disappeared to an East London dive bar where she asked a beautifully androgynous man if he would like to buy her a drink. He did. Of course he did. She knew he would. Nathaniel. An aspiring painter, working in advertising sales.

Not all psychopaths are high achievers. Not all are killers. Not all work alone. But all are narcissistic. They are interested in their own self-gain. Wealth, position, power, a partner to share their ways.

Lailah and Nate drank and laughed and fucked, and she hung

around longer than he thought she would, but she was captivating and encouraging of his art, and sexually liberated. And while she never told him that she loved him, he knew it from the way she looked at him and held him, and he felt it, too.

Both of them considered themselves the alpha, they were the one who was desired, they were the one in control. But it was fairly evenly matched. An oddly egotistical co-dependency that relied on a feeling that went beyond love and into obsession.

Somehow, it worked.

Lailah hung around so long that the bed soon seemed too small and the frying pan too narrow. They found a place to be together. It was affordable. The lower level of a maisonette owned by the widower upstairs.

Five months in, Lailah pushed Nathaniel to follow his dreams. To put his painting first. To go for it. Take the chance. Take the opportunity of youth.

WTF was he doing working in advertising sales, anyway? LOL.

Her passion made sense to him.

He did as was being suggested. Or told. Or forced. Or manipulated. YOLO.

If it worked out, it was Nate's idea. If it came crashing down, he could blame Lailah.

And the money soon ran out and they argued about what to do.

Fighting and passion are often misconstrued as being the same thing. With Lailah and Nate, the fighting always led to passion. That was their cycle and they were happy stewing in it.

'He's reasonable. We just go up and explain that we are a little late with payment, we can take up half the money,' Nate had suggested.

'Or we could go up there and kill him and have the entire place to ourselves.'

There's a smaller story from her childhood that explains why she is like this.

And another one that explains why Nate shrugged this off and held her hand as they entered Saul's flat.

22   THE SPORTSMAN (AND THE LITTLE, RED BUTTON)

The sportsman wakes up and screams.

At first, nobody reacts, there's a lot of screaming in this place.

He blinks his eyes open and shut several times then opens them as wide as he can. Nothing.

'Fuck,' he shouts.

He closes his eyes tightly then opens them with a start.

Still the same.

He presses that little red button by his bed. And he moves his body to get up, forgetting about those six breaks in his right leg. And he screams again as the needles of pain shoot from his heel. It hits the floor with the full weight of his limb and the heaviness of the cast that wraps itself around his soon-to-be withered muscles. The pain travels up through his thigh and torso, before piercing the brain in his head, which is telling the sportsman that everything he can see is now in black and white.

A monochrome nurse arrives and fusses around the sportsman, lifting his leg and turning him back into the bed. She hits a switch behind his head to stop the call to the nurse's station made from his little red button.

'Sir, you can't get out of the bed without your crutches.'

'I can't see...'

'They're on the other side of your bed.' She points towards them and continues to tuck the blanket around him.

'Not the crutches. I can't see...' He falters again.

'You can't see?'

He takes a deep breath. The pain from hitting his broken leg on the floor has subsided. He shuts his eyes one more time as he composes himself. He opens them. It's still the same.

'I can see. I can see everything in here. But there's no colour. It's all been washed out.'

'No colour?'

'Everything is in black and white and ... and ... various greys.'

'How many fingers am I holding up?' she asks, holding up three fingers.

'Three. Three grey fingers. I told you. I can see them.'

'I think I need to bring a doctor around to see you. Are you comfortable? Do you require any pain relief?'

'It was a shock. It is a shock. My leg is constantly throbbing. You think maybe the drugs have done this?' He's not really listening to her questions.

'I wouldn't like to say. This isn't something we see very often. I'll get the doctor now. Will you be okay to wait here?'

'I'll be fine. Just ... just don't be too long.'

'As quick as I can, I promise.'

She walks off through the greyscale landscape of the hospital ward and out of view. The sportsman shuts his eyes again so that he can only see black.

23   THE SON (AND THE PAIN IN HIS CHEST)

Ash was close to his father. But a distance had grown between them since his mother had passed. It's not that he had been especially close to her, but Saul was no longer the dad that Ash had known and idolised while his mother was still alive. He had watched that sadness and longing envelope the old man, and he thought, selfishly, that it made Saul hard to be around.

Saul had loved Ada. When she fell pregnant with Ash, Saul loved her more for making their dream of becoming parents come true. And when Ash finally arrived, when Saul should have loved that child more than anything in the world, he was amazed at Ada's strength, how she had brought that beautiful boy into being.

Saul loved his boy. He adored him. He loved being a father. But the way his passion grew for his wife was unparalleled. It was a once-in-a-lifetime love. Scour the universe and you would find nothing that comes close.

It never affected the relationship Saul had with Ash, they were close, it only affected every relationship that Ash would have with a woman, as he tried desperately to recreate his parents' devotion, failing at every attempt.

Before Ash had his own children, he and Margaret would eat with his parents once a week. Sometimes, on a Sunday, Ada would make a roast dinner, or Ash would pay to take everyone out for lunch – also on a Sunday – once he started earning a decent wage. This fell away when Ash had his own dependents to think about, as is so often the case.

Their visits became sporadic, but Saul and Ada were active grandparents and spoiled their grandchildren just enough to not make any lasting damage. But when Saul lost the one person he depended on the most, Ash should have stepped up and repaid his father for the lifetime of support and affection.

Grief is such an odd thing. In this situation, for either man to take on the weight of the other was to deny themselves the proper mourning period they required.

Their sorrow was separate.

Saul wept for Ada.

Ash had lost his wonderful mother. It was sudden. That was probably better. Because seeing his father like this, losing him gradually, was too painful.

So he stopped calling as much, when he should have been calling more. He stopped dropping in, when he should have been taking his children over to see their grandfather. He didn't call. Or message back to symbols and misspelt words that Saul would accidentally text while the phone was in his pocket. He just let him float off.

Ash was an only child but he had three children, himself. Two girls and then a boy, who hadn't saved the relationship. And his wife was not kind. She did not light him up. She wasn't what he wanted. She had no soup stories. There was no mischievous smile.

He had idolised his parents and then disregarded everything they had shown and taught him to be. They were a tough act to follow. A perfect example of how love can damage just as much as hate.

And then he drifted away from the old man.

But when one of those wannabe angels burned that letter that was meant for only Ash's eyes, the injustice manifested itself as a pain in that man's chest. A pain that worried him; it did not feel the same as the usual throb of boredom and burnout and self-sabotage he had become accustomed to.

It made him think of Saul. His father.

So, Ash picked up the phone and began to punch in the numbers.

24 THE NOTHING

The hospital bed is empty. It's supposed to be Saul in there. Groggy and churning on the inside from having his stomach pumped, and yearning for his wife, feeling like he failed his family by trying to take his own life, and failing himself for screwing up something so simple.

But the old man is not there.

Nobody at the hospital feels anything about his absence. It's difficult to have an opinion on something that has not happened, something that is not present. Only Vashti senses the disquiet. Only she notes the sensation that fate has been tampered with in some way. She doesn't know exactly what it is, but it feels like something is missing. And, sometimes, something that does not happen can be as important as something that does.

But the nurse is not here either.

Doctor Hayward is. He's looking at the results of a CT scan, which shows, clearly, a large, probably grade-four brain tumour on the frontal lobe. He knows that this part of the brain controls personality, emotion and the ability to regulate behaviour. The doctor is acutely aware of how a tumour this size can not only cause a patient to behave inappropriately towards others, it can make them irritable, aggressive, anxious, depressed, confused and apathetic. These are the things that the Daves need to hear and be prepared for.

But the Daves are not there.

The Daves are at home. One is experiencing a severe mood swing that sees him hurling obscenities at the other, who cowers in the corner of the living room where there once was a sofa but is now just a wine stain.

They love each other.

They loathe each other.

And neither knows what the Hell is going on. They cannot

identify the emotions within themselves or the other Dave who shares that locked flat. The neighbour hears everything.

Vashti's shift will start in a few hours. By that time, the empty bed will be filled by the wrong elderly man, who will cough so much in the night that those sharing the ward will all wish him dead and each will blame themselves when he is wheeled out in the morning.

She will encounter the sportsman and the issue with his vision. But now, she finishes a dream, tossing uncomfortably in her bed as the burning in her shoulder blades starts to affect her neck and will eventually wake her up.

And Saul is in a drug-fuelled haze. And his captors are hungry and horny and the sickness in their minds is growing faster than any brain tumour could. And none of them are there at the hospital where the sportsman sees only in black and white, for now.

So many things that are not happening. You'd think that events and occurrences are what's important, rather than their absence. Their intangibility.

Yet there is a great power in nothingness. In stillness. In silence.

In having the right questions rather than pretending to know all the answers.

And He continues to ride around and around on that train line. A ticking bomb. An act of God.

25 THE ANGELS (AND THE MESSAGE)

The phone rings. The pretend angels are young. Millennials. They have heard about landline phones. Plugged into the wall, sitting on a side table by the sofa, but neither has used one. They've always known about the internet, and the idea of a phone with a wire seems comically outdated.

They are worse off for it, of course.

The doomed generation.

The depressed generation.

The trick-a-suicidal-pensioner-into-believing-he-has-died generation.

The phone rings and they freeze.

At first, they don't know what it is. Then something clicks, but they can't find it. And Saul is drugged up in his Purgatory but in need of a top-up. The ring seems to be getting louder the more they panic and throw cushions from the sofa. The phone is on the floor, obscured by the bottom of a curtain.

Then the phone clicks. Saul's voice says that the caller has reached him and Ada – he never changed the answering-machine message, perhaps because he hoped that his wife was still there with him somehow – please leave a message and we'll get back to you.

The fake angels are paralysed.

'Hey ... Dad. It's me. Ash. Of course. Who else calls you Dad? I just ... I just wanted to check in and see how things are. I know I should be doing that more. I've not been good ... since Mum ... Anyway, I'm going to try harder, be better. Look, I hope you're okay. Please give me a call back when you get this. If I don't hear from you, I'll pop by. Not tomorrow. The next day, I think.'

Ash wanted to say that he was sorry but it felt weak to do so over a recorded message.

'I had a feeling tonight that you needed me. It was weird. Maybe it wasn't that. Maybe I needed you. Call me back. Or I'll see you in a couple of days. Okay. It's Ash, by the way. I think I said that.'

He hangs up. The worry and embarrassment gave way to frustration at his own inadequacy. It was uncomfortable to listen to.

'What do we do now, Nate? That's the son. He sounds worried. He's coming here. He probably has a key.'

Nathaniel holds Lailah by the arms.

'Nothing to worry about. We have time.'

Two days.

Or fourteen months in Hell.

He pulls her in close. She feels comforted. Nathaniel is tall and slender, his hold does not feel like protection, they just tesselate. And they're both thinking the same thing.

26   GOD? NARRATOR? TERRORIST?

What if they just killed the old man? Wouldn't that solve their problem? Do you think they've even considered it? If I asked you which of the angels had thought about giving the man an overdose, who would you choose? It would be the male one, wouldn't it? He seems like the one who is in control? Have you underestimated the woman? Why is that? She was only joking when she suggested killing the landlord, wasn't she? That was before she knew he'd even taken the pills, right?

Have you not noticed that she has compassion for Saul? Has she shown this side of her yet? Where are we in this story? Is it so hard to believe that any of these things happened?

What if I told you that it was all true?

They say that if you stay in the same place for long enough, everyone you have ever known will pass you by, so, if I remain on this train carriage, will all the people I have ever seen come back round again? Will I see that man a few seats down with the orange book? Will the angels climb aboard? Does it matter that we have never met? I know about them, but that isn't the same as knowing them, is it?'

Is life a circle or does it stop? If there is an end, then what is the need for a God? What are the faithful working towards? If it's not a circle, then I can't be God, can I? God couldn't have a breakdown or amnesia? Could He take a holiday?

It must be the narrator thing, huh? The terrorist thing is still on the table, though?

Do bombs really tick? Why don't I just look inside my backpack? Am I afraid of what I might find? Do I want the confirmation?

If I stay in this spot, when will I see the nurse?

27   THE NEIGHBOUR (AND HIS GIRLFRIEND)

The neighbour and his girlfriend have been drinking in the flat all evening. Three bottles of prosecco and half a bottle of gin. They are sitting on the carpet, watching something mind-numbing but funny, and made hilarious by the amount of alcohol flowing through their systems.

It's become something of a routine.

Next on the agenda is sex. They're a couple who prides themselves on having sex sober more than they do drunk. They enjoy it. The want is still there. They like to remember it.

Not tonight.

He takes a little longer to get there than he usually does, but that isn't necessarily to any detriment. She is always vocal, particularly towards the end, but more so when inhibitions have been dissolved by Tanqueray.

They are both sweating and panting as they collapse. He is still inside her as they look at one another and smile.

'Fuck, I was loud there, wasn't I? There was no way your neighbours didn't hear me.'

'It's fine. It's late. Their TV is always turned up to the max. Don't worry.' He brushes the hair that has fallen across her face back behind her ear. He looks into her eyes and knows that he loves her. He's drunk but he knows the way he feels is true and real and right. And he wants to tell her. And he can't help himself.

As he goes to speak, he is interrupted by a sound in the space between his front door and the Daves' front door.

'Well, why don't you go and fuck yourself?'

A door slams.

It's much louder than his girlfriend's orgasm, but she still cringes that she may have been heard saying something in the moment that she has already forgotten.

Neither of them moves. They listen. The fire door swings open, and one of the Daves makes his way downstairs. They don't speak because they know what is coming. Not even a minute passes and the sound of Dave's footsteps can be heard as he despondently shuffles his giant tumour up the stairs.

They hold their breath.

Dave turns the key, opens the door, speaks. 'Not there.' He says this at a normal volume, which the neighbour's girlfriend hears clearly, and it makes her cringe.

Another empty post box.

The couple falls asleep, still entwined.

28 THE SPORTSMAN (AND HIS ANGEL)

He is awake anyway, but the screaming is still annoying. And the coughing. Even the sound of the curtain rings scraping against the rail as another patient is closed off for privacy is as aggravating as chalk on a blackboard.

He isn't inherently ill-tempered or malign, but he has no time for those wallowing in their pain and misery, though it is exactly what the sportsman is doing. Blinded by his own failing, as people often are.

He hates this kind of behaviour because, right now, he hates himself.

How can he be The Sportsman when he can no longer play his sport?

Having the colour taken out of his world is truly making him see everything in black and white.

The man opposite, in the bed that was meant for Saul, has been coughing for hours. A deep, hacking, painful and dry cough that the sportsman wants to stop. Whether the man is medicated in some way or somebody holds a pillow over his face until he stops breathing, it doesn't matter. It seemed that everybody was leaving him alone.

Maybe they don't want to get close to him. Maybe it is contagious.

The sportsman finds himself praying for an embolism or a lung to be barked up just to make it stop.

But it still wouldn't be quiet. Because there is a wall behind him and through that wall is a child, and they are screaming. It sounds like a murder. He wants the noise to go away and, though he feels lower than he ever has, though he begs for the wheezing bag of phlegm opposite him to croak his last croak, though he feels lost and alone and with no purpose, he cannot bring himself to wish a child ill. The competitor in him makes him want to find a solution to the agony in the adjoining ward.

He wishes he could have lost his hearing rather than having the glorious spectrum of colour washed from his vision.

He tries to read because the pages of his books are always black and white and it makes him feel like things are normal for a moment. A regular monochrome page of words with the sound of a child being operated on without anaesthetic and a dying man who has seemingly swallowed razorblades.

A drink. Part of him wants a drink. That might settle him, knock him out. There is no way that was happening in there, but he could complain about his leg. His stupid, worthless, twisted, broken, never-going-to-play-again leg. If he tells them that he is in agony, if he tells them quietly and calmly, so that he doesn't look like a junky, maybe they will top him up, give him some of those industrial strength pills he had when he first got there.

The sportsman presses his red button to summon the nurse and he waits.

He waits for his angel.

29   THE NURSE (AND HER COLOURS)

Vashti is doing her rounds when a call comes through from the ward that had made her feel uneasy the day before. She'd helped the sportsman out, got him some crutches early because he'd had stage fright about crapping in a bed pan. She wonders what it could be now. He was mobile. He was healing. His pain meds had been lessened.

As apathetic as she has become, she finds herself worried about the sportsman and cannot fathom why.

Her shoulder blades itch.

'I'll take this one.' She scratches at her back, turns off the notification and goes to her patient.

He is reading when she enters. He doesn't look in particular discomfort. Sometimes they need companionship. She knows his story. His leg is broken, yes, but inside his heart is where the real damage lies.

'Someone's up late,' she quips.

He glances up, his eyes widen, and the book he is holding drops to the floor.

The sportsman is staring at Vashti like she is the most beautiful thing he has ever seen. Like he has fallen head over heels in love with her. Like God has entered the room or he's just discovered that Father Christmas is, in fact, real.

'What?' Vashti blushes.

'You.'

Neither of them moves.

'Me ... You pressed your buzzer.'

'I can see you.'

'That's great. I'm here. Is there something wrong.'

'I can see you.'

'You said that.'

'But I can't see anything. It's all washed out. It's black and white. And grey. Everything. Everything but you.'

The sportsman is paralysed. His nurse has arrived and brings hope with her. She is in glorious technicolour. She is a ball of light and energy. Luminous and four-dimensional. There is no pain in his leg. He could get out of that hospital bed and walk over to her. There is no coughing or screaming in the background, there is only her.

Vashti.

She will save him.

30 GOD?

What if you've been here from the beginning?

What if you have been on Earth forever?

What if you are God or an angel or one of those *Turritopsis dohrnii* jellyfish, that can, essentially, turn back time by reverting to an earlier stage of its lifecycle? What then? How many times would you change who you were? And, more importantly, could you forget who you started as? Could you completely lose yourself in the vastness of time?

Could you recreate?

Or create?

Or forget that you created everything? Could you lose your faith and live a life of apathy because you have seen that your God has turned His back on humanity and the humans are now being blamed for screwing it all up?

Isn't it devastating when you find you've been lied to?

What's worse, being told that God is watching over you when he's decided to take an eon-long sabbatical, or being offered visions of paradise, where rivers of milk and honey await in exchange for giving one's life for the cause? Isn't the idea of forty willing virgins more of a motivation?

Even if you are told that your sacrifice is your religious duty and that your parents will definitely enter paradise as a result of it, even if you are given a key to hang around your neck and you're told it will open the gates of Heaven when you complete your task and cross over, wouldn't you still have doubts as you sit within a crowd of strangers, who you have been told are the enemy (but not told why)?

Wouldn't you have thoughts about pulling out, knowing that the nails were going to rip you to shreds before embedding themselves in the flesh and eyes of the other people in that club in India or that embassy in Beirut or that Buddhist temple in Java or on that bus in

Tel Aviv or at the World Trade Center in New York or on a flight from Manilla to Tokyo?

Or in this London Underground train?

Wouldn't you sit and watch the people and ask yourself a million questions?

31 DAVE (AND DAVE)

Dave is sitting in the corner of his lounge. There's no three-piece suite or entertainment unit. The television picks up almost no channels now. There is a coffee table, but it's really a foldable camping table. The top is tacky with spilled wine and beer and juice.

He sits in the corner on a single mattress. The stains look like shit and blood but they're not. He doesn't know what the marks are because they were (probably) there when he got it, though he can't ever remember buying or finding or stealing it.

It's just there.

Like Dave. There. On that mattress. There is no sheet but he has taken to sitting on a plastic bag because he's pissing himself in his sleep more and more, recently. Could be the imaginary tumour or the very real Pinot Grigio.

Dave is there. Drinking and staring at the wall. He's telling it to 'fuck off' like he can see somebody he doesn't like.

He's there.

He's also out in the hallway by the front door. He's added another bolt, and a long screw splinters through the door on a diagonal and fixes it to the frame. This Dave has also hammered a flat-headed screwdriver into the wood as a final layer of protection.

Nobody coming in. Not his bothersome kids. Not his landlord. Not the noisy neighbour who is always having sex and listening to loud music so that he can't hear the Daves shouting their obscenities in his direction.

Dave at the door stares at Dave in the corner of the lounge.

'Who the fuck are you looking at, eh?'

Dave in the lounge, peering through the wall, takes a mouthful of wine and whispers to himself, 'What's it gonna be then, eh?' And he laughs at himself. And he drinks some more. And he doesn't answer the other Dave, who tuts loudly, opens the cupboard next to the front door where the vacuum used to live and the half-sized ironing board that came with the rented property. He opens the door and looks at the three pillows on the floor, steps in, pulls the door closed behind him and lies down.

He's not tired but he can't sit with Dave when they can't even watch Channel Four. The only one they can get now is Channel Five but it's ghosting the History channel.

The neighbour is singing again. At least it's just him. Two weekends ago, he went through every duet in the complete back catalogue of musical history while his girlfriend tried to harmonise. Piss-drenched Dave hated it, but sleep-in-the-cupboard Dave half respected their tenacity, if not their talent.

One in the cupboard, hiding from the outside world, in the dark, alone and afraid. And one in the lounge, sitting on a plastic bag, drunk out of his mind and laughing at the faces he sees in the wall and the words he hears in his mind. The Daves are there, and they're not.

There's a tumour and there's not.

There's fear and there's not.

Hope. And not.

And the neighbour sings, '*I don't wanna know 'bout evil, only want to know about luh-uhve.*'

And Dave in the cupboard hums along, though he has never heard the song before in his life. And that hum resonates in the other Dave's head, pulsing across the synapses of his brain and electrifying the inoperable growth as the inside of his skull desiccates with every new swig of cheap vinegar.

He looks up at the skylight, and his vision blurs. There are no more faces in the wall. The weight of his head and his troubles pulls him backwards onto the mattress. He looks over at the cupboard by the front door.

'What's it gonna be?' he whispers, as he wets himself again before falling into drunken slumber.

And the neighbour sings, '*Yes, it's getting hard to listen. Hard for us to use our eyes.*'

And the other Dave is asleep, too.

And he's not.

32   THE OLD MAN (AND THE DOOR)

Saul wakes up early. Sore head. Guts wrenching. Hell looks a lot like his bedroom. But there's no fire, no choking smell of sulphur. It's not like they say in The Book.

He stares at the ceiling.

There's no Ada.

Of course. Why would she be in Hell? She was perfect. She was kind. She couldn't help that she died. Even when she was frail, Saul thought of her as the strong one. She would never swallow down a bunch of pills. How stupid?

He feels like crying but he can't. Too dehydrated. There's no liquid in Hell.

Then he turns his head to the side and sees a glass of water on the bedside table and two pills. And he remembers. It's not Hell. It's somewhere else. The in-between.

For the undecided.

The unsure.

The unworthy.

Saul hoicks his failing body to a seated position. He drinks the water and blindly swallows the pills he assumes are for the pain in his head. He finishes the glass and hopes there is enough moisture in his body to produce a tear for the wife he longs to see again.

The place is silent. Saul's hearing is not what it used to be, and he strains for some sign of life other than himself – he isn't sure whether he is technically living but he doesn't feel fully dead yet, either.

Birds tweet outside his window and cars drive by, but Saul wants to hear something so much that it can never happen.

He stands up. Still in the clothes he was wearing when he dizzily writhed around on his kitchen floor, his body convulsing to evacuate his stomach of the poison he had ingested, his mind fighting to keep it down and follow through with the plan to end everything.

The old man needs to wear glasses all the time. It's difficult to see things far away and he needs a different lens if he wants to read. He can't hear the traffic outside but his nose still works and he knows that the smell in the room is definitely him. If only there was sulphur to obscure it.

The pills have not kicked in yet.

The old man gets to his feet. He has no socks or shoes. If his eyes could focus on the state of his feet, he'd know that they are responsible for at least thirty percent of the putrid aroma of his Purgatory.

It's difficult for Saul to comprehend how long he has been in this state. Days? Weeks? How long until they decide? He recalls waking up before and calling out for help or guidance, but he doesn't want to do that again.

The bedroom door opens as easily as it always did.

'Where on Earth did I put my glasses?' Saul chastises himself, inwardly, feeling around the door frame to steady himself.

There are two figures in the living room, entwined in one another. Saul remembers them and how they have been there for him and he doesn't want to disturb them now and he needs more water and the pills are starting to take effect. His head still hurts, because they are not painkillers, though the old man will forget about his pain soon enough.

He walks past the sleeping angels and out into his hallway. Then down the stairs, which leads to his front door and the world outside. And he fumbles with the chain and feels around for the bolt as spots of colour dance inwards from the periphery of his already blurred vision.

'Hello?' he asks out loud as though he can see somebody on the other side. 'Hello?' he repeats, his voice croaking. He drops to his knees and pushes the letterbox open. He calls out a little louder. The old man wants to shout for his wife but is paralysed by the fear that she won't answer.

It looks just like the world out there. The way it has always been.

Grey London sky. Blurred buildings. Yellow spots creeping in from the edge of his vision. The pills doing their job.

Then a hand on his shoulder.

Saul, still on his knees, looks up. The male angel extends a hand, which the old man takes and is led upstairs. There is no threat, no anger that he went to the front door. It is gentle. Kind. Gracious.

This time.

Just a few more pills and Saul wouldn't be here. He would be surrounded by fire. Or he would be in an eternal nothingness. Perhaps he would be reunited with his Ada. He can't know without talking to God.

Later, when his vision sharpens and his consciousness returns, he does know one thing, something he unearths from deep in his drug-addled brain: he would be better dead than stuck within this endless purgatorial loop of misery and monotony, yet there is a door that will lead him out.

33   RODS (AND CONES)

Achromatopsia is a disorder of the retina – the tissue at the back of the eye, which is sensitive to light. It is a result of a change in certain genes. The doctor goes through the names of these genes. A series of numbers and letters that mean nothing to any patient, but the professionals like to show that they know what they are talking about.

Then there's some simple science for the layman.

The retina contains two types of light-receptor cells. Rods and cones. Rods provide vision in low levels of light, and cones do the same in brighter light. Imagine that one is for night and one is for day.

A mutation in any of the genes the doctor rattled off to the sportsman will affect the cones and their ability to react to light. In some cases, these cells become entirely non-functional. The result is a complete lack of colour vision.

Total colour blindness.

'So, I'm a mutant?' the sportsman bites.

'That's not what I said.' The doctor is scrambling. Achromatopsia is not a common condition, and he has not had a great deal of practice explaining the intricacies. If you need him to inform a family that a loved one died on the operating table, he is well versed.

'You poked and prodded me and you've tested things. So you're saying that one or more of my genes have changed and now I can't see properly?'

'There are no identifiable mutations that we have found.'

'So, how did I end up like this?'

'We don't know.'

The sportsman recalls a story about Bob Marley and how he was playing football one day and stubbed his toe during the game. The shock to his body manifested itself in a cancer that killed him. Something like that.

And he thinks that perhaps the same thing has happened to him. One moment he is young and fit and his athletic life is spread out ahead of him. The next, his tibia is protruding through his leg and his foot is facing backwards. That's a shock. Psychologically and physically. He doesn't have cancer and he may never play sport again, but there is no colour in his life.

It's all washed out.

Black. White. Greys.

Except for Vashti. Technicolour Vashti. But he doesn't want to tell the doctor about that now. Because if it isn't a mutation in his genes and there is no medical explanation, then it could only be a gift from God.

34 VASHTI (AND THE FADING COLOUR)

Then Juned phoned.

'Vash. There's a call for you. Some guy ... Ned.'

Vashti took a moment to realise who that could be – it had been almost two years since she had spoken with her brother. The other nurses were throwing teasing looks her way as though she had another man on the go.

'It's my brother,' she mouthed, walking towards the nurse who had taken the call.

'Ned?'

'Vash. Hi. You okay?'

'Ned, is that you? Where are you? What have you been doing?' She wanted to scream at him, *TWO YEARS AND YOU ASK IF I'M OKAY?*

'Slow down. Slow down. I'm fine. I'm fine. I just wanted to let you know that I'm doing alright. But I'm moving again.' He was speaking to her as though they were still close, like they had kept in touch and his sister knew anything about his life.

'Moving? Where are you moving to? I don't even know where you are.' She knew that she should stay calm, not alarm her brother, who had shown himself to be impulsive and prone to outbursts, but handling him with care hadn't worked before, so why would it now?

'Calm down,' he instructed. 'I shouldn't even be talking to you. I just know what you're like – you worry, that's all.'

The problem was that Vashti used to worry. She used to care. She used to think about the welfare of everyone around her. She used to feel compassion and hope. But he took that all away from her.

So she didn't want to *calm down*. And she wanted to know why her brother would think that he shouldn't be talking to her, a career nurse, a guardian of the sick and broken. What had she ever done that was so awful, her own brother would treat her this way?

She told him this. All of this. With other nurses watching her and listening. Vashti couldn't contain it. She needed to vent, to get it out. Somewhere she thought it might jolt some sense into her wayward sibling.

'I shouldn't have called. I won't again.'

That was the end.

And all the progress she had been making evaporated. She started smoking. Because if she didn't care about anyone else, then there was no need to care about herself.

It has been three years since that call.

To Vashti, it feels like thirty.

35 NARRATOR?

If everyone is just waking up and taking pills or getting medical advice, how am I already on this train? Did I leave? And if this backpack contains a bomb, why did I not detonate it yesterday? What am I waiting for? Do you think it is because I am scared? Aren't all suicide bombers scared? Is it only in that moment before death that we find the courage to question things we have ignored in life?

What is the route back from apathy?

Is it fair to say that people assume the way to a brighter existence is through empathy? But are we asking too much of a doomed race? Could we start with something smaller like compassion? It's too difficult to make people care but could we make them understand?

Should we aim lower?

Could I reduce all that is wrong with the world into 140 characters? Should I film a twelve-second dance, ending in jazz hands, saying, 'Give a fuck about somebody else'? Should I monitor my food and work out every day, get a six-pack and start preaching? Would people listen then? Or would they only take in part of the message because their attention span can't even last the length of a Ramones song?

Does anybody see me here?

Can I be stopped?

If a butterfly can flap its wings one day and the result of that seemingly insignificant moment is a tornado a week later, could a sportsman losing his vision of colour somehow impact what I plan to do? Could an envelope in a letterbox shrink a brain tumour? Could an exploding tongue set an old man free? Could a nurse remember who she really is? Could a broken sportsman run once again?

Could they all be linked?

Could we all be linked?

If that is true and a child falling over and grazing their knee in Burkina Faso results in depleted corn crops in Iowa, how do we stop this generation from believing they are the centre of the universe?

Are these the kinds of questions that a God would ask?

Where is the commuter with the orange script and the pencil? Will I see him again today? Is he significant in any way? Does the turning of his pages cause disruption to the stock market or rig a political election? When I looked forward and two seats to the left, should I have been paying attention to somebody elsewhere?

Who will step on the carriage to interest me when we reach Farringdon?

Are these the questions I should be asking? Is it the time to be reflective or philosophical when my job is simply to hit a red button and move on to my next life?

If a butterfly can cause a tornado, if something so small can have such a giant effect, what, then, is the effect of the tornado? What happens when I blow up everybody on this train? Could I make the world end?

Would that be such a bad thing?

36   THE NURSE (AND THE MEMORY)

People with insomnia end up forgetting things. Their powers of retention aren't what they used to be. Because when we sleep, that is when we consolidate our memories.

Vashti does not have trouble with sleep. She works night shifts, goes home, and she sleeps in the day. If she works all day, she sleeps at night.

But Vashti doesn't have an issue with her memory.

She wants to forget.

And she's a nurse, so she knows how.

Identify the triggers. Memories require these. All the bad shit isn't constantly sitting in the forefront of your mind. It often requires some outside intervention. Identifying these triggers, and their associations, is crucial because you can then suppress them. You break the link with that bad memory. Police who worked the Potter's Bar crash aren't triggered by seeing trains, but the sound of a mobile phone ringing sparks a similar distress of hearing family members trying to reach loved ones who had died on that train.

Talk to a shrink. They don't all want to fuck you or make a mask from the skin on your face to lay over their own. Many want to listen. And they are trained to aid in memory reconsolidating. You can actively recall the trauma you wish to forget, in a safe space. It doesn't get deleted but you are rewired in a way that makes it less painful, therefore, more forgettable.

Suppression through interruption. Exactly what it sounds like. An individual can use reasoning and rationality to obstruct a memory from being completely recalled. Essentially, you shut down the incident before it starts to fully form.

Exposure therapy takes talking to a psychiatrist to a new level. It's most common with people suffering from post-traumatic stress. They talk about the issue. They confront it head on. But they take things further. Patients retell their stories but are then forced to visit locations they have been avoiding as a consequence of their trauma.

This is the opposite of suppression. This is confrontation. This helps you handle what happened to you. Because by making it manageable, you make it more forgettable.

If you are a nurse, there's the possibility that you can get your hands on some drugs. Propranolol is effective. You may see it as Angilol, Bedranol, Beta-prograne or Half Beta-prograne. It is prescribed to help with anxiety or migraines or high blood pressure. It's a beta blocker. It stops the physical fear response.

So, if you are about to enter into a conversation with your therapist about how the priest used to invite you to his chamber after communion, and that memory is as painful mentally as it was physically, popping a propranolol ninety minutes before your session can help. Because it removes the fear response from the trauma, so that eventually, you can remember it without the pain.

The nurse, Vashti, can't remember which of these techniques she used, perhaps a cocktail of each. It doesn't matter to her. She knows that she has access to the medication and therapists and the leaflets and knowledge, but she has no idea what she was trying to forget. She has pushed away some of the things she has seen. She has suppressed the thought of her brother leaving or going missing or moving across the country or whatever it was.

So it worked.

But it has left the carer apathetic.

And the trigger to make people care is something that scientists are yet to discover.

37 THE DAVES (AND THE DOORS)

Dave wakes up in the bedroom wardrobe. It's the place he goes when he's most afraid. But he's confused. He doesn't remember getting here. There are pillows laid out and a blanket that has kept him warm.

He remembers the cupboard by the front door and the mattress in the lounge. He can smell urine but he's not wet. Part of him knows that the smell is him, though. His head hurts like he has been drinking but he knows that he hasn't.

That was the other Dave.

He pushes the door open, cautiously, and waits for a sound. Some kind of a reaction to his movement. There's nothing. Not stirring from the other room. The neighbour must be asleep. Sometimes, Dave can hear the annoying alarm on the neighbour's phone. He changed the sound about three months ago and it's worse than before.

It doesn't go off every day at the same time.

It's so irritatingly unpredictable.

He's wearing one sock. He rubs his pus-filled brain. The goddamned tumour feels like it's growing teeth. Where is the other sock? Why does it suddenly feel so uncomfortable. Dave rubs his foot backwards a few times against the carpet until the sock he is wearing starts to move its way down his foot, eventually falling off the end of his toes so that he doesn't have to bend over and use his hands. So that the blood doesn't have to rush to one of those spots that showed up on his last hospital scan.

And Dave walks out into the hall and looks in the cupboard by the door.

Nobody there.

The other Dave is snoring in the lounge. He smells the piss again and turns up his nose.

Then Dave is wiggling the screwdriver to get it out of its divot.

He's unlocking the bolts and taking the chain off. Dave didn't set an alarm but he does this at the same time every day. He doesn't need an annoying beeping sound. He's not an idiot. His brain still works.

Now Dave is unclicking the latch so he can open the door. He hates that sound almost as much as the neighbour's phone alarm clock. The tiniest snap of metal to release the catch, but it echoes down the corridor.

He watches to see if the other Dave stirs.

He does not.

This Dave unlocks the door, clicks the button to keep it on the latch and tiptoes his way downstairs. He doesn't look back. Has to be quick. Doesn't want anybody to see him. Doesn't want to talk. Doesn't want to be seen. He reaches the ground floor and runs over to his post box. He unlocks it easily with his hand – the key never really worked – and he checks inside.

Nothing. No letter.

The post doesn't ever come at this time. He doesn't even know why he goes to check so early, but it is habit now.

Maybe he's testing himself. Seeing if he still has some bravery within him. It's not a risk because nobody in the building is up at that time. The postman has only just got up. But Dave is out. Out of that flat. Out of that Hell. Out of the confusion of falling asleep in one cupboard and waking up in another.

Away from the other Dave.

The Dave who makes the place stink like a cat marking its territory.

The Dave who drinks so much that they both end up with a hangover the next day.

The Dave who is still asleep on a mattress in the lounge. No covers. No pillow. Just a plastic bag underneath his body to prevent further staining. But it hasn't helped.

Sleep-in-a-cupboard Dave shuts the post box, mumbles something under his breath – his tongue still hurts – and sprints up the stairs as fast as he can. Three flights. He picks up some speed in the middle and jumps two steps at a time but is exhausted by the last flight.

He pushes open the door to his flat and clicks off the latch. He's safe. Back inside with the other Dave, who still hasn't moved.

Wardrobe Dave slams the door as hard as he can then replaces all the bolts and the screwdriver.

He waits. A smile on his face. Cupping a hand behind his ear.

The neighbour stirs and swears.

Dave wins today.

He laughs to himself. When he turns around, the other Dave is there and it startles him.

'No mail today?' the Dave asks.

'Nope. You stink. Let's get you clean.'

38 THE SPORTSMAN (AND THE BLACK-AND-WHITE NURSE)

He was supposed to leave today. The six breaks in his leg had caused him so much pain, the industrial strength painkillers weren't doing what they were designed to do. He was moved to a morphine drip and lost two days of his life to a beautiful haze.

People visited. Family. Friends. Teammates. His coach almost cried when he heard the news that a full recovery was a long shot and chances of returning to the game he loved so much were somewhere between zero and never.

The sportsman doesn't recall any of this. Apparently he spoke with these people, but he feels like he was knocked out for the operation to set his leg in plaster and then slept for a couple of days.

He was due to leave the next day but woke up with no colour. And now he has to occupy a hospital bed while they run some tests.

He presses his buzzer and some black-and-white nurse walks in with her stupid monochrome face. White skin and grey lips. Even whiter teeth as she throws a smile at the unresponsive patient.

'Is everything okay?' A soft Scottish lilt. She leans over and presses a button to turn off the red light by his bed, which indicates he has called for aid.

'Where is Vashti?'

'I'm sorry?'

'Vashti. Where is she? I need to talk to her.'

'She's still on shift. She may be at the nurses' station. Can I help you while I'm here.'

Vashti is outside the hospital, smoking a cigarette and wondering why she seems to care about things, all of a sudden. She has got by for so long by being removed. Now she feels things. She sucks the smoke into her lungs, and her shoulder blades burn.

'No. You can't help me. You've got no colour. I want to speak with Vashti. She's the only one.'

The nurse identifies his agitation. She would love to help, but experience tells her that anything she tries will be unsatisfactory. She can see that he is on the edge. He looks as though he might cry from those innocent and broken eyes.

'Let me find her for you. You want me to refill your water before I go?' She looks over at the tray at the bottom of his bed. He could do it but it's a pain with the cast over his leg.

'Er, yes. Okay. Water would be great.'

She has to smile on the inside so that he doesn't notice her counting the win. She fills his glass and pulls the tray closer to him.

'There you go. I'll find Vashti and get her to come to you.'

'Thank you.' The sportsman takes a swig of his drink and lies back into his pillows. He's grateful to the greyscale figure heading out into the hallway.

He waits.

When he knows that she is definitely gone, he starts to cry.

39 THE SON (AND THE KEY)

Guilt only has an immediate power. It's fleeting. It cannot endure.

Take a look at Ash. When Ada passed away, he was sad at losing his mother, of course. Devastated, in fact. Perhaps more for Saul than himself, but he certainly had his own grief to deal with.

He also had guilt.

There were times towards the end where there was an opportunity to see his mother and he chose the ease of his daily routine. He opted for time with children who were not fulfilling him and a wife who existed in the home they had tried to build that was now nothing more than a house where their clothes and electronic goods were kept. Sometimes, he even prioritised his work; the job he had grown to hate almost as much as he hated himself.

Then, when his father's mental state was in clear decline after losing the great love of his life, as Ash saw that vibrant, passionate man slipping away, he told himself that he wasn't going to make the same mistake again. He would not put anything above seeing his father and ensuring he got as much as possible out of whatever time he had left. But, of course, that was guilt talking.

So it never happened.

He needed compassion.

Guilt is fleeting. Passion endures.

But today, something clicked. Saul hadn't answered the telephone and he had not called back, so Ash was worried. And, while worry can be as debilitating and useless as guilt, it can promote more immediate action.

Ash stands at his father's front door for a few moments, breathing deeply and composing himself. He rings the doorbell a couple of times and bangs his fist against it as an encore because he knows that his father doesn't hear as well as he used to.

Saul is the centre of a blur in the Hell that is his sweat-drenched bedroom. He thinks the doorbell is a sound within his dream.

The fake angels sit on the edge of the sofa, holding hands and waiting so see what happens. The door is locked. Nobody is getting in. Or out.

Ash tries again. The bell. His fist. He crouches down and pushes the letter box open, shouting through: 'Dad. It's Ash. Are you there? I wanted to check on you because you didn't return my call.' Ash puts his ear to the open letter box. The lying angels do not make a movement. 'Dad?' he calls again. A moment later, the letter box shuts and Ash is lost.

But he has a key.

Ash looks through the bunch of keys in his pocket. There are two that he doesn't recognise. He tries the first one. It scratches around the keyhole but doesn't go through.

'Fuck it. Not that one,' Ash talks to himself.

Nathan panics and stands up. Lailah keeps hold of his hand, her squeeze telling him not to blow this. His eyes saying, 'He has his own key to get in.'

Ash tries the other key that he doesn't recognise. It goes into the hole but won't turn. He gives it a wiggle in case it is stiff through misuse. It isn't. It's the key for a padlock, which secures a storage box that holds a bike Ash was going to use every day to get fit but only used twice.

He checks the time on his phone. He's going to be late for work. He's annoyed but partly proud that he chose his dad over his job, for once. Ash thinks about calling his wife now, she will know where the key to Saul's place is. She's good at that sort of thing. But he places the phone back in his pocket, drops to his knees, lifts the flap on the letterbox again, and listens for a sound.

Something.

Anything that will let him know that his father is okay.

He waits for the tell-tale sound of shuffling feet, but there is nothing. He can't hear the held breath of the pretend angels.

He thinks about trying one more time. Shouting a little louder. Instead, he tells himself that he will call his father again tonight, and if there's no answer, he will have to speak to his wife and get the key, so that he can come back.

Unless his worry fades or turns back to guilt. And he leaves his father to wither away in an opiate-fuelled departure. Perhaps his father's death would be the catalyst for change, this time. Maybe he would work harder at his marriage. Or give his children the attention they require and deserve.

It is more likely that he will walk the path of self-reproach. A journey that ends in stagnation. The long road to the middle.

What matters to Ash at this moment is, simply, this moment. Whatever is driving him, whether it be guilt or compassion or the need to prove something to himself, he wants to get one thing right. And maybe things could snowball from there. Start with something small. A flutter.

He resolves to return with the key.

Ash would help his father, this time.

He leaves for work and the angels let out their breath.

40 NARRATOR?

Are you keeping up? Wouldn't it have been easier to tell each person's tale in its entirety before moving on to the next? How boring would that have been, though? Wouldn't the stories lose some of their tension? Would your brain have wandered or switched off if you hadn't had to constantly think and analyse and remember things?

Do you have a favourite? Is there someone you look forward to hearing about more than the others? Are you intrigued by the Daves? Do you wonder about the significance of the neighbour? Is the post box important or just a character quirk?

Have you stepped back to notice the similarities? Is there a way that all of these people could be linked?

Do you ever step back in life? Do you try to listen more than you speak? Has it become more difficult over the last decade? If you see a picture or a status that you like online, do you ever hover over the button and wonder what your double-tap could mean?

What motivates you?

Have you been contemplating the difference between guilt and compassion and how it leads to action or inaction? Are you worried about Saul? Do you want him to get out? Where would he go? How do you feel about justice? Do you hope something happens to the fake angels? Do you have one that you dislike more? Is it Nathaniel?

If I tell you that I feel most drawn to Vashti, does that impact your opinion of her story?

Or is it me that you're waiting for? And have you realised that you are answering every question as you read them, at the speed of thought?

If I am not on that train and am merely the narrator of a novel, then who is going to blow it up? Where is God? As jobs go, narrator is much better than suicide bomber but surely not as good as God? Could He end up hating His job the way that Ash hates his?

If I look around the carriage and don't like what I see, I can reach into my backpack and press the red button, but why do I hesitate? What do I need? If I press it now, do the other stories end? Is that it? Or would we carry on without a God? Isn't that what we are doing, anyway?

41   THE SPORTSMAN (AND HIS GIFT)

The sportsman cries because he's lost.

And sportspeople, true competitors, never like to lose.

He had a gift. A talent, for those who believe in such a thing. Yes, he had always been able to run faster than anybody else, but being fast doesn't make you the best. It doesn't even make you good.

His coach had said to him, 'It's not a case of being able to go from nothing to top speed, you have to be able to go from fast to even faster.' He was right. It was coaching talk, but he was right. It was more than that, though.

It was about balance.

With an open pitch in front of you, it is not difficult to push into the ground and really open your legs to pick up speed. When there is ten inches of room down one side and you have to tiptoe along the side line without setting a foot into touch and still maintain your blistering pace, that's the thing that sets you apart.

It was about your lines of running. Knowing when to take an opponent on the outside or whether to cut back in and go against the grain. It was knowing when to sidestep or drop the shoulder or dive for the line. These are the things that a coach can talk to a player about, they can draw on a whiteboard or revisit some old video footage, but it can't always be taught. And, with the sportsman, it never had to be. It was there. He looked at that pitch and he knew.

He knew.

Somehow, he could see where the ball was going a split second before it happened. He understood the possibilities and the lines he could run that would make him look faster than his opponent, even if he wasn't.

And that is just the beginning.

The talent isn't enough. It never is for those who need true success. Skills can still be honed. It becomes about hard work. And there are always other players working hard to get close to you, so you have to work even harder to keep that gap between you and the chasing pack.

And it's harder because you have less room to grow.

You are in the top percentile.

But the fact that very few reach your level means that a slight increase in your ability to read the game and act accordingly can take you further than others can even dream.

The sportsman had all of this. The gift, the drive, the work ethic. He'd had it since childhood. But none of this prepared him for that small section of the pitch where the ground was a little softer, where the mud could grip your boot so firmly that your foot would stay locked as the rest of your body twisted in the other direction and the bones in your leg snapped and splintered and poked through the flesh.

And that's why you cry in your hospital bed.

You did what you were supposed to do. You gave it your all. You didn't owe it to the world to use the gift you had been blessed with but you owed it to yourself. It was everything.

And then it was taken away.

When everything is taken away, you know what you are left with.

So you cry in your bed. Because you worked hard and you succeeded. Because your body was strong and now it is broken.

Black and white.

You no longer see.

42   THE NURSE (AND HER SPORTSMAN)

Vashti throws three pieces of mint-flavoured gum into her mouth to disguise the smell of her habit and returns to the nurses' station.

'There you are. I've been looking for you. Your boyfriend needs you.'

'What? Did he call? Is everything okay.' Vashti: Caring.

'Oh, no. Not your actual boyfriend. I'm joking. The sports guy. I think he's got a thing for you, Vash.' Her smile and soft, Scottish accent are immediately disarming. 'Doesn't want to see anybody but you.'

'Oh, give it a rest. He's a good kid and he's going through an ordeal. I was just there when he woke up.' She feels herself start to blush and feels stupid for doing so. But she has agreed not to mention that she is appearing in colour to the man who, apparently, can only see things in black and white. It was his idea. He doesn't want to be prodded any more. He just wants to know where the rest of the colour has gone.

Vashti steps out from behind the counter, there are sick people everywhere. It's as though she is only noticing this fact for the first time.

'It's busy today, right,' she states.

Another nurse shrugs. 'No busier than usual.'

The Scottish nurse grabs Vashti by the arm and leans into her, speaking quietly, 'Be careful with him. He looks fragile today. I think it's all coming home that he might not play again. He's either going to blow or break down.'

Vashti nods in understanding and takes off down the corridor, noting how noisy it is with patients outside the x-ray room, and visitors wandering around, and doctors and clipboards and vending machines and water fountains and pain and anguish and heartbreak and cancer and it is overwhelming, and she needs a distraction. Something to dampen her senses.

He is propped up by a few pillows, so he is neither lying down nor standing up. Vashti can see that he is staring at the ceiling, perhaps searching for a God who is not there, his body shaking slightly as he lets the tears run and fights off the sobs.

The sportsman can sense his angel immediately and turns towards the entrance to his ward. Across from his bed, a middle-aged woman is closing the curtain to give the man she is visiting some privacy. She looks at the sportsman like she knows him but also like she hates him.

He is just relieved to see some colour.

'Vashti. They found you.' His face tries to brighten but his eyes are red and bloodshot, and he looks awkward as he tries to sit himself up. For someone usually so in control of every part of their body, Vashti empathises with how difficult that must be.

She has to check herself before blurting out that she was just outside smoking a cigarette or three, her insides held together by nicotine.

'They did. Why did you call for me? Are you in pain?'

He is in physical agony. The bones in his leg wanting to fuse back together stronger at the points where they have broken. A dull and constant ache from his ankle to his knee. But he is two hours away from his next dose of co-codamol.

'Of course. It's constant. But that's not what I need you for. I just feel so incredibly ... shit.' Silent tears fall from the corners of his eyes. 'I know it's happening. It's weird. I know that I feel something like depression, like, I know it's there, but there's nothing I can do about it.'

'It could be because of the morphine. We are still waiting on the results of your scan, but this may be some side effect to the thing that's going on with your vision.'

He begs her to get him something. He can take the pain in his leg but he can't take this. Just a little something to lift his mood.

'I can't just get hold of prescription medicine, I'm not a doctor.'

'But you know where they keep it.'

'Yes. In the pharmacy. With the pharmacist. Locked away.' She can see the desperation through the tears.

The sportsman has spent his entire life feeling special. He has something that others did not.

Direction.

So many people never find this. They coast through life, no ambition to go higher, go further, do better. Do good. They're content. Part of having a talent is never feeling truly satisfied. Wanting to do more. Be more.

Suddenly, he is not special. He cannot move fast. He can't even walk. He is worse off than somebody who is average. That's quite a fall. Add an opiate comedown into that mix, no wonder he feels so worthless.

'I'm not talking about the hard stuff, just something to take the edge off this edge.'

The nurse takes a seat next to the patient. She places both her hands over his and looks at him deeply and with nothing but concern and the most profound compassion. And she speaks softly but severely, telling him that he does not need medicating, that he is strong, stronger than he understands. That his leg will heal. His mind will heal. And his heart will heal. That it may take some hard work but he knows what it was to work hard.

And he feels her warmth and what seems like love. And part of the weight lifts. His leg even seems to stop aching in that moment.

'You're here for me, Vashti. You're going to save me, I just know it.'

She knows it, too.

43   DAVE (AND THE WIND ON HIS FACE)

Not everyone can be saved.

One of the Daves buys bread, ketchup, four packets of smoked back bacon, no fruit or vegetables, salt and vinegar crisps, a packet of pork pies, two litres of semi-skimmed milk and a jar of bolognese sauce. He manages to squeeze it all into one carrier bag and walks home.

The air on his face, the sun in the sky, Dave feels a sense of freedom. He doesn't feel scared like he does in the flat. He spends most of his time afraid to leave the confines of his home, but when he does it – out of necessity – the anguish and anxiety that plagues him dissipates.

He's alone.

Only one Dave.

He forgets about the giant tumour on his brain and his exploded tongue. For a moment, he is himself. Alive. There are no thoughts about the future, there is no hope or desire, it is just about now. A brightness. Clarity.

He crosses the road, turns the key that opens the front door to the building and sees the neighbour descending the stairs. Something pulses under his skull and everything unpleasant about his life returns. The hallway darkens. He senses the other Dave. The smell of his neighbour's aftershave forces him to hold back a dry retch.

'Morning, Dave. Out for an early shop?'

Dave lifts the bag up. 'Ran out of the essentials.' The six-pack of crisps pokes out the top of his bag and the neighbour can't help but grin. Not in a judgemental way, more as an appreciation that Dave considers snacks as essential.

At this point, Dave could have said nothing. It would have been a cursory exchange between acquaintances. A 'Morning, how are you? Good, you? Yeah, good, thanks' moment. Over. Get on with your day.

But you can't have such a meaningless chat when the person you are talking to knows about your condition. When you have heard the noise his girlfriend makes when she is brought to fruition. They are neighbours, and a lot of the time they each despair at the irritating existence of the other, but they can't just blow past.

It is Dave that takes it further.

'Off to work?' He realises at this point that he doesn't know what his neighbour does for a living. He has heard him throw up in the night, defecate, sneeze, cough and fuck, but he's never asked what his job is. And the reason is that Dave is a talker.

'Just heading out for a bit,' the neighbour responds, offering no information.

'Yeah, well, you might not see me much soon.' Dave can't remember whether he has already said this to the neighbour or not.

Bigger lies lead to a deeper, darker pit.

'Oh?' the neighbour offers so that Dave can continue his lie.

'I have to go into the hospital for a week or two.'

'That seems like quite a long time.'

'Yeah, I need to be monitored and they're trying something new. The doctor said that it could take a week, maybe longer, I've got some time off work but I might have to leave altogether.'

It is at this point that the neighbour realises that he has no idea what Dave does for a living. He has seen him, on occasion, with a tool belt and toolbox, wandering back from the train station, swaying slightly from side to side as though he has been drinking all day. One time, Dave walked right by him without acknowledgement, which seemed odd because he usually has an elaborate story to tell.

The neighbour has heard Dave swear at himself, shout at the other Dave, play his music, cough, hack, spit and slam doors, but he has no idea what he does for a job, whether he even has a job, what he keeps in that toolbox. And the reason is that Dave is a liar and the neighbour enables him.

'God, Dave, that sounds intense. I've got my fingers crossed for you, man. I guess you have to try everything, right?'

'That's the idea. Anyway, I won't keep you. Going to make myself a decent breakfast.' And he lifts the bag of sliced pig, cow juice, processed sauces and white carbohydrates again.

'Sounds like a plan.' The neighbour walks down the remaining two steps and past Dave. 'See you soon, okay?'

'Sure thing.' And Dave slumps back into a hunch as the door closes behind him. He carries the bag up the stairs, the handles cutting into his hands, and he wonders whether the neighbour feels as free as he did for being outside in the world.

By the top, Dave is panting and his forehead is sweating. He opens the door and is hit by the smell. He looks into the lounge. Nothing. Then to his right, where the other Dave is standing in the kitchen doorway, wearing only a T-shirt and socks.

'Where the fuck have you been? I just shit a pint of blood.' He is the worst of Dave.

'Across the road to the shops to grab us some food and milk.'

'It doesn't take that long. Are you sure there isn't something else?'

'Something else?'

'I heard voices.' It's accusatory. The other Dave wants to make a joke about sanity but bites what is left of his tongue.

'Where did you hear voices?'

'On the stairs. Downstairs, on the stairs.'

'Just now? I was talking with the neighbour. There's no getting around it if he's coming down when I'm going up.'

'You talk too much. You'll get us caught. You'll get us kicked out.'

'He's harmless. He doesn't care about us.' He starts to take the shopping out of the bag and line things up on the kitchen worktop. 'I'm going to make bacon sandwiches. Do you want one?'

'You're trying to change the subject.'

'I'm just moving on because there is nothing to talk about.' Dave continues to unload the shopping. He puts the milk in the fridge.

The other Dave doesn't like it.

'Don't turn your back on me.'

'I'm just putting the milk away.'

The other Dave, the angry one, the drinks-three-bottles-of-wine-and-shits-blood Dave, grabs calm Dave by the shoulder and pulls him around so they are facing each other. And he repeats, 'Do not turn your back on me. I'm talking to you.'

'The neighbour is fine, I—'

Sleeps-on-a-plastic-bag Dave grabs sleeps-in-a-cupboard Dave by the throat and pins him to the fridge. The carton of milk drops to the floor.

'You don't know him. You don't even know you. You think you're so clever with your conversations and your lies and your bacon sandwiches. If we get thrown out of here, I'm going to kill you.'

Strangled-against-the-fridge Dave tries to push strangler Dave away.

'You idiot. I'm the strong one. I push you. Not the other way around.' And he slaps the other Dave around the face. And the other Dave doesn't like it. And he pushes again. And he swipes the hand from his throat. And then he is punching and rolling around on the floor in the spilled milk and shouting, and no neighbours can hear him.

And when he is finally exhausted, he remembers the breeze on his face and the freedom he felt outside. Then he's hammering the screwdriver back through the door frame and imagining the sweet release that his own death will eventually bring.

44 THE SON (AND HIS TUNNEL VISION)

Ash contemplates his own death, too, but feels he has so many problems, so many issues, that dying still wouldn't solve them all.

As soon as he rounds the corner from his father's home, Ash stops worrying about him and starts thinking about himself. He's already late for work and he still has half an hour of travel left. Maybe he could call in and say there is traffic or rail issues or someone has jumped off a bridge onto the tracks. It could be a thing, there were those people on Chelsea Bridge the other month and then another two at the Millennium Bridge.

Dropping like flies.

He's anxious. What if he gets sacked and then can't afford to live in the house he bought. The one with all the space to get away and the room to hide. The one with two lounges. The one that used to be a games room and a quieter room for reading and relaxing. The ones that are now separate living areas for Ash and his wife, so they don't have to be around each other all the time.

They don't like the same kinds of TV shows any more.

They eat at different times.

They go to bed hours apart.

What if he loses his job, loses his money and loses this lifestyle?

Ash slows down.

What is he really hanging on to?

He puts the phone back in his pocket, deciding that he doesn't need to explain himself at this instant. Besides, if his boss or his team were worried in any way, they'd have phoned him by now.

Ash descends the stairs. He taps his wallet against the yellow circle and the barriers open to let him through to the underground station. He stands to the right on the escalator and lets the ones in a rush strut past him. The posters on the wall that line his descent are all for the same show. A film from the eighties that has been raped and bastardised and turned into another god-damned musical. Are people not writing any new plays?

He stares over at the other side. The people ascending, going up in the world. He catches a glimpse of a woman. Mousy. Wearing glasses. He thinks she makes eye contact but quickly adjusts his thinking and believes that she was disgusted by his appearance.

And he'd have to agree with her.

There's only so many times you can get beaten down. There's only so long you can put up with being treated without respect.

Ash isn't doing anything to help his situation. He is dwelling on things. Ruminating. Taking root. And it is this kind of selfishness, this apathy for anything that gets in the way of him basking in his own misery, that prevents him from seeing the wonders around him.

Being so self-absorbed can often mean that you miss the important things that are directly in front of you.

Ash doesn't usually travel to work via his father's home and has to stop like a tourist to see which platform he should use. He waits next to a giant poster advertising a novel ghostwritten for some celebrity that other, genuine writers have quoted as being 'smart' or 'funny' or 'a thing of pure joy', not because it is smart or funny or joyous, but because they want an association with some drivel they know will be marketed to bestseller status.

The train pulls into the platform, and Ash spots a woman a little further down wearing some kind of headscarf. He doesn't know if it is a hijab, a khimar, a niqab or a burqa, he has no idea what religion the woman may be a part of, but he doesn't care. It is just something he notices before he steps onto the carriage. A moment when he forgot to worry about himself.

Then he's looking around for a seat because he knows there are another eight stops before he has to get off. He would usually remain standing but it's already been a taxing morning. There's a seat right in the centre, between an elderly woman reading a book and a young man with ridiculously large headphones.

Ash sits down, tilts his head back and shuts his eyes. He can feel the old lady close to him. But he cannot hear the music from those giant headphones, and, with his eyes closed and his mind on himself, he cannot see what is directly in front of him.

1st April 2023

<u>Surveillance</u>

This document will be available in the public domain once completed. As such, the ISC will not publish information that is to be redacted. However, there are instances where certain information will not be shared as a matter of national security and to safeguard the extent of MI5 capabilities with regards to levels of surveillance and other activities.

The phone records of the attackers have been examined and cross-referenced. There are no instances where one bomber called, messaged or emailed the other. None of the phones were on a monthly contract. Most made calls to family members on 20th July – the day before the attacks. (The families are being re-interviewed.)

Two calls were made to the same number several minutes before detonation. One from the Jubilee Line bomber and another from the bus at Holloway Road.

Eyewitness and survivor statements have a common thread regarding the flash of white light that came before the chaos, and those who recognised they were under attack speak of a 'glazed' or 'dead' expression and how the bombers seemed 'removed' from what they were doing. These descriptions, however, are inconsistent with those for both the Jubilee Line and Holloway Road detonations.

Immediate thoughts suggest possible second thoughts, followed by coercion on the calls.

The number dialled was also a 'burner' phone and shows a link between the separate attacks.

No evidence has been uncovered regarding the possibility of an alleged accomplice who opted out of the attack.

45 GOD? NARRATOR? VOYEUR?

Who just got on? And what is he doing? Is he looking at the ceiling? Are his eyes closed? Did he see me when he stepped into the carriage? Is he avoiding my gaze? Could it be that he is suspicious of me?

If I was the narrator, wouldn't I know that the man directly opposite me is Ash, the son of Saul? I definitely would if I was God because He knows everyone and everything, right? So, He would know that Ash's father was on the other side of that door, in no fit state to answer or be heard? Why would He allow that to happen? Why would I? And if I am God and I appear to be caring about injustice and the lives of others, does it seem plausible that I am here to take the lives of as many of these people as I can?

But then, if I am a common pickpocket or terrorist – as I suspect mostly likely I am – then how would I have known that Saul's son is sitting opposite me, that he is contemplating his own demise and that he has not noticed me yet?

Does God know more than a narrator?

Why am I focussing on Ash when almost everybody else on this train is more interesting than he is? If he gets the key from his wife and manages to make it inside the flat, what happens then? Can he save someone, like Vashti is trying to save the sportsman?

If I tell you to imagine a racist, what image springs to your mind? Is it somebody real who is known, globally, as a bigot? Or do you make somebody up in your mind? Are they a man and are they white? How old are they? Are you, yourself, falling foul of stereotyping?

Do you know the difference between a hijab and a niqab? Or, like Ash, do you not care? And when you say that you do not care, do you mean it in a they're-all-the-same-kind-of-thing way, or is it more that you don't care because you are happy for people to go about their business, dressing and believing whatever they like?

What if everyone could feel as free as Dave does when the wind is on his face?

If everyone was free, what would happen to fear?

Would it die? Or can it not be killed?

Is everyone being free too much of an extreme? And does 'extreme' always mean 'trouble'?

If I told you now that two men have stepped on at the next station and will not stop staring at the woman, sitting on her own, minding her business, wearing a hijab, would you fear for her safety? Can you already feel how intimidating they are? Can you really empathise with what she is going through?

What do they think they will achieve by trying to frighten her like that? What has happened in their lives that they think it is normal to behave in a threatening way to anyone? Is anyone else on the carriage seeing this? There is an air in here now, am I right?

Why are Ash's eyes still closed?

If somebody else sees what is happening and does nothing, aren't they just the same as Ash?

Why are people who care called snowflakes?

And what's the deal with people saying things like, 'I say what I mean, and if you don't like it then you can fuck off?' Is freedom of speech now freedom to be a dick? Do you have to say and share, in some way, everything that goes on in your mind?

Was the staring not enough? Do they have to take it further because she was too brave? What do they mean with the pig noises? Are they saying she is fat or ugly or smells like an animal? Are they calling her an animal? Is it something to do with meat or the foods they think she cannot eat? Am I overthinking the actions of a couple of Neanderthals who don't even know why they allegedly hate her?

What am I feeling now? Is it anger? Pity? Confirmation?

Is she going to get off at the next stop even if it's not the destination she had planned? Can somebody tell them how ridiculous they sound saying that stupid word when they have no idea what country she is from? It's possible that they are from the same country, isn't it? Would they listen if you told them that? Is it only a matter of seconds before they tell her to go back to where she comes from? Is it this kind of behaviour that got me here, on this carriage, in this seat? Or am I more aware of it because of the reason I am here?

Why is everybody sitting still? Why will nobody step in and help her? Should I do that? Is this what they call bystander behaviour? Or is it pluralistic ignorance? Are they the same? Are we all just waiting for somebody else to step in? Do we all want to be saved? Does charity start at home?

Why am I shaking so much? Is the sweat from my anger or my adrenaline? When did I flip that metal upwards with my thumb? Why is that thumb now hovering above the red button?

It isn't time yet, surely?

Is killing them the right thing to do or am I wasting my opportunity on a couple of nobodies?

What would Jesus do?

If He does come back, will we kill him again?

46 VASHTI (AND THE COLOURS)

She sees everything in bright technicolour now. As if the entire spectrum of light that the sportsman is missing has been added to Vashti's vision. Every person has an aura, a colour that is specific to them and their situation and their outlook and their personality. She is yet to decipher what they mean but certain people on the same ward have a similar pigment.

She assumes this is sickness.

This is disease.

The horror.

It feels like something she has experienced before. One of the things she has forced herself to forget. It reminds her of war. She can't quite recall the sadness she felt at losing her brother.

Wrong crowd.

Wrong ideas.

Vashti can see everything in front of her: the patients in the hallways, lying on their gurneys; the ones screaming in their beds, calling out for a nurse, any nurse, begging for an end to their suffering; the hospital staff weaving through the carnage, trying to appease everyone; doctors and clipboards and bad food on trays and plastic cups of water next to paper cups of pills, and the rainbow of signs showing which direction to walk to get to paediatrics or cardiology or neurology or, Vashti's least favourite, oncology.

But that is only what is there.

She can also see the things that are not there. Or perhaps they were once there. Maybe they haven't yet happened. An image of a wartime hospital that overlays reality. She looks back at the sportsman. He is lying on his side, staring in her direction, a smile on his face. She soothed him. She helped. And it felt good.

What doesn't feel good is the sight of the burned and broken soldiers. Blood and bandages. And in the empty hospital bed that was meant for Saul, there's a beautiful, young American man, gauze across one eye and his head wrapped in a white dressing.

She knows him. Somehow.

She sees him when nobody else does.

Vashti could help him, she could help all of them. And then she remembers something. Not everything. Nothing specific. But she remembers helping and caring and wanting the world to be a better place.

And how tiring and thankless that can be.

And how it makes you want to not care.

And forget everything.

47   THE FAKE ANGELS

Nathaniel and Lailah see each other. And that is enough.

He sits on the edge of the sofa, she straddles him and wraps her legs around his back. They look into each other's eyes as she slides herself back and forth, slowly.

They don't need anything else. They are wrapped up in one another. They are entwined. Their bodies. Their souls. Their collective fate. They have started something and they have no idea where it is going to lead them. But they are not even thinking about that.

Blinkered millennials.

Decisions are made in an instant. Everything is now. How do we feel *now*? What are we doing *now*? What can we have right *fucking* now?

They know the old man is in the room next to the one they are having sex in. They are not thinking about whether he will wake up or if he can hear them. He was passed out earlier, and they left some food on the side with water and more pills.

He could choke or overdose or slip and crack his head. They will deal with events as they happen.

In some other version of things, Saul is really dead.

They're not worried about Saul's son calling again because they have unplugged the landline phone. If he comes back with a key, it's not a worry because they have put the chain on the door and Nathaniel had the idea to hammer a screwdriver through the frame. The son left. If he was that worried, he'd have stayed and waited for the police to arrive.

Nathaniel tells her that she 'feels amazing' and that he is 'close'. Lailah puts her hand between her legs and tells him to wait. Hold on. 'Let's get there together.'

In that moment of orgasm, when you are, for a moment, nowhere, with no thoughts, but the purest sensation of pleasure coursing through you, that fleeting moment of purity, that everything and nothingness, where nothing else matters but that point in time, that is how the fake angels always feel.

And it is wise and healthy to live more in the moment, to put the phone down and stop scrolling through lies, but these two, young and in love and stupid, they have messed with the natural order of things. They have saved a man who was not supposed to be saved.

He wanted to leave.

He wanted to see if he could be with Ada again.

They stopped it from happening. And now they are just winging it. Which is fine. If they hadn't cheated fate.

Their unwavering focus on one another has left them blind at the periphery.

48 THE COMMUTER (AND THE RACISTS)

Thomas Davant steps onto the train. His face is buried within that orange-covered script he is always reading and scribbling in. Two white men in suits get off the carriage, walking either side of him. They deliberately bump their shoulders into his to knock him off balance. But they don't get the reaction they wanted, because Thomas Davant is focussed on his work.

He also saw it coming. He's not an idiot. He could see them approaching him and braced himself for impact. Just as he saw the man the day before, one seat in front and three to the left, taking a particular interest in him and what he was reading. And just as he heard the two Neanderthals croak some phlegm from the backs of their throats and spit at one of the carriage windows.

There's an empty seat immediately to the right. Beside it sits a woman whose head and neck are covered with a black material; she looks nervous.

'I'm sorry, would you mind if I took a seat here, next to you?' Thomas asks, though he is perfectly entitled to sit wherever he likes. He sees the relief wash over her and he sees the mucus dripping down the glass behind her, and the two idiots on the platform, laughing with each other.

The meek and clearly disturbed woman nods at Thomas Davant, almost imperceptibly.

'Actually, it's okay. I forgot something.'

Everybody on that carriage saw what those two racist bullies did to a defenceless and innocent woman and they looked on. They waited and nothing happened. Thomas Davant hadn't seen it but he knew what had happened from the fear and resignation in the young woman's eyes. And he didn't like it.

Just as silently as he had entered the train, he exits. He steps off, minding the gap, and then he runs. His orange script in one hand, a pen in the other, he runs. Straight at those oppressive imbeciles.

Nobody hears what he says, but those vermin turn around to see who has said it, and before they can register, Thomas Davant has hit the biggest one on the chin and sent him backwards. The smaller racist, in shock, freezes to the spot. Davant gives him a chop to the throat and kick to the stomach. It isn't fluid martial-arts movement, Davant has no idea what he is doing. It is adrenaline and anger and instinct.

There is a beeping on the tube and the train doors start to close. The passengers look on and just manage to see the larger bigot sucker-punch the theatre lover from behind before his partner wades in with some wild punches and kicks to the ribs.

People on the platform walk on by. Just as they had not got involved on the carriage, they do not get involved on the platform. They are late for work or are scared or don't want to spill their coffee. Or they are checking texts. Or, worse, they stand and film it. Great for evidence or identifying the perpetrators, but it isn't helping poor Thomas Davant as a size-nine loafer stamps on his elbow and snaps his arm.

That's not being a bystander. That's not waiting for somebody else to intervene. And you're not doing it to help the police. It is morbid fascination. It's counting up your 'likes' before you've even posted. You are part of what is happening now. You're on the inside. You are every kick to the head and stomp on the stomach.

If you let things happen, you're saying that it's okay that it happened.

If you don't speak up then you can't speak out.

The train pulls into a tunnel.

A commuter, talking into a Bluetooth headset, steps over Thomas Davant's lifeless body as though avoiding animal excrement on a footpath.

The cowards have gone, and Davant lies on the cold concrete, his script still in his hand, bleeding and broken and waiting for his Good Samaritan.

49 TERRORIST?

Did I just see what I think I saw? Is there good in this world? Are there people who do not sit idly by and, instead, are compelled to action? There are 450 deaths per day as a result of cancer in the UK alone, twenty-one percent of people are obese and, therefore, at a higher risk of heart disease and other illnesses related to their weight, but how many die as a result of apathy, of not caring, of accepting?

When did people stop caring about other people? When did they become okay with their misfortune?

Does there always have to be a balanced view?

Should Thomas Davant have left the situation alone? Should he have sat down next to the woman from a culture very different to his own and talked to her? Should he have tried to confront her or console her in any way?

Does violence beget violence?

Are their people looking at him and thinking that he should not have stopped so low? That he was in the wrong? Was there another option? Could he have tried to reason with them? Educate them?

What do the other racists think?

Should we care about what they think? Are they below us? Could they have been taken in by an idea at a time when they were feeling low and alone? Why would a God create so many races and diversity and not have them be thoughtful and embracing of one another?

What if I am just like those two? What if I am one of the disenfranchised youth, drawn into an ideology because I want to feel a part of something? What if I have been brainwashed to hate a certain group of people so much that I am willing to take my own life in order to make a statement as I end theirs?

How are you picturing me now? I'm still a man, right? Have you narrowed down my ethnicity, yet? You're either thinking brown-skinned Muslim or white skinhead, a tattoo of a swastika on my chest, hidden by the clothes I am wearing, is that correct? You don't hear about too many female suicide bombers in this country, do you?

But think about those two men in their designer suits and ties, did they look like the people who would oink at a stranger before hocking whatever was in the back of their throat in her direction? Did they seem like the type to rain down blows on a smaller, weaker man until he blacked out?

Could I not be a woman? Could I not be a straight-laced, homophobic, Christian woman?

What has happened? Who has their claws in us? Where is free thought? Why did nobody try to help that woman on the train? Why did people walk around Thomas Davant? If you were God and your project had gone so terribly wrong, would you not have given up by now?

If the great love of your life had been wrenched from existence by illness, would you have waited two years to try and end it because there was a possibility you would be reunited?

If you had seen war and destruction and needless killing in the name of profit or religion or oppression, would you not find a way to forget it? Would you not try to disappear and make a new life for yourself where you wouldn't have to think about it, you wouldn't have to care any more?

But if that was your intention, why would you choose a profession like nursing, where you would undoubtedly be jolted from your indifference at some point? If you didn't care, why, in all the world, would you choose to work in that particular hospital?

If you had a low chance of survival from a brain tumour, would you try everything you could? Would you blast it with radiation and try any experimental drug or treatment? Or would you live hard? Would you make use of the time you had left?

Or would you lock yourself away in a cupboard?

When is it right to just … give up?

And how is Saul's son still asleep through all this?

50 THE SPORTSMAN (AND THE HOPE)

The toes on his right foot have turned blue. (A darker grey.) The cast is too tight around his foot and is cutting off the circulation. The sportsman manages to reach a hand down and pull at the opening of the cast. Immediately, he feels the blood pool into his foot. It hurts. Not like normal pins and needles where there's a fine line between the pain and the tickle, this is all agony.

Through the blur of discomfort, the sportsman can see that the bed across from his has finally been filled. A man, similar age to him, perhaps a couple of years older, lies sleeping. His eyes are puffed and purple, his lip is cut, there's a bandage on his head, his elbow in plaster. Even in his slumber, he looks uncomfortable. Like there are further injuries that the sportsman cannot see.

But the sportsman is mesmerised by what he can see. It's not a lot, it's not vibrant, it's not everywhere, but it's there. A glimpse. A glimmer. Of colour.

Only around the edge of the injured man. The sportsman tells himself that he can see a faint green colour. Everything else is still black and white, but this new patient, he looks pretty beaten, but there is some green there, he's sure of it.

If you believe there are seven chakras that deal with trust, sexuality/creativity, wisdom, love, communication, awareness and spirituality, any sight of a green hue would suggest peace, compassion or healing. And if you've just been kicked half to death by a couple of racists, you would hope to have an aura that suggests you are getting better.

But other beliefs are not as positive. Green can also mean deceitfulness or jealousy. It's difficult to believe that somebody deep in medicated sleep would feel those emotions, though.

Isn't the joy of faith and belief that there are so many to choose from? We decide what it is that we believe in. Even choosing not to believe is a viable option.

There is beauty in diversity.

One of the problems with faith and belief is that there is so much choice. Like anything that is given away for free, it is abused. People pick and choose. You can decide to love thy neighbour and also decide that you are not required to love them if they are two people of the same sex who happen to share a bed.

But there is a power in having the freedom to decide how you want to believe and what you want to have faith in. What's missing is the compassion to accept and even embrace the differences.

The sportsman doesn't think there is a God, he is not a person of science, nor does he worship trees or meditate to such an extent that it opens his third eye.

The bones in his legs have been broken, his dreams have been shattered and his vision has altered, but he thinks that he is seeing some colour. Colour that isn't just his nurse, Vashti.

And that's enough.

Even if it is his mind playing tricks on him, even if he is seeing what he wants to see, the sportsman believes it. He has faith in it. And in his faith, green means hope.

51   SAUL (AND THE WAY TO AIR)

Purgatory is no fun. It's the soul's equivalent to being put on hold when you call your internet service provider.

You can't see a way out.

But for Saul, there is. He saw it yesterday and he will see it again today. It's a door. His front door. Just walk through it, Saul. Step into the light. Feel the air on your face.

He does the same thing. First, he notices the stench in his one-room palace. Then he sees that he is still wearing the same clothes. Then he registers that the smell is him.

He feels the pain in his skull, his brain rattling around inside, it feels dry. He spots the glass of water and the pills. He knows he shouldn't have them on an empty stomach but he seems to recall eating something the night before.

Then he's on his feet and trying not to make a sound and stepping out of his confines into the kitchen he'd promised Ada he would decorate but never quite got around to finishing. And he sees the naked angels, seemingly innocent in their lack of attire. Pure. Yet something tells Saul that it is best to tiptoe past and not disturb.

Experience.

Instinct.

The drugs start to take effect.

He slides the chain across, clicks the latch upwards to unlock the door, turns the handle and pulls.

Nothing.

It won't budge.

He tries a little more force. There's some wiggle but the door does not open.

Yellow spots creeping in from the corners of his eyes. A colour that can denote optimism in some beliefs and indecisiveness in others. Saul is somehow both.

He looks down and sees the problem. A screwdriver has been hammered through the frame and into the door, wedging it shut. From the outside, it would be easy enough to kick the door and force it open. The motion of pulling is much harder and requires a strength that the old man does not possess.

He leans down to try to remove the tool from the wood but Nathaniel grabs his crepe-paper-skinned hand before he can get any further.

'Got yourself lost again, Saul,' he tells the old man, as orange hexagons dance across his eyes. Orange: ambition for some, lack of will for others. 'Let's get you back upstairs, shall we?' He places his hand tenderly on the old man's back and leads him up the stairs.

Saul obliges. This is his routine now.

Wake up. Feel like death. Drink water. Take tablets. Creep past naked angels. Failed escape attempt. Led back upstairs with stars in his eyes and a nice male escort. Back to bed. Pass out. Wake up to a sandwich on the side, its corners starting to curl. Repeat until Heaven or Hell is ready to take you.

Or the old man can change something and hope for a different outcome.

He decides that, tomorrow, he won't take the pills.

The patient opposite the sportsman wakes up, his head pounding, his eyes throbbing and a stabbing pain in his ribs as he tries to push himself up to a seated position.

'Ah ... fuck.' He exhales his words through gritted teeth.

'You okay over there? Need me to call a nurse for you?'

'That's very kind of you but I'm almost there.' He pushes the pillows together behind his back so that he can rest against them. 'It seems I have a broken arm and possibly bruised or even broken ribs. They weren't like that when I was last awake.'

He's so matter-of-fact it takes the sportsman a moment to register.

'What happened to you, if you don't mind me asking?'

'Couple of racist idiots. I got a few decent hits in but I guess I never really stood a chance?'

'You were beaten up for being white?' the sportsman asks, genuinely.

'Oh, God. No. Don't. It hurts to laugh. I can see how you got the wrong end of the stick there.' He laughs again and grimaces. Then, Thomas Davant explains what happened in the Underground station.

'It wasn't anything to do with you and you knew you weren't going to win...' The sportsman trails off.

'Yeah. Sounds about right. I mean, I didn't think I'd end up in hospital, of course.'

'I'm sorry you got hurt, but what were you thinking?'

Thomas Davant explains that he wasn't thinking, he was doing. He was acting. That there are so many people with opinions and solutions but remain passive. 'They don't march against injustices. They don't campaign for rights. They piss and moan about everything that's wrong with the world and let it stay that way.'

The sportsman is captivated.

Davant continues. 'If you're worried about fish dying in the ocean, stop using plastic. Better yet, stop eating fish. If you're tired of hitting all those potholes on the way to work, write to your local councillor. If you're worried about homeless people in the winter, get out there and help serve some soup or volunteer at a shelter. Just. Do. Something.'

And he explains that when it registered what had happened to that poor, frightened woman on the train, that everyone in that carriage must have been thinking that it was atrocious behaviour, but they just sat there, hoping it would go away, he couldn't do the same.

He hadn't heard what the men had said to her or the noises they had made, but he saw them laughing and he saw her cowering and watched as their spit trickled down the window behind her head, and he couldn't be a bystander.

'I'm not a violent man. I'm not a big man. I don't know how to fight. But if you let bad behaviour go unchecked, it will continue. And it will get worse. And when it comes to bullies and bigots, there is no reasoning with them. They only respond to bricks and baseball bats to the head.'

'You're a regular fucking hero, man.'

'It's a sad time in the world when doing the right thing has been elevated to the status of heroism.' He looks saddened by such a concept. Like he doesn't understand where or when humanity went so wrong. Davant's thoughts are simple, perhaps naive; it still troubles him that Eve took a bite of the apple.

'I'm not talking about trying to jump two guys on your own, that was idiotic, they could have killed you. I mean your outlook. I think we'd be better off if there were more like you but, sadly, it seems that, everywhere you turn, there are more like them.' He nods his head to the side as though gesturing towards the racists in Davant's story.

They talk across the ward for the next hour like they're old friends. Both equally enthralled by the other. The sportsman has to bite his tongue about Thomas Davant's green glow and feels like he is lying.

Thomas Davant sees something within the sportsman. No glow.

No aura. But something he admires. Perhaps the will to listen, perhaps the unwavering self-belief and drive. Both of them, in different ways, men of action.

They're disturbed by a nurse and not the one the sportsman wants to see. Not the one with the soft Scottish accent, either. Another one. A harsh one. She tells the sportsman that the tests are inconclusive and they cannot determine the cause of the recent loss of colour in his sight, but his leg has been set and he has his crutches and they will prescribe him with some extra-strength painkillers.

He has to leave. Or, as the harsh nurse puts it, 'You are free to go.' What she means is, 'Get out, someone else needs this bed.' She asks whether he would like someone to take him in a wheelchair when he leaves. He politely declines, saying that the crutches are all he needs. The sportsman had been brought in an ambulance, and the hospital would pay for a cab to take him home.

Then she leaves.

'Looks like they want me out. Back in a week for a check-up on my eyes and three weeks to go down to a half cast.'

'That's not what you wanted to hear?' Davant asks.

'It's fine. I was expecting it. The pain is subsiding in my leg and I can get around on these things.' He picks up the crutches. 'I just wish it hadn't been her. I was hoping to see Vashti before they pushed me out the door.'

'Vashti?'

The sportsman tells Thomas Davant all about the magical nurse, how caring she is, how extraordinary she is, how she seemed to take away his pain with her soothing touch. And, because he felt a connection with Davant, so didn't want to lie any more, he says, 'She's the only thing I can see in colour.'

Davant understands.

53 ASH

Apathy is a slow death, but who cares?

Action can mean that you get beaten up at a train station or break your leg in a sports game, and your death may come quicker, but at least you have lived.

Ash is not a doer. He has stagnated. He's like a tick in suspended animation, frozen as life passes him by. He somehow managed to zone out on a train carriage during a racist confrontation, a fight, and the death stare of God (or the terrorist in the seat opposite his.)

When he gets to work – late – nobody even notices. Ash's colleagues care about him as much as he cares about his place in the world and his impact upon it. He could have used the excuse of the disruption on his journey, but there was no need, the sales director at DoTrue comes in whenever he likes. He will put his feet up on his desk for half an hour, go and talk to the sales team and make some inappropriate jokes that they have to laugh at, then maybe he makes his way to finance and customer care.

The finance director is just as bad. He is conscientious enough to get the first tee time at his golf club in the morning, but it still takes a few hours to get around the course. Then shower. Then, apparently, bath in old spice before turning up in the middle of winter with a bright-orange tan.

Of course nobody notices that Ash was half an hour late.

He is of no consequence.

It's the same when he gets home. His kids don't come running out of their rooms to greet him. His wife is on autopilot. She's not happy to see him but she's not disappointed. She doesn't want him to hitch up her skirt, right there, and give it to her in the hallway, but she's also not dead between the legs.

They are functioning.

Through dysfunction.

And this is entirely common.

Ash's wife kisses him hello and asks him how his day was at work. Because that is what she is supposed to do.

He doesn't answer her question. Instead, 'Do you know where Dad's key is?'

'I'm sorry?'

'The key to Dad's place. We've got a spare. I popped over to see him this morning before work and there was no answer.'

'Before work? You didn't tell me that you were doing that.'

In her mind she's thinking, *And what else aren't you telling me?*

In his, *Fucking hell, Margaret, what has that got to do with the location of the key.*

He chooses not to respond straight away. Take a breath.

'I mean, I'm glad that you made the effort with him, I'm always saying that you need to speak to him more. He's not getting any younger. You used to be so close.'

Ash doesn't want to hear that.

'So, you know where the keys are, then?'

'Yes. They're in the cutlery drawer. There's a pot of keys in there for various things.'

Ash makes his way over to the drawer, while his wife continues to blather about nothing.

'They've got a red plastic keyring with his house number on.'

The first helpful thing she has said.

He pulls out three sets of keys he's never seen in his life and throws them on the kitchen counter. And there, at the bottom, a red plastic keyring. He turns it over. Number forty-two.

'Got it?' Margaret asks.

'Yes. Thanks.' He puts the unknown keys back. He'll never use them.

'Dinner will be about thirty minutes.' She knows when her family is due home and she prepares things accordingly. It may sound outdated but it's important to her. It's the way for her to show that she cares.

Ash thanks her again and says that he just needs to freshen up. It's not much but he has a plan of action. It's not much of a plan, and it doesn't involve that much action, but it's a start. Ash will eat whatever gluten-free, superfood-enhanced concoction his wife has been slaving over for hours, then he will leave his family at home and head across town with the number forty-two key.

And this time, he will help his dad.

This time he will speak to him; he will be a good son. Worthwhile. He will get into that flat. Even if he has to kick the door down.

54   THE COMMUTER (AND THE VISIT)

At the moment Saul's front door gets kicked open, Thomas Davant is talking to Vashti, the nurse that the sportsman said was 'magical'.

'Some of the nurses think you are very brave but I have to say, I think it was a pretty stupid thing to do.' She doesn't sound judgemental, she sounds like she cares.

'You know, I get that comment a fair amount, too.' He smiles and disarms his nurse. It's not the first time he has done something like this. It's all so simple to him. Black and white. He wants to be a good Christian, but over two thousand years have passed, and it no longer pays off to be a Christian who tries to act as their Christ would.

Davant doesn't think of himself as brave or heroic or even stupid, he was acting how he would expect other people to act, seeing a person in distress. In his mind, doing nothing when you see something is wrong is worse than trying to help and making a mistake.

Love your neighbour as yourself.
Do unto others what you would have them do unto you.
The opposite of love is indifference.

What if that person receiving abuse was you, would you want help? What if it was your friend, your child, your sibling? Would you want somebody to step in and say something rather than step over them?

Times have moved on, perhaps too quickly. There are handfuls of believers who would do the Christian thing, who stop, who would help, but there are many more who would step over or walk on by.

You can't just tell people to 'be kind'.

You can't *tell* them anything.

'The guy who was over in that bed with the broken leg, he called me an idiot.'

'He was a smart guy.' There's a knowing glance between them.

'He wanted me to give you this.' Davant leans over to his orange script and pulls out a piece of paper that Vashti assumed was a bookmark. 'It's his number and his email address. He said he knows it's unconventional, but you helped him so much and if you could at least speak to him before he comes back next week…' He trails off, not knowing how to finish, hoping she will fill in the gaps.

'I know how to get in contact with him.' And she places a hand on his. And he feels a release in the stab of his ribs. And she burns up a little on the inside, though you couldn't see it on her face. And Davant tells her, 'He mentioned about his sight.'

'A very rare condition.'

'I'd say. There can't be too many people who see everything in black and white but see the colour in you.'

Vashti takes her hand away from his.

'He told you about that?'

'And he said that you were magical.' A moment of silence. 'I think maybe he had a bit of a crush.'

The tension eases.

'That's what the other nurses tease me about.' Vashti fake rolls her eyes. 'Now, get some rest, you've got a sponge bath tomorrow unless you can show some movement on your own.

Thomas Davant watches her leave the ward. His vision is fine, even with two black eyes, but he still sees Vashti's colour.

55 GOD?

Did Thomas Davant stand out for me on the train that time because he would eventually become entwined in the story at a later date? Or was it simply that his orange script caught my eye? Is there such a thing as destiny? Is the path laid out? The story already written? Or did I affect things? Did I bring Davant into this by noticing him?

Have you heard about the law of attraction? Doesn't it make more sense to have faith in that, faith in yourself, than throwing it away on a God who is out of touch, and lacking motivation?

If I am a parent, gossiping in the school playground, waiting for the children to go inside to learn, isn't it obvious that my behaviour will attract other gossips? If I am prattling on about the intricate details of my recent home extension, isn't it only right that those with something interesting to say will not form a part of my group?

Do we only mix with our own kind?

Why, then, do they say that opposites attract? When you see a couple and one is conventionally beautiful while the other is not, what does this prove? That physical attraction fades or becomes insignificant? Does courage play a part?

Does anybody grow up to be the thing they wanted when they were six years old? Why do people define themselves by the job that they do rather than the kind of person that they are? What use is it to tell somebody that you work in HR or finance?

Would you not rather be defined by your passion?

And do the people with no passion congregate? Do they meet up and have passionless conversations about nothing? What's wrong with that?

And if you have been blessed with vigour and a lust for life and justice and honour, would you not, somehow, through no effort on your part, merely by putting that out into the universe, be greeted by others of that same ilk? Could you bring that out in another person? Do we all have these qualities inside, lying dormant, waiting for the right person to open them?

Could a colour-blind sportsman unleash something forgotten within his dispassionate nurse? Could he be a catalyst for change? Could he remind her that she is magical? That she could make more of a difference?

Are these things really linked or do we force the things that we want to see onto a situation?

What's that called?

And will everybody wait and say nothing if I stand up on this train right now and say that I am going to blow myself up at the next platform? Or will there be someone like Thomas Davant, who will try to stop me?

Can I be stopped?

Is it already written?

He doesn't say where he is going, only that he is going *out*. Ash is fumbling with the number forty-two keyring in his pocket and is anxious to get to his father. And it's nothing to do with guilt this time.

He takes the tube in the opposite direction to that morning. It's almost empty.

No terrorist.

No God.

No narrator.

Just Ash and another guy with oversized headphones. A man around his age is flicking through a *Metro* newspaper that somebody left on their seat when they got off. And two women are reading novels he has seen posters for on bus stops and train platforms.

It's dark but the light is on in his father's lounge. It wasn't on in the morning, Ash would have noticed. His father must be at home.

He taps lightly on the door. Five seconds later, one of the fake angels turns the light off.

'Dad.' Ash knocks louder. 'I know you're in there, you just turned the light off. What's going on?' He waits, thinking he sees a shadow coming down the stairs to open the door.

Nothing.

'Dad?' he tries again. 'I'm coming in. I need to know that you're okay. You can't keep avoiding me.'

Ash pulls the key from his pocket and twists it in the lock. It turns with ease but the door won't open. He pushes harder against it. The top half of the door is moving but the bottom appears to be stuck. Ash pushes harder, holding the top half so that he can look into the flat through the gap. He wants to see his father.

Something is holding the bottom of the door. He knows his dad's place. There's no bolt on the door, just a chain. Why would he have had a bolt fitted? Unless he felt unsafe for some reason.

He pushes the door again and feels the bottom loosen, slightly. Maybe his dad screwed the thing in himself.

'If you don't come down and take the bolt off, I'm going to push my way in. Dad?' He waits. 'Dad?'

Nothing.

Ash pushes the door hard, but only the top moves and it feels as though the wood might snap or splinter in the middle. He doesn't want to leave his father with a broken front door, especially if the bolt is there because he is worried about his own safety.

He kicks at the bottom where he thinks the bolt is. It isn't a bolt, it's the screwdriver, wedged into the wood. And, with each kick, it loosens slightly until Ash gives it one final thrust, making the door swing open wildly as he loses his balance and lunges into his dad's flat.

Ash manages to stop himself from falling by placing his hands against the wall. When he steadies himself, he turns to the stairs. There's somebody there. He expects to see his decrepit old dad. But it's not. A young man lurks in the shadows.

'Who the hell are you and what are you doi—'

Before Ash has time to finish his sentence, Nathaniel pounces. He's slight and wiry but manages to push Ash to the ground and get on top of him.

Now what?

Nathaniel instinctively places his hands around the intruder's throat. And he squeezes. But Ash, though older and out of shape, is a naturally bigger man. He moves his weight around all day. He has the strength to do that and has more than enough strength to bat away the fake angel's hands, reach up, grab a clump of his stupid long hair, pull him down and roll himself over to have the advantage.

Ash's own instinct is to hit the stranger trespassing in his father's house. But he's never really punched anybody before. He screws up both fists and starts lashing at the angel's beautiful, androgynous face. Sometimes connecting with the knuckles, others with the fleshy part of his hand as he hits downwards like he is trying to hammer in a nail.

He doesn't hear the woman. She is not wearing any shoes and she descends the stairs at pace but with light feet. The screwdriver that was kicked out of the frame is lying on the floor at the bottom of the stairs. All Lailah can see is the back of a large man, he is kneeling on Nathaniel and hitting him repeatedly.

Her instincts kick in. She doesn't strangle or hit or jump on Ash's back. She doesn't kick or shout or speak or scream for help. Lailah picks up the screwdriver and, with two hands, thrusts it deep between the shoulder blades of the man beating down on the love of her life.

He screams a scream to wake the dead, to wake an old man dosed up on opiates. Saul stirs in his bedsit Purgatory as his only son reaches behind his back – a futile attempt to save himself. Lailah kicks him forwards. His face smashing into Nathaniel's below.

A voice inside her: *But you, take courage. Do not let your hands be weak, for your work shall be rewarded.*

She lifts her foot, her right knee come up as high as her chest, before it comes crashing down on the back of Ash's head, cracking his face into the floor. She does it twice more and then he stops moving.

Lailah closes the front door to Saul's flat and slides the chain into place. Nathaniel has been knocked unconscious and lies on his back with a middle-aged man spread over his front, bleeding and dying or dead already.

She needs a moment. To collect herself.

The fake angels will eventually manage to drag Ash into a corner and throw a blanket over him. A cotton-pad solution to the stab wound of their predicament.

57   THE DAVES (AND THE SCREWDRIVER)

And then the Daves.

The neighbour is listening to music while he makes dinner. Dave sneaks out, runs downstairs, checks the post box, finds it's empty – as it almost always is – runs back upstairs and into the flat.

Lock.

Lock.

Lock.

Screwdriver.

The other Dave is getting an early start on the cheap white wine in the living room. He has laid out his plastic bag on the mattress in case there are any accidents again.

'They don't deliver at night, idiot,' drunk Dave says under his breath.

'What are you mumbling about, now?'

'I said you're an idiot.' There's a bite to wine-swilling Dave's words that the other Dave doesn't like. He's sick of the venom and backchat. He's sick of living with the drink and the piss-stained mattress and shitting pints of blood and the threats and the pushing him up against the refrigerator and being told to fuck off all the time.

He doesn't want to live with this Dave any more, he has enough to deal with.

End-of-his-tether Dave leans his head into the lounge and says, 'Hey, Dave, why don't YOU fuck off?'

It's so out of character that pessimistic Dave is taken back for a moment.

Then he clicks into reality. Their reality. Their form of warped, tumour-fuelled reality.

'What did you just say?' He stands up, the wine bottle in one hand, staring intently at doorway Dave.

'I said, why don't YOU fuck off, this time.'

The neighbour can't hear. Onions are sautéing, guitar is playing, a man's voice, low and hypnotic, sings, '*There's got to be a way for a lazy face to get up, start loving the human race. There's got to be a way for a crazy face to get out from under this paper chase.*'

Wine-bottle Dave attacks, running straight at the doorway. Hallway Dave braces himself for impact. They collide, just as they did in the kitchen, when both had got their hits in, spat their vitriol and seemingly got the poison out. But things are boiling over again.

Next door: '*There's a man in the station and a train in the rain, there's a face in the mirror that's showing the strain.*'

They roll. They punch. They bite and scratch. The bottle breaks. Glass digs into fed-up Dave's back as he looks up at the housemate he no longer wants, straddling his chest with a shard of glass in his hand.

He freezes. The sharp edge pressed into his cheek.

'I hope you've learned your lesson, Dave. Talking like that to me. I should cut your throat.' There's saliva forming in the corners of his mouth. It's disgusting. He pushes the glass into the cheek to make Dave start bleeding.

'I hope you're sorry. I hope you're going to get me some more wine after making me break that bottle.' He runs the glass down the other cheek as though tracing the tear tracks he envisions on his vanquished foe.

On-his-back Dave says nothing. He just looks up and stares. He doesn't want to show any fear. He doesn't want the other Dave to know that the cuts hurt.

'Are you going to cry?' Drunk Dave teases. 'I can see something in your eyes but I don't know what it is. You want to hurt me? You want to try your luck? Come on then, coward. Give it a go. I'll let you have a free shot, you sad little waste of space.'

Then, a voice from the kitchen. 'Hey, Dave?'

Violent Dave takes his eyes off pushover Dave for just a split second to see who is talking. Which is long enough for cut-cheeks Dave to reach back towards the door, pull the screwdriver from its hole and jam it through the temple of the bully on top of him.

Dead Dave releases the glass and flops to the side, the screwdriver poking out the side of his head. Killer Dave gets to his knees, both cheeks bleeding, and he bends over to whisper in the other Dave's ear.

'Why don't YOU?' he hisses, holding back a smile.

Then the voice again from the kitchen.

'Dave?' He steps into the doorway. 'What are you doing on the floor? I just wanted to know if you wanted a cup of coffee?'

Another Dave.

Friendly Dave.

Helpful Dave.

Home-economics Dave.

It will all become clearer over time.

Just-killed-a-Dave Dave looks back for the corpse. There's nothing there. Just a screwdriver on the floor and some broken glass.

'Er, yes. Coffee would be great. I'm just clearing this up.'

The new Dave nods and goes back into the kitchen, the sound of the kettle already coming to the boil.

Old Dave picks up the screwdriver – no blood – and pushes it back into the hole in the door frame. The voice in the neighbour's kitchen comes through the wall.

'There's one more circle I'm dying to try. There's a piece of my heart that's asking why.'

Dave goes into the kitchen to meet his new flatmate.

58 NARRATOR?

You don't feel sorry for the Dave that's gone, do you? Is that because he was evil or because you think he was never really there? Which is better? We are not supposed to celebrate the death of anyone, are we? Not even the tyrants and despots of the world? The serial killers? Those who have hurt children? Can we, at least, not feel relief that they are gone?

What about Ash? Maybe you hadn't bonded with his plight enough to feel real sorrow at his inevitable passing? Isn't there that thing where you have to have sympathetic characters within a story to make the reader care? But, if somebody dies, no matter how little we know or understand them, should we not care a bit?

Is not caring at all just as bad as celebrating the death of somebody responsible for human atrocities? Was it not frustrating that Ash was on the verge of discovery? Is your heart with Saul? Because he is old? Because he is being mistreated? Because of Ada?

Do you crave answers to your stories? Does everything have to be packaged perfectly at the end?

What was the song that the neighbour was listening to?

Are the Daves not that strange, after all, because most people now have two or three sides to them, anyway? Can we be who we want to be online? It's much harder in real life, isn't it?

If you could die and come back as any other animal, why would you even bother?

And what's with the screwdriver thing? Do you want to know why they both did that? Are you searching for the link? Will everything be ruined if you never find out what Dave was waiting for in the post box?

What if you thought about everything in this way?

Shouldn't there always be more questions than answers?

Are we all just trying to find out who we are?

A way out of the dark?

PART TWO
THE LIGHT

1   THE NURSE (AND THE HEART)

He traces his fingers along the length of the scar on Vashti's left shoulder blade. She lies, naked, on her front, half satisfied and half distracted by thoughts of her own place in the world. Of the sportsman who lost all the colour from his life. Of the young man who ended up in the bed that could have been meant for Saul.

'What are you doing?' she asks. She knows what he's doing.

'I don't know. I guess ... I like them.' Vashti's boyfriend is genuine. Coy, but genuine.

'You like those giant pink scars that run down my back?'

Basking in afterglow, he responds positively. Enthusiastically.

'Yes. Yes I do. They're ... you.'

They've been together for several years. Vashti appreciates his simplicity. He's more like a dog than a boyfriend. Loyal and trusting and protective. He doesn't push her or pry into her past. She met him at the height of her apathy. And, though she never cared for him in that way, she never fell in love, she found that there was something comforting about being around him or having him around.

And the sex was great.

But on that bed, she sees through him. He is not lying. He loves the scars because they are a part of her. And he wants a child that is made from both of them but is largely Vashti.

She lies there, staring through the man who is drinking her in. He has just finished inside her. He's hoping that one of those swimmers gets through, but Vashti knows they won't. She can't have children. And that's always been something that she has understood. It's the reason she lets him finish that way. There's no danger. She didn't care.

But now she does.

Now she is in colour. Now she feels. Now it is all coming back to her. And she can't allow him to hope. She can't let this kind, tolerant, going-nowhere nothing of a man love her. There's no future there.

She winces.
'Are you okay? Sorry. Did I hurt you?'
Her scars burn.
She can hear his heart beating with compassion.
And the kindest thing she can think to do is break it.

2   THE ANGELS (AND THE FACTS)

Some facts about real angels:

It has never been proved that angels exist. Not even the so-called guardian angels.

That's a fairly important piece of information.

In San Antonio, Texas, near the San Juan Mission, there is a train-track intersection. On 1st December 1938, a school bus filled with children allegedly stalled in the winter fog and was hit by an oncoming freight train. Thirty children were killed.

None have died there since.

People travel from far and wide to drive their car onto the track and wait. They wait to be saved. If they sit there for long enough, the car will start to move. The road is not slanted or angled in a way that would cause the car to roll. It is being pushed. Pushed by the children who perished in that unfortunate accident, just before they were forced to live through a war.

The phenomenon has been tested time and time again. To the extent that a car was covered in flour, stopped on the tracks and, as always, moved by itself to safety. When examined after, there were children's handprints all over the back of the car where it looked to have been pushed.

Some cite the occurrence as ghostly while others hail the children as guardian angels.

However, according to the Bible, God created all angels. And he did it in the beginning, before he even thought about humans. There's no word that He turns dead children into angels, and no scripture that states these heavenly beings should be put to work as a sideshow amusement, pushing vehicles around all day, every day, for the sceptical and curious among us.

Angels do not experience death. They may witness it on an astonishing scale, but they will never feel it. They may also never marry, which is possibly their greatest blessing, particularly for the Catholic angels, who could find themselves stuck in an eternal relationship with someone they never really liked in the first place.

And they may never reproduce. Though there is nothing that says they may not enjoy the perfectly formed body of another angel after taking too many sips at the Eucharist.

While being intelligent and certainly much faster than human beings, angels are not all-seeing, all-knowing and present everywhere. But the true scale of God's army is still unknown. Angels could be walking among the humans. And they have their own will. They can express emotions and take an interest in human affairs.

There could be billions of them.

Watching.

Listening.

Everywhere.

One place they are not, is a South London flat with the number 42 screwed to a door that has splintered near the bottom where a screwdriver was once jammed in.

Another fact, angels do not trick elderly, suicidal men into believing they are dead. Or in Purgatory. Angels do not drug old men and make them wait for God. Or Jesus. Or a sign.

They don't give this to anyone.

Just after the war that the schoolchildren of San Antonio missed, Theresa Munto of Caserta, Italy, experienced an ecstatic moment. This is to say that she was in the presence of something holy. In her case, the Virgin Mary. She was five years old and her father had just given her a beating. Apparently, Mary appeared to inform the young girl that her father meant no harm with the physical abuse.

In a life plagued by illness, Ms Munto was also visited by a saint who loved her, she made statues and paintings weep blood, and developed stigmata on her hands, replicating the wounds of Christ at the crucifixion.

These are signs.

Signs of a higher power. Signs of drug use. Signs of mental-health issues. Of loneliness and torment and the wish for something to be true.

Saul's stomach is empty. He is drugged and doesn't know whether he is hallucinating or he is asleep and dreaming, but he hears a voice that he thinks he recognises. His son, Ash. And he is calling for his father. It is muffled like the angels but it is him.

And Saul smiles because it gives him hope of hearing Ada's voice.

He lies on his back, his wife's face in front of his and his son's voice in the background. It's the first time he has been happy in Purgatory. He is still smiling as the female angel stabs the screwdriver into his son's back.

When her partner comes to, he thanks her and helps her. They drag Ash into the corner and throw a blanket over his lifeless remains.

Of course they are not real angels. They may be faster than the humans they have encountered but they are not more intelligent. They are old enough to marry and physically capable of reproducing.

They have emotions. They can take an interest in human affairs. And they certainly work to their own will.

But they are not angels.

And, the greatest of blessings is that, at least, it means they can die.

3   THE SPORTSMAN (AND THE COACH)

Being solitary physically doesn't make a person alone. One way to define loneliness is in terms of what help a person might require. So, if you look around and can't find a friend or your brother is too busy or your father is too dead, you know you have to do things by yourself.

Dropping off a punnet of grapes at the hospital is one thing, but who will help the sportsman carry a plate of dinner from the kitchen to the lounge while still using his crutches? How will he get in and out of the bath without getting the cast on his leg wet? He would much prefer Vashti to be there with her sponge and warm, soapy water.

He calls his coach.

'You're out already?' He's shocked. 'And what have the doctors said? They didn't seem hopeful when I was in there visiting.'

'Three weeks in this full cast, then they cut it down to below the knee and give me some weird shoe, so I can try to start walking on it and strengthening it again.' This is true. It is the plan. But it's not quite as simple as that, and the real diagnosis suggested the sportsman will never be able to participate at the highest level again. Yes, he will walk again, he may even run, but if he takes a knock to that leg or is hurt badly again, it may require pins through the bones, which will hinder his mobility for the rest of his life.

But he doesn't say that.

Because the sportsman has belief.

Not in a higher power, not some god or deity. Not even in the National Health Service. But in himself. In his drive and his utter need to succeed.

'They always give the worst-case scenario at the start. But they said that I am young and healthy and fit. It's a bad break, but if I do the right things, it could grow back stronger.' Possible. But this was never said to the sportsman. 'I'm going to have to work with the physio, of course. Probably some pool time to begin with, so there's not as much impact.'

'I'll get it set up. This is great news. I have to say, I was worried when I came in. Everything seemed to be pretty black and white.'

The sportsman pauses, looking around, searching for a spot of colour.

'I've got a check-up in a week. I'll call you after and give you an update. I want to get back before the end of the season, coach.'

They speak a little more, and even though the sportsman knows his coach is present, it isn't entirely due to friendship, it is because the sportsman is a commodity. The club owns him. If he's broken, he's no good to them, not important.

He hangs up the phone, grabs his crutches and makes his way to the bottom of the stairs. And, because his upper body is supporting his entire weight in order to move around throughout the day, at least half of him is remaining strong.

The sportsman rests the crutches against the wall and balances his weight on his left leg. He focusses. Takes five deep breaths, and goes. He hops up the stairs as fast as he can. When he reaches the top, he does sixty push-ups. Then he hops back down and does fifty push-ups, the cast resting over the back of his other ankle to keep the weight off it.

Then it's back up the stairs. Forty push-ups.

Down again. Thirty.

Up. Twenty.

Down. Ten.

And he takes back the crutches, makes his way into the kitchen and fixes himself a pint of water.

He will not be beaten by this.

He is determined to make the lie he told his coach the truth.

There is still a lot of work to be done but, he thinks, if he can minimise the loss of fitness by training on one leg, it will cut down the recovery time. If he can stay strong, he can fix his body. Then he can worry about his mind and the lack of colour. No colour but that one nurse, who has left a hole in his heart that he can't worry about fixing.

Vashti knows how to get hold of him but hasn't been in touch. The sportsman isn't one to wait around for something to happen, he makes things happen. He controls his destiny. He thinks about Thomas Davant, in the opposite hospital bed, beaten but positive. Everything he said had resonated with the young sportsman. He should say a proper thank-you.

Tomorrow, he will visit.

So that Thomas has somebody. So that he is not alone like the sportsman.

Perhaps Vashti will be working.

28th April 2023

Why were the bombers known to security services not brought in sooner?

Several of the bombers from the 21st July attacks were known by the authorities and intelligence services through a separate investigation. The investigation in question regarded the plot to detonate explosives in areas of mass population. Eavesdropping and surveillance uncovered talk of the Westfield Shopping Centre in Shepherd's Bush, Stamford Bridge and The Emirates stadiums and Ronnie Scott's club.

Arrests were made before an attack could happen with subsequent trials and sentencing. A large number (in the thousands) of contacts were revealed using phone records and all had to be investigated, many of which were in no way involved. Several of the eventual 21st July bombers were on this list.

Each had been in contact with the police at some time but not for any possible terrorist activity – details can be found in the section 'Who were the 21st July bombers?'

At the time, they were monitored and categorised as '*other* – may be associated with individuals who are directly involved in or have knowledge of plans for terrorist activity'. They operated on the periphery but were not part of a facilitation network. These men were not even seen as *desirable* at that time.

After the failed mass-population plot, with the information available, it was the decision of the intelligence community to continue to gather evidence rather than make further arrests.

4   THE CIRCLE LINE (HIGH STREET KENSINGTON)

Is today the day?

There are plenty of free seats, so why have that couple opted to stand and hold the same pole? Is it because they want to be close? They want to stare at each other, soak up the other person? Is that what everybody wants?

Have you ever met somebody in your life who changed everything? Someone who made you stop, breathe for a second and then see the world differently?

Isn't it always the case with love? Isn't that why love is such an unquantifiable and mind-boggling emotion? And don't you find that one of the interesting things about love is that it happens in an instant; a snap of the fingers and your entire state of mind alters?

What may seem like brainwashing could simply be a case of feeling listened to, couldn't it? Maybe that's what people want most?

Are you scared of change?

If you can change your entire outlook as a result of falling in love, then why can you not do it for other reasons? Can you find a way to quit the job you have hated for the last five years? Can you actively tell yourself that you are feeling better than you are?

There's advertising space all around the carriage for broadband and vegetable boxes and newspaper subscriptions, but what does the one above the lovers' heads mean?

You don't hate Mondays, you hate capitalism?

Has anybody ever looked at one of those motivational posters on an office wall and been moved to action? Don't you hate it when people quote somebody famous in an attempt to portray that they think in the same way but clearly do not have the eloquence to put their thoughts across in such a rousing manner? Has somebody ever said to you, 'As long as you tried your best', and you know, deep down, that it was nowhere near that level of effort?

Can all of this be manipulated?

Do I ask these questions to keep from the truth?

Is it easier to make a difference to the life of somebody else when they are at their lowest? Is that how Alcoholics Anonymous converts so many drunkards to Christianity?

What if you are a young and lonely kid – not quite an adult, but on the cusp – deep into reading and praying, maybe scribbling some poetry, and your faith is important to you but you also feel like an outsider? What if somebody, a leader, someone well versed in the teachings and wisdom of your faith takes you under their wing? What if they convince you that the world you are living in is not right, that you are being oppressed, that the white man is the enemy, that women are worthless?

What if they were the person that changed everything for you? What if they altered the way that you think? What if they washed your brain? What if they got in there with their ideas and hatred grew inside your mind, spreading out like an inoperable tumour?

What if they gave you a vest and a trigger and told you to sit on a train, wait for the carriage to fill, then press the button?

What if you were stupid enough to say yes? Or honoured enough to say yes?

What if you sat on that train and started to have some thoughts of your own?

Would there be a way out?

Would you take it?

Is it too late?

Am I watching every passenger and hoping that one of them will notice me, speak to me and, *SNAP*, change everything?

5   NEW DAVE (AND THE ABSENCE OF FEAR)

New Dave is so nice.

Maybe the best one yet.

He's so positive that it's almost as if he has blocked out the fact that the growth on his brain will eventually kill him.

New Dave is helpful. He's always making cups of tea or coffee. He loves cooking and keeping the place clean. He reads a lot, so the television isn't always blaring out something inane like the home makeover of the fifth-place contestant of some love-at-first-sight car-wreck TV show.

He's quiet and polite and understated, and he even checks the post box twice a day.

But, like drunk Dave, he never goes out. He never sees the sun unless it's through a window, and he doesn't feel the wind on his face or smell the grass.

That's only for the other Dave.

The other Dave, who hasn't slept in a wardrobe or cupboard since his new housemate arrived. They've been sleeping together in the double bed. It's comfortable and platonic. And, for now, means that original Dave is not afraid.

Perhaps the medication is working and that mass in his skull is shrinking.

There's a twenty-five percent chance he could live.

Or so he told the neighbour.

'In the morning, I will make us some bacon,' says the new Dave as he pulls the duvet over his legs and finds the last page he read in his book.

'You don't have to do that.'

'I want to.' He watches as the other Dave gets under the covers. 'Just going straight to sleep?'

'I can't read like you, it makes my brain hurt.'

'That's just it expanding with knowledge.' He smiles. So positive. Annoyingly positive.

Original Dave always gets annoyed with the new Dave, eventually. They look at each other as though they might say 'goodnight' or 'I love you'. And it's not weird but it totally is. And Dave doesn't really remember how many roommates he's had since his diagnosis. And he is starting to miss his pillow and blanket in the cupboard by the front door.

6   MARGARET AND ASH (AND THE DEVILS)

Ash's pocket vibrates for the fifth time as his wife tries to get hold of him. He didn't say where he was going, and she thinks it's unlikely that he will be at Saul's but Ash had been searching for the spare key and he'd been talking about his father a lot, recently. She had noticed. She notices everything.

When he doesn't answer, she tries Saul's landline phone. It rings and rings. He's had the same answering-machine message for years and suddenly there's nothing. She doesn't like it. She feels ill. There's an apprehension inside that she can't explain but also a sense, a certainty, that something is wrong. She can't call the police yet and she doesn't want to leave the house in case Ash comes back.

Ash isn't coming back. The screwdriver is still hanging out of his back and he is crumpled beneath a blanket, pushed into the corner at the bottom of the stairs.

At the top of the stairs, Nathaniel and Lailah are discussing their options.

Lailah is calm.

Nathaniel is panicking.

'I can hear his phone buzzing. Someone is trying to get hold of him.'

'Get the phone and see, then.'

'I'm not touching him.' He shudders.

'Leave it, then.' She doesn't want to roll her eyes but she can't help it.

'How are you so fucking calm? There's a dead man at the bottom of the stairs, his dad is drugged up in the bedroom and thinks he's on his way to Heaven or Hell, or whatever.' The anxious angel points down the stairs. 'I mean, he's got a screwdriver hanging out of him, babe. And we're just supposed to keep living here? We need to get out. Move on. Find somewhere else.'

She takes the suggestion and turns it over in her mind.

'What if it's his wife and they have that "find my phone" thing?'

'It's not that accurate. It can't pinpoint his exact location.'

'Pinpoint his exact location? Who are you, right now?'

She places her hands on his shoulders and steadies him. Tells him that he needs to get a grip and calm down, stay rational.

'I think we are in way over our heads now, that's all. Slipping the old guy a few pills is one thing but it's gone past that.'

She pulls him in to her. Their love for one another is usually so passionate and intoxicating but he is not as strong as her, she knows that, and occasionally he needs to be mothered.

As they embrace, she pats his back a couple of times in a *there, there* way.

'It's going to be okay. We are alright, and that's what matters.' She kisses his cheek. 'But you are right, we have gone past it here. It's almost time to go. We can't leave things like this, though. As blurred as it may be for him, the old guy has seen our faces.'

Nathaniel pulls back from her. 'What are you saying?'

'Come on, Nate, he tried to kill himself the other day. He doesn't want to be here. We need to tie up any loose ends.'

'You want to kill Saul, too?'

'It shouldn't be too difficult, he's old and frail. We can hold a pillow over his face or drop him an extra couple of pills. That's how he wanted to do it, anyway.' She is cold and removed and in complete control.

And Nate bows down to her command. He doesn't want to kill the old guy. He doesn't want to kill anyone. He hasn't yet. 'Okay, so a couple more days and then we run.'

She is pleased by his compliance and kisses him again. This time on the lips. Then her hands are running up and down his slender arms. His hands move to her hips. Hers to his belt buckle.

He doesn't want sex. He's not turned on. He's afraid. Of the situation. Of the ease at which Lailah deals with these stressful circumstances, but he obliges. They slip down to the floor, and

Nathaniel eases himself inside her. Sandwiched in space and time by two desperate, longing souls. Dead and half dead.

At first, he can't get them out of his head, but Lailah makes a noise that suggests pleasure and he looks down at her. Beautiful. Luminescent. She may not be a real angel but, to Nate, she glows. She is everything to him.

And he lets go. He loses himself in that moment.

Margaret tries Ash's mobile phone again. She wants to tell him that his father's answering machine appears to be unplugged. She wants to know exactly where he is and what time he will be coming home. She wants to say that he can't do this, he can't just leave the house and not tell her where he is going and who he is with. She wants him to pick up the damn phone so that she can say, 'I'm going to fucking kill you when you get home, Ash.'

The screwdriver went into Ash's back. Through the fat and muscle. But it missed the spine. It wasn't sharp enough to slice through his thoracic vertebrae, instead decided to hit bone and bear off to the side.

It still hurt, of course, but it was never pulled out. That's when the real pain comes. That's when you bleed. That's when you die quickly.

The phone vibrates in Ash's trouser pocket again. It was freaking out his male attacker. And a stressed captor makes stupid mistakes. Rash decisions. So Ash slides his hand into his pocket and flicks the switch that keeps his phone silent.

7   THE COMMUTER (AND THE NURSES)

All of the nurses love Thomas Davant.

He has cast a spell over them.

It's an easy crowd. They've already proven that they care about others.

It begins with Nurse Chappelle. Exhausted and distracted but realising that she is far more fortunate than the people she is tending to, her bedside manner remains. Cautious. Conscientious. Davant watches her move around the ward. To the nurse, it feels like a slog, dragging her feet across the floor from bed to bed, to Davant it is a ballet, elegant and refined. She could have done it all with her eyes closed.

When she reaches Davant, he tells her that he thinks she is magnificent.

'Well, I don't feel it, I can tell you that.' It's difficult for a lot of people to take this kind of compliment but, for Nurse Chappelle, it is harder. She spends most of her time thinking about and taking care of other people. This results in her paying less attention to herself, then caring less about herself, then pushing through to a place where she now thinks very little of herself.

It's easy to do.

'I've watched you tend to everyone in this ward and you give them everything they need. Even the difficult ones. But you also have to look after yourself, you know?'

She is pottering around at his bedside, tidying things away, propping up pillows, keeping busy, but she stops.

'That's it,' he tells her. 'It's important to take a breath once in a while. If you are at your best, then you can give your best.' He places a hand on hers. She is not entirely comfortable with it but doesn't push him away. Davant locks his gaze with hers. He tells her that she is important, that she matters, that she has been blessed with the gift of compassion. It's preachy but not godly, and the nurse finds it supportive.

He places his other hand underneath the one he is holding, so now she is wrapped in his grasp. Nurse Chappelle feels something. A rise in energy perhaps. A warmth. A flutter of something akin to sexual pleasure – but it isn't a sexual moment.

'Take a breath,' he repeats.

She does so, and Davant lets go of her hand.

'Start there. That breath, that short moment is yours. It is something for you. To rest, to regroup. Give yourself that time and attention.'

He places his hands on the mattress and moves himself up against the pillows, letting out a noise as a pain in his ribs stabs against him.

'Let me help you.' The nurse helps but notices that the bruising on his face and swelling around the eyes has almost disappeared. She can't help herself. 'You are a miracle.'

'You can't let somebody call you magnificent and then try to beat them with a bigger compliment.' Davant smiles.

'I can hardly see the wounds on your face. They were very pronounced when you arrived.'

'What can I say, I'm a quick healer.'

'Apart from those ribs.'

'Indeed. I wonder whether you could pass me my book.' She does so. It's only slightly out of his reach and she wonders whether he is doing it to make her feel useful or to distract her.

He thanks her. And she walks away, dragging her feet a little less.

They notice something at the nurses' station and tease Chappelle about how she is 'glowing'. It's as playful as usual but some of them are jealous that it wasn't them.

She stops.

Takes a breath.

And laughs with them.

The same thing happens with another three nurses that day. Davant sees something in each of them that others do not see or they cannot see in themselves any more. He draws it out of them with his words and musings, his touch. He is not a faith healer, he is not solving their problems, he is merely facilitating a change. He's a catalyst. Sure, his patter is a little dated, but his intentions are honourable. Solid and simple Christian values.

Not all people are born to be great, but Thomas Davant realises that everyone has the opportunity and duty to be the best version of themselves. And it is a very specific gift that allows one person to bring this out in others.

Davant is the director of his own play.

He struggles to get comfortable – the pain in his ribs is still very real and not healing as quickly as the rest of his body. Even if they do start to feel better, he is thinking of continuing with a pretence that he is still in agony, so that he can spend more time with Vashti. She is the antithesis of the extremist's bomb. Davant seems best at helping people one at a time but, if he can get through to her, Vashti is the positive explosion that could affect on a greater scale.

She is magical.

The sportsman was right.

Thomas Davant smiles to himself at the thought of his favourite nurse and the young man who seemingly had a crush on her.

Davant reads a couple of pages of his play and scribbles something in the margins. The next time he looks up, a young man is hobbling towards him on a pair of crutches.

8   THE SON (AND THE SHUFFLING FEET)

Ash wakes up. Even though the blanket has been thrown over his head, he can tell that it is morning. He has been asleep. There is a screwdriver still in his back. He doesn't want to move.

There are no voices, no music, no white noise from a TV channel that was watched until the end of broadcast and now only shows black-and-white flecks until it's time to start everything again.

He knows that he is not alone. He remembers those Devil's rejects attacking him. But they, too, make no sound. They're sleeping upstairs, lying lengthways on the largest sofa at number forty-two.

For some reason he remembers his female attacker more clearly, even though she came at him from behind. He wants to hear her voice.

But there is nothing.

Not even their breath.

And then, a creak. The fourth step from the top. Somebody was coming back downstairs. He would have to be still, not draw attention to himself. Find the right moment to drag himself to his feet. One last chance.

The man was weak. The girl caught him with a sucker punch. If he could surprise them, maybe he could overpower them. Maybe he could just leave while they slept.

The footsteps come closer.

They don't seem young. Shuffling across the floor. Closer. Closer still. How an older person would walk.

Closer.

Ash is not the healthiest or most flexible person when he doesn't have a screwdriver hanging out of his back, but the human body is capable of amazing things when the brain takes over. He would be ready.

Closer.

Then nothing.
Silence.
Whoever it was, they were not there for Ash.
The sound of the chain.
Whoever it was, they were trying to leave.

9   THE CIRCLE LINE (BAYSWATER)

Why am I here? How did I get here? Not this physical location, but this point in my life? Do I have anyone? What about family? Do I care? Should I say goodbye? Should they know where I have been, what I have become? Is there a reason I can't seem to press the button and put an end to all of this? This feels like one long day to me but it isn't, is it? Am I confused? Troubled? Impressionable? Was I somewhere else this morning? Do I have friends? Is there a question I have missed?

Is there still a way out?

Where am I now? Bayswater? Two stops until Edgware Road, right?

Will I have to change?

Have I changed too much?

When did you last feel vulnerable? Do you think it is in that state that we are most malleable, most able to alter who we are, the way we think, or do we need to be strong to make those much-needed alterations?

Is Thomas Davant in the right place to do his best work? The sick and the injured and the dying are easier for him to affect, aren't they? Is that such a bad thing? Is it always so stupid to have hope? And the nurses are tired and underpaid and overworked and under-appreciated and forgotten, so when they are told that they are magical or magnificent, are they not going to feel suddenly positive even if their self-esteem is so low that they can't quite believe it?

For anyone who was alive at the time, they remember exactly where they were, who they were with and what they were doing when man first landed on the moon, but this is also the case when John F Kennedy was shot or Elvis was found dead or a plane flew into the Twin Towers in New York, and all of these events seem to galvanise a nation, but how do you quantify which was more successful in bringing people together?

Are we awakened as a group, a community, through positivity or negativity? And when did that change?

Does Thomas Davant's mission to help one person at a time make sense when I could probably achieve more and stimulate the group social conscience by blowing this carriage and the people on it into pieces? What is the point of me?

What happened to the woman in the hijab? Why don't I remember her getting off the train? Am I losing my mind? I guess, if I think there is a possibility that I am God, that goes without saying? Will that woman's experience taint the way she feels about people? Or will she feel heartened by the actions of the stranger with the orange script? Is it another person that Thomas Davant has improved?

Was she Muslim? Is that what you thought of me when I said that I had a bomb? Why did you think that? Are the media to blame? Have we been conditioned? If I said that I had a gun, would you imagine something a different? A radical Christian, perhaps?

Why aren't they doing anything about the school shootings in America? How stupid does 'guns don't kill people' sound? Just because you have the right to do something, does it mean that you should do it?

When did freedom of speech become so dangerous?

If a law was passed 250 years ago, should it not be reviewed to ensure that it is still in line with the way that we live now? If you can abolish slavery, why not abolish guns? Is this the same with holy books? Should devout believers be living their lives according to the principals that are two thousand years old?

There is no chance of abolishing religion, but could they not have an update? If your computer or mobile phone starts running slowly, don't you delete a few files and check for the latest version of the operating system? Could this not be applied to everything?

Are there people in your life who are not fulfilling you in the way they used to? Do you have friends who offer nothing of interest? Are *they* slowing *you* down? Have they been around for so long that you don't want to cut them out of your life? Is it easier to think that you can still love them but that you need to let them go? Is it worth running that update?

Have you ever bothered to read through the terms and conditions?

How many people do you know who have a picture in the house that says, 'Live. Laugh. Love', yet fly in the face of that very sentiment?

If you read, 'Wherever you go, no matter the weather, always take your own sunshine,' doesn't it make you feel sick rather than motivated?

What is the point in positivity? Where does it go and how far does it really reach?

Am I just trying to help myself quit?

Are we stopping?

Is that Edgware Road?

Are they getting off the train?

Am I?

Is it time?

Should I change direction?

10   SAUL (AND THE YELLOW DOTS)

This time, he remembers not to take the pill.

Of course, they could be putting something in his sandwiches that messes with his mind and makes him sleep. But he notices that he has made it to the door without coloured spots starting to cloud his vision. He hasn't quite made it through the door yet, but if he is quiet, he won't alert the angels.

He doesn't really believe that they are angels any more but, sometimes, it is easier to go along with something you no longer believe in than fight for something better.

Saul doesn't like the male one. There's something about him. He doesn't think that they want to hurt him, but they are keeping him around for too long, keeping him away from Ada. He wasn't an evil person. He never beat Ash. He was devoted to his wife. He worked hard. What could be taking so long?

The angels are naked again, this time on his floor. They hardly ever wear clothes. Saul wonders whether that is how God intended it to be.

He tiptoes. His head hurts, just as it does every morning. He drank the water but placed the pill underneath his mattress. He doesn't feel drowsy yet.

Slowly, he edges towards the only exit. In the corner is something that wasn't there the day before. He's old and his mind is playing tricks on him, but he would have noticed a pile of blankets that big. It may not be a pile but there is certainly one blanket on top that is covering something beneath.

Closer. He shuffles.

Closer.

But he stops. Saul is not interested in the pile in the corner.

He wants to get outside.

Feel the wind on his face.

Saul carefully takes the chain off the door, as though an alarm will sound if metal touches metal. He looks up the stairs. No movement. Then he turns around to the pile in the corner. It looks like it moves. Perhaps it's not the morning pill that affects his mind. He rolls his eyes from side to side, looking for the yellow dots. But there's nothing yet.

He wants to cough, or something, to cover up the clicking sound he anticipates when he unlocks the latch, but realises that would only make it worse.

Click.

Nothing from upstairs.

The pile in the corner moves slightly, he's almost certain.

But Saul doesn't have time for that. He's getting out. He turns the lock slowly. Deliberately. Down by his shin, he notices that the door is splintered. Cold air rushes in through the gap. There's no screwdriver. His vision is fine.

He pulls on the door. And Ash groans.

Saul is not a bad person. Yes, he was going to kill himself by ingesting a handful of pills, but love and pain often make us do stupid and impulsive things in their name. He could leave right now. The door is open. But that noise was the sound of a person. Another human in despair.

And Saul can't just leave them there.

He shuts the door and turns around to what he thought was a pile of fabric. This is not the action of someone who deserves to be locked in Purgatory.

A deep breath. For courage.

A cautious shuffle.

Closer.

A held breath.

Closer.

Saul reaches out towards the blanket. But before he can get a hand to the material, another hand is on his shoulder. He lets out a yelp.

'Saul. Saul. Shh, shh, shh, shh. It's okay. It's just me.' He tries to keep the old man calm but also guide him away from the body of his son. 'You've got lost again. Did you take your pill and drink your water?'

Saul nods. He sees the female angel standing at the bottom of the stairs. But there's no blur now. No light around her face. She is half in shadow and she is not looking at him. Her gaze is fixed on the thing in the corner.

Male angel puts the chain back on the door, knowing it won't do any good. And he ushers the old man back to his room.

Saul pretends he is feeling the effects of his drugs in the way he has for the past few days.

One month in Hell.

And downstairs, Ash cries in his mind. He's stuck in his own Purgatory. He's alive, barely. And he can't move his legs. But he knows that his father is in the house with the two people who did this to him, and, if he didn't have a purpose before, he has one now. Somehow, he needs to get his dad out of that door.

11 THE CIRCLE LINE (EDGWARE ROAD)

How did I get outside and what do I do now? Have I been going around under the ground for so long that I have forgotten the feeling of air on my face? Do you travel on the tube? When you come back to the surface, do you show gratitude for the air you breathe, no matter how polluted? Is it good advice to tell somebody to stop and look up at the clouds once in a while? And how many books could you sell by repeating that platitude over and over again?

Am I trying to distract myself with questions because I am afraid? Because this is different? Why would God not want to be seen? Would it not be simpler to show the world that you exist? If you could create a world in one week, what would you drink to celebrate?

I know I'm not God, don't I? What am I stalling for? Do I ask inane questions to prevent myself from realising what I have to do? Is it working? If I don't think about it, maybe I won't do it?

Who sits down to compose the chants at sports matches? Do you have to feel sad to write a sad song? Do you have to be in love to write a love song? How many people want to be famous more than they want to be a successful singer? And should they be labelled as artists?

Speaking of labels, has anybody ever told you that peeling the label from the front of your beer bottle is a sign of sexual frustration?

And why am I following this crowd to the other side of the platform?

Do they see me?

Am I here?

Does this feel too real?

It is said that estate agents and recruiters are the worst kinds of people? What then of a person who recruits suicide bombers? If I don't remember the recruitment process, is that a sign that they have done their job well? Has my brain been washed? The fact that I am about to change trains is an indication that they may have backed the wrong horse, is it not?

Can I be the one who walks away?

If you eat pig meat and cow meat and chicken meat, why does the idea of horse meat turn your stomach? If I talk about roasting a dog or barbecuing a cat, what is it that makes eaters of flesh so angry? Would they eat less lamb if it was labelled 'baby sheep'? If the Lord is your shepherd, are you not a sheep?

Can I keep myself distracted until the doors on this new train close and we set off in another circle? Is this the right train? Am I going around the other way? Have I given myself longer to decide? Can I find enough questions to keep me from the answer I'm not ready to hear?

Can I ask anything? Will I always come back to what is important?

Why won't these train doors close?

The platform is almost empty and there is one spare seat, but I don't like to draw attention to myself by taking it, however, it makes me anxious to stand up knowing that I am strapped to a bomb, so what should I do? How am I already back to thinking about the bomb? Did I not spend long enough talking about nothing to stop myself panicking? What else can I think about?

Do you feel awkward when people tell you jokes? How do you feel about riddles? Have you ever looked at a painting and been moved to tears? Who is it that decides that the awful art should be popular and why do we buy into that?

They say that being shot in the stomach is a long and painful death, but how long can an overweight man in his forties last with a screwdriver hanging out of his back?

The doors are finally closing but when should I take over that empty seat? Is it best to just grab it now so that I can settle in for another revolution or should I wait until the other passengers have their eyes in a book or on a phone screen?

Do I really want to be seen, because it seems like I'm trying not to hide from everyone?

Have you ever heard of the term 'Golden Age Thinking'? Which point in history do you think was the best socially, artistically and ideologically? If you had the chance to go back there, do you think that the people of that time would be feeling exactly the way you are now? That they would wish they could travel back to something better because what they have is so god damned awful?

Doesn't it worry you that people, in thirty years, will wish they could be in this time? How bad does it get in the future?

Is there a benefit to always seeing the worst in people?

Wait, who is that? What is she doing? Can I say something? Isn't there something about mortals not being able to hear the voice of God? Who does she think she is? Is she pregnant? Oh, great, I have to let her have the seat now, don't I?

I can feel myself shaking, can they see me shaking?

What if I just blow this place sky high?

12 THE FRIENDS

Handing Vashti the sportsman's contact details was a gesture of friendship from Thomas Davant, but the entire ceremony was redundant. The sportsman had managed to find Vashti before heading out of the hospital on his crutches.

He had seen her, thanked her and marvelled at the colours that were dancing around her. He had then passed on his details and asked her to call him.

He had hugged her goodbye, dropping one of his crutches in the process. His arms were wrapped around her and his hands were dangerously close to the scars running down Vashti's back. They heated up, not burning like they had been, it was a comforting warmth.

In that moment, Vashti felt a love for the sportsman. Not love. A love. A kind that is somehow both maternal and platonic.

The sportsman's feelings were as muddled as his vision. He wanted to be near Vashti, with Vashti, inside Vashti. He wanted her colour and magnificence to overwhelm him.

They had shared a moment. Both of them getting something different out of the exchange but, nevertheless, getting something.

So, Davant didn't have to give his favourite nurse the note from the sportsman, he could have kept her all to himself, but he had done it because he said that he would.

And then the sportsman walked in the next day to, 'Come and visit a friend.'

'Bull shit,' laughed Davant, deliberately splitting the word in half for effect.

'What? What do you mean?'

'You are not here to see me.'

A look of knowing. They seem like old friends.

'That's not strictly true. I am here for you but ... Is she working? I thought she might have been in contact by now.'

'It's very proactive of you to take the initiative to come here, but sometimes you have to wait these things out ... It'll happen. She is good. Better than you or I. And better every day.'

The sportsman misses the last part of the sentence because he is looking around the ward for his technicolour angel. He seems despondent when he finds that everything is black and white.

'She's here. Don't worry. Only recently arrived, but I have seen her about.'

There's visible relief in the athlete.

'So, tell me, what have you been doing with your freedom from this place?'

'Training hard.' The sportsman regales Davant with his stairs workout and explains how he has recalculated his macros and planned his meals to stay in shape. He says his coach is arranging some pool training for when the cast comes off.

'That's mighty optimistic of you. I had thought the prognosis was a little bleaker...'

'I think I have to thank you for that. You really lit a fire under me. I need to make things happen and...' He pauses and stands up straight, not turning around, his ears pricking up as though trying to hear something behind him.

Vashti.

'You could feel that she was here, couldn't you?' Davant asks.

The sportsman smiles a smile that confirms.

He could feel her.

They both could.

13 THE CIRCLE LINE (NOTTING HILL GATE)

Do you ever persist with a novel that hasn't gripped you within the first twenty pages? Is there some intrinsic reward to this persistence? Is it another case of how we all need instant gratification?

Am I delaying things to gain more pleasure from the ending?

Remember video shops? Did you ever walk in, knowing exactly which film you wanted to rent out, yet still walk around the shop for half an hour, pulling at boxes and reading the words on the back? Were you one of those people who would straighten things as you went? How unlucky are people today that they no longer have to rewind a film after they have watched it?

What am I hiding among the inanity?

Is this obfuscation?

Do you want to work less but earn more? Why do you think you deserve that?

What does it feel like to die? What's the best way to go? Most people think it's falling asleep and never waking up but, if we really do crave everything in an instant, how about a gunshot to the head or explosion on a train carriage?

Did I misdirect you, make you look the other way?

If I think about where the human race is, right now, and the place that they are heading, it makes my decision about the bomb so much clearer, but isn't all this my fault if I created these monsters and then gave them free will?

Isn't it more effective to destroy something beautiful?

Shouldn't I be punished?

How do you discipline God?

Surely I am the only one who can do that?

What should I do, write lines? Should I scribble on a piece of paper one billion times, *I must not give up on humanity ... I must not give up on humanity...*? Am I supposed to ground myself and send myself to my room without any dinner? Maybe I could take my mobile phone away for a hundred years?

Or, perhaps I could force myself to sit on the same train for a decade, travelling around in an endless loop, watching people waste away and fade, and devolve? Should I force myself to see what people have become with their fighting and spitting and status updates?

Could I witness some kindness?

How much is left?

14 OLD DAVE AND NEW DAVE (AND BAD DAVE)

Dave and Dave are eating dinner together.

Still no mail.

Although a dining table for two has been delivered. Old Dave put it together, he's the handy one, good with the tools. He had to take the screwdriver out of the door frame for half an hour but, luckily, nobody came knocking.

New Dave prepared the food. Curry. Nothing too fancy, but homemade, from scratch, and that counts for something. He also opened a bottle of wine. Said that it would help with the spice.

And this is where it starts.

At first it was gratitude and graciousness. But the wine kept coming. And the curry wasn't even that spicy. And it seemed that the new Dave, while helpful and domesticated, could not handle his booze. He was laughing too enthusiastically. Everything was funny. Even his own jokes.

Particularly his own jokes.

The neighbour could hear. All the neighbours would hear.

'Maybe you should slow down on the wine a bit.' Old Dave tries to make it sound as light as possible. Nobody that far into a night of drinking wants to be told they've had too much.

'You've had exactly the same amount as I have.' New Dave picks up his glass and takes another swig. There's no acrimony, he's merely pointing out a fact.

'I know, but I'm not...'

'You're not what?' New Dave places his glass on the table. Something changes in his eyes, in his demeanour.

'I'm not ... being loud.'

New Dave laughs again. A raucous cackle. 'Being loud? Ha! We're the only ones here, David.'

Old Dave surrenders his point, and they go on drinking and

laughing. Their feet are touching beneath the table. It's friendly again. Tender, even.

'I think there might be one bottle left in the fridge. Let's get down from the table and get more comfortable, eh?' new Dave suggests.

There is no sofa in the lounge area. Once, there had been an old computer chair in the middle of the room. One of the Daves used to love spinning around on it while watching the television. Nobody remembers where it went.

Now all that is left is the mattress. The stained mattress that bad Dave used to drink on and piss on. And shout from.

Helpful Dave goes into the kitchen to fetch the last bottle of wine. A Riesling.

He re-enters, talking to himself, 'You know, I've never really understood these bottles. They're so thin but they're tall. So it feels like you're not getting as much but it's exactly the same.'

Quietly drunk Dave waits a beat in case his new flatmate found his own observation as hysterical as the joke he told earlier about a nun and a prostitute in a bath with a bar of soap. *One had a soul full of hope and the other had a hole full of...*

It wasn't funny or conversational or observational. Patient Dave waits as slurring Dave pours another glass each then takes the bottle over to the mattress and sits down, leaning his back against the wall.

'Come and sit over here,' he pats the mattress with his hand, 'It's more comfortable.'

Unsure Dave does as is suggested.

But he's nervous. He's been here before. When he'd had a drink and was feeling things that he shouldn't be thinking. That his parents would never have approved. That God would look down on. He'd got himself into a similar position with the last Dave. They were drunk and laughing and messing about, and that turned into something else. They were still and looking into each other's eyes. And now-dead Dave snapped himself out of it and said, 'What are you? Fucking gay? You want to kiss me, is that it?'

The accusation turned into confrontation, developed into a fight and ended with one Dave lying on top of the other.

Old Dave didn't want a repeat of that, so kept a little distance between himself and new Dave.

New Dave passes out before the bottle is finished. Old Dave stays on the mattress and looks at him, watches him sleep while he continues to put away the Riesling. He strokes gently at his hair.

A patch of wetness appears near new Dave's lap and spreads out as he pisses freely into his pants and onto the mattress.

Dave's tumour taps against his skull.

It's happening again. But quicker this time.

He doesn't want to hear what it is saying. Everything was going so well. He has a new friend. One that he likes. They get on. There's no shouting. No threats.

But now, Dave is scared. He doesn't want to wake the other Dave, he's made that mistake before, too. Instead, he fills his glass with the last of the wine, goes into his bedroom, lays the quilt and the pillow inside a wardrobe, steps in, and shuts the door behind him.

This is the fear.

He sees no way out.

So locks himself away.

15 THE CIRCLE LINE (SLOANE SQUARE)

Two men just got on and are sitting next to each other, and I see that they are holding hands, then I spot a woman look up from her book and smile at them, then another does the same but screws up her face in apparent disgust, and I want to ask, why does she feel that way? How is it her business? What's not to like?

What sense would there be in me telling the world that man should not lie with another man? It's not a belief I hold but, also, surely that would harm sales of THE book? And, if my greatest gift was to provide man with free will, can that will not be used to love whomever they so desire? Why would a God prevent the spread of love? Why must my words be so misconstrued?

Should I, as God, have added restrictions to free will?

When I say, 'Do not use your freedom to indulge the flesh; rather, serve one another humbly in love', what do I mean? Can you twist that to fit into your distorted view of existence? Should I have been more explicit? Would anyone listen if I said, 'Do not use your free will for hate'?

Does anybody listen, any more?

Are they too busy hating?

Are they preoccupied with talking and posting and boasting and lying?

Does everyone feel so awful because things have become so negative or are they negative because things have become so awful?

If I created a virus that ate away at the world's population, and I made sure that it could not be combatted with medicine, that there would be no vaccine, but that it could be eradicated with kindness, how long do you think people could keep it up? And would they go back to their ways as soon as it was gone?

Should I smile at those men to cancel out what that woman did with her face? It still matters, even if they didn't notice, doesn't it?

If I wanted to wipe everyone out in one go and start again, and I directed an asteroid at the planet that could not be blown up by rockets, missiles or nuclear bombs, if I said the only way to change its course was through compassion for others, who would bother?

If the leading scientific minds of the world put out solid data that human beings were the biggest threat to life on Earth, that they were quickly reaching a tilting point where the damage would be irreversible and that humanity was going to be stamped out, who would even hear it?

How many people would pay attention and alter their selfish ways?

Would more people read and share the words of Mary, fifty-two, from Stoke (originally) but now living in Salford, two 'O' levels – one in art, the other in home economics – who says, 'It's all a hoax. The ozone layer repairs itself over time. They just want us to spend more money on metal straws'?

Isn't it easier to read something and make it fit your existing views than absorb what is being said and change the way you think?

Can being positive make a difference or are we all just positive that we've screwed everything up?

Is it not that I think I am God, but simply that I feel that way because I hold so many peoples' lives in my hands?

Do we ever hear about the failed suicide bombers? The ones who walk away and do not detonate?

I smile at the gay couple, and one of them screws his face up in the same way the homophobic passenger did, and you wonder why I'm here and so confused?

16 THE NURSE (AND THE WOUNDS OF CHRIST)

When all the kids get a medal or a sticker or a bag of sweets, when every layer of pass the parcel has a prize, not just the last one, when we are told that we can be anything we want to be in life but it is not explained that we will have to work hard and make sacrifices along the way, when people say things like, 'happiness is found within' or 'smiles are contagious' or 'things always get better with time' – when these things are thrust in our direction at a time when we feel low or despondent, they are not welcome, they are doing no good.

That may be their intention but the result is the opposite.

This is toxic positivity.

This is poisonous to humanity. And humility.

What Thomas Davant does that works is combine his positivity with realism and truth. It's not even hard to do.

Be honest.

Get the facts.

Have compassion.

He is talking to Vashti when a man starts screaming in the bed across from his. The one where the sportsman once lay and lost his ability to perceive colour.

Last week, last month, last year, Vashti would have rolled her eyes at the drama. Last week, Vashti had no colour. Nobody called her magnificent or magical. She was liked but she didn't stand out. She didn't want to.

She looks at the sportsman and then at Thomas and says, 'I have to go. It sounds like he's getting worse. I'll be back, okay?'

The sportsman nods.

Thomas Davant grabs Vashti's hand and doesn't let her leave.

He could say something like, 'Some people cannot be cured but everyone can heal.'

Or throw out, 'Life isn't about waiting for the storm to pass, it's about learning to dance in the rain.'

What good would it do?

This kind of flowery rhetoric resonates with nobody.

Davant stares deep into her. 'It's not just about fixing them. You can take away their pain but they need to know that you care.' She doesn't look away. 'Show him that you care.'

The sportsman is still. For that moment, everything is still or slowed down. All but Davant and the nurse.

The two men watch as she makes her way across the ward to the screaming man. His wife is visiting and looks to be in shock.

'Oh, thank God. He was fine and then he started complaining about a stabbing in his stomach. And he doesn't sound like himself. Help him, please. Please.'

Vashti pushes towards the bed, excusing the wife as she does so.

The patient seems manic. He's loud and obnoxious.

'Don't you put your filthy fucking hands on me, get me morphine.'

The cynical side of Vashti wonders whether he is an addict who has been brought in for something else and is now in withdrawal. Another part considers him a possible racist. But pain can change you in an instant. Like love.

The chart hanging over the bottom of his bed confirms he is the victim of a stabbing. Another London statistic. Vashti sees blood on his hands. She's worried.

'Sir, I need you to take three deep breaths.'

'I'm not giving birth, I've been fucking stabbed.' And he lifts his hands to show those bloody palms.

Vashti wants to fix him. She wants to take away his pain.

She needs to show him that she cares.

'Mr Branford, I need to check your wound. I think you may have popped some stitches. Please take a deep breath.'

He ignores her again, delirious and hysterical, he holds up his bloodied hands like a vision of deep Catholic guilt.

Her words are not getting through to him.

Vashti grabs his blood-covered hands and holds them still.

'Look at me,' she tells him. 'I need you to breathe.' She has to ignore her now-bloody hands. She has to ignore her own pain as the red-hot needles poke at her shoulder blades. She has to tell herself that she is there because she cares.

She holds his hands, her thumbs pressed into his palms, and she looks the patient in the eyes. He is silent. He is taking deep breaths. His pain is receding. Slowly, carefully, she lowers his hands, never taking her eyes away.

'I care,' she speaks in her mind. 'I care.'

Mr Branford's breathing slows. He is calm. Vashti lowers his hands to the bed and then releases her grip. The point on his palms where her thumb was pressing looks darker than the rest of his hand.

'I need to take a look, okay?'

He nods.

Calm.

Cared for.

The nurse can already tell from the dressing just above his hip that he has not been bleeding from his wound but she lifts it anyway. It's clean. Stitched perfectly. He wasn't bleeding from there. Vashti is confused. Where did all that blood come from?

She looks back at the man's hands.

'Did you cut yourself somehow?'

He shakes his head this time. Exhausted by the situation. His eyes start to close, and Vashti worries that he has lost too much blood. His head droops to the side and his arms relax on the mattress, slightly splayed, palms up. Vashti checks his left hand. She knows she saw a darker spot on his palm. A hole. Perhaps that is where he is cut.

She wipes the blood away and thinks she sees the wound from which he is bleeding. She looks at the other hand. It's the same. But, when she returns to his left palm, anything resembling a wound seems to have closed up and disappeared.

She checks his right hand. It's the same.

Where the hell did all the blood come from?

'What did you do?' Mr Branford's wife. 'Did you give him something to calm him down?'

Vashti doesn't answer. She is looking across his body for any marks that could have produced the blood over his hands and hers. The sheets are stained. His dressing will need to be changed and he will need to be cleaned up.

She can't find a thing.

'Excuse me, nurse? Did you up his morphine? I didn't see you inject him or anything. Is he going to be okay? Nurse?' Branford's wife calmed when he did, but now she is agitated.

'No. I ... I didn't give him anything. I just got him to focus and breathe.'

And placed her hands on him.

And showed that she cared.

Vashti looks back at Thomas Davant, who is smiling. He was right. How could he possibly know? What was happening to her?

'Is he okay? He's bleeding.'

'He's fine, Mrs Branford.' Vashti can see that his breathing is steady. 'It looks like his wound opened a little and was bleeding. I think the sight of the blood may have panicked your husband.' She lies. 'We see it all the time.' That part is true. 'I'm going to get him cleaned up and the wound redressed. It's perfectly okay if you want to stay here, but maybe you want to get yourself a drink or snack...'

Mrs Branford nods. She stands and leans over to kiss her husband on the cheek before heading out into the hallway to find a vending machine.

Vashti's back feels warm and numb. She is sweating.

The sportsman is in awe. Everything still black and white but the woman who cares.

Davant sees it all. He picks up his orange script and scribbles something in the margin.

17 ADA (AND NO REGRETS)

Ada had been what Saul called 'a tough old broad' her entire life. She'd grown up poor, in a house full of kids with a father who was never afraid to raise a hand to any of them and a mother who wasn't afraid to raise a bottle to forget.

She was plucky. Scrappy. Full of fight. You couldn't keep her down. It was something that Saul loved and admired about her. She was fearless and adventurous. And alive.

But, damn, that disease kicked the crap out of her. It was relentless and remorseless and disrespectful of the life Ada had led.

When they first found out, everybody said to Saul, 'If anybody can beat this thing, it's Ada.' And they weren't just throwing platitudes his way, they all believed it.

But Ada went fast. No energy to fight. Beaten down. Scared. Annoyed with God and science. However, unlike many who are faced with their own demise, who look back with regret at the things they never got around to, all those things they had never done, Ada was thankful for the life she had led, the child she had birthed and the man she had fallen in love with, married and stayed with until the end. She was gracious until the last moments.

Her mind had gone. The cancer invaded her body and it was aggressive. There were many drugs in those final days. Saul has the date that she died lodged into his brain, but he had lost her before that day, even though he could never admit it. He was grieving for her while she was still alive.

The woman at the end was not his Ada. She was old and sweet, but it wasn't who he wanted. And it wasn't how he wanted to remember her.

And he couldn't be like Ada. He couldn't think about all the great times they'd had because he wanted to dwell on the things they would never do together. There was torture there and Saul wanted to sit in it.

Ada was dead.

Dust in the wind.

And here's the real kicker, she's not waiting around for Saul. She's not in Hell, at least, but she's not in Heaven. And she's certainly not in a Purgatory that looks like the flat she lived in for most of her life. Because, to Saul, there couldn't be a God who would extinguish such a star. Yet, still, he holds out some hope that there is something after. Something better than the guides he's been lumbered with.

Maybe Ada is waiting for him.

Maybe she still has that same fire and spirit, and when Saul finally gets to her, she is going to have something to say about him making her wait around for two years. (Fourteen in Purgatory.)

Saul won't know until he gets there.

Or doesn't get there. Because he can't be sure about Heaven or Hell. It's most likely that there is nothing. Eternal nothing. Which means there is no more Ada and there certainly is no God. And, if there is no God, that explains why a disease could strip him of his love, but it doesn't help to determine the identity of the man on the train.

18   THE CIRCLE LINE (WESTMINSTER)

If Ada is dead and there is no afterlife, then I can't be God, can I? I must be the narrator of this twisting tale that refuses to bring all the stories together, is that it?

Is it going to be worth it?

What's with the bomb, then? Why can I feel the weight of it?

Surely I could find her? If I can create all the animals of Earth in one day, surely I can find one of the women I created? Do you think she is waiting for Saul? Can you imagine a love that strong? Do you have a relationship like that? Do you want one?

What's the point of procreation? Aren't parents always moaning about their kids? Why do we look so confused when somebody says that they don't want children? Is marriage outdated now, too? Aren't the divorce statistics daunting? What is it, one in two marriages fail? Are these made-up numbers? Could it be worse? Two in one?

Would you rather sue a charitable organisation for a lot of money and win, or sue a corrupt organisation for a lot of money and lose? It seems like the answer is obvious, right? You wouldn't take money from a charity, would you? Would you like to know what percentage of people would take the money rather than expose corruption and end up with a clearer conscience? If I told you it was over sixty percent, would you be shocked?

How did we get here?

Can I skip to the end to see what happens?

Do I already know?

What's the best funeral you've ever attended? Have you ever dipped segments of a Granny Smith apple into peanut butter? Is there a better combination of foods that exists? Who told the world that chocolate and orange belong together?

Did you know that, in America, six people a year are killed because they were shot ... by their dog? Would you wear a T-shirt that said,

'Guns don't kill people, dogs do'? Why do people on *the left* use satire when right-wing idiots have trouble understanding knock-knock jokes? Is it to show that they are more intelligent? When will they realise that punching down doesn't win an election?

Do you think I will run out of questions at some point and be forced to ask myself the one that will unlock everything?

Or am I stalling until all the pieces are in place to press this red button?

Why are they always red?

19   THE NEW DAVES

Old Dave sleeps soundly after a night of drinking wine. He is curled into a ball with a blanket wrapped tightly around his body and tucked between his legs, his head on a pillow and the wardrobe doors closed, blocking out any light from the new day.

The other Dave wakes up in the lounge, on the mattress. It doesn't smell good in there. He gets up, goes to the toilet and goes back in to the lounge. It smells worse on returning.

Both of the Daves missed the usual run to the post box at 6am.

Stinking Dave takes the screwdriver from the door frame and quietly unlocks the door. He doesn't like going outside at all, that's for the other Dave, who likes fresh air on his skin.

He opens the door, cautiously, peering outside to see if anyone is there. It's clear, but he can hear the neighbour closing his microwave door and setting a timer. He's singing along to a song on the radio that Dave does not recognise. He rationalises things in his brain. If the neighbour is waiting for something to heat up then that will give him a minute to run downstairs. It is breakfast time so it's probably something he is about to eat, which would give Dave much longer.

He stops rationalising and starts running, pushing through the heavy fire door that leads to the stairs. He holds the bannister and moves his feet as fast as he can, jumping the last few steps of each flight.

He can see through the small plastic rectangle on the front of the post box that there is mail in there. One letter. White envelope. Blue stamp. NHS logo. This is what the other Dave has been waiting for.

Piss-drenched, hungover Dave takes the letter, folds it in half, puts it in his pocket, takes a deep breath and runs back upstairs. The neighbour is still singing as the microwave pings to inform him that his oats are hot. Dave mutters something under his breath and goes back into his flat, replacing the locks and screwdriver. Everything as it was before.

Everything the same but the letter in his pocket.

Dave tiptoes into the lounge, heads back to the corner where the putrid mattress awaits, and he lies on his side with his back facing the door and takes the letter out of his pocket.

It's urgent. Dead Dave unplugged the telephone weeks ago and the hospital have not been able to get hold of alive Dave with the results of his test.

He requires treatment.

Autoimmune encephalitis.

Not a brain tumour. Many of the symptoms are similar and can cause a misunderstanding. The neuroimaging results have removed any doubts. But the key to surviving is detecting early and acting swiftly. A course of steroids or intravenous antibodies can clear things up, though recovery can take anywhere from a week to two months.

Not a brain tumour.

Dave doesn't have to die.

He isn't going to die.

He just needs to get to the hospital or call the surgery immediately. He would need to stay in hospital, though. Dave looks back towards the door at this realisation. He would have to be at home alone. Cooking for himself. What if he needs to go outside to buy something, stock up on milk, maybe?

No. No. This would not work.

That can't happen.

If Dave goes to the hospital, they will give him drugs to make him better. He'll stop thinking the way that he does. It would fix his mouth and face. They would cure him. And if they cured him, he would come home to an empty flat. There would only be one Dave.

Dave number one.

Happy. Healthy. And alive.

Dave number two doesn't want to stop existing. He doesn't want to disappear. So he can't let the other Dave see the letter. It is probably too late for him now anyway. He'll just have to die.

So, Dave takes the letter into the kitchen. He folds it in half twice and holds it over the flame of the cooker and watches as it turns to ash.

The other Dave appears in the kitchen doorway.

'Something smells good,' he says, noting the scent of burnt paper.

'Yes, I'm just whipping up some breakfast. You want bacon?'

'That would be perfect. Thanks.'

'Okay, well I'll get that done. Why don't you go and check the mail?'

20 VASHTI AND THE SPORTSMAN (AND THE HEALING HANDS)

Stigmata. That's what Vashti was thinking. She saw the holes in his palms, she was sure of it. There was nowhere else the blood could have come from. That wound was sewn up tight. There were no other marks.

Only the marks of Jesus Christ.

It was a sign, she was sure of it.

Somehow, so was Thomas Davant.

The nurse washed the blood from her hands. Two other nurses came to help her move Mr Branford and sponge him down. They, too, could find no injuries other than the part of his stomach where he had been stabbed. They changed his sheets and asked no questions.

They were doing their jobs and that was enough for them. No sense in stirring things up. No point in asking questions. No reason to care. He was clean and quiet and breathing. On to the next patient.

Vashti scratches at her back. It won't stop itching.

She sees the sportsman heading down the corridor on his crutches.

'Hey,' she calls. But he doesn't hear. She goes after him and calls again. He turns and she sees his face light up at the sight of her. She can see what he is seeing. Colour. Glorious colour. It warms him. She feels that, too. 'You were going to leave without saying goodbye?'

'I could see how busy you were with that patient and I didn't want to get in the way. You seemed to calm him down pretty quickly.' He stops himself from saying that he was only there to visit Thomas Davant, because he knows that she would see straight through that.

'Sometimes you just have to look them in the eyes and focus on their breathing, and they forget about everything else.' She stops herself from saying that she thinks that laying her hands on him did something. That, perhaps, she cared so much it healed him in some way. But she knows that nobody in their right mind would believe that.

Vashti knows what the doctors said about the sportsman's leg. They thought it was over for him. A career-ending injury. She could see how determined he was to recover. And damn it, she just couldn't care any more about getting him back to health. Stronger than ever. And she believes that she can help him.

'I'm sorry I haven't called. I have been meaning to.'

She wants to help him.

She needs to.

'You're busy.' He tries to sound understanding. The sportsman is captivated by Vashti. He has had a pain below his kneecap all day but, as he stares at the nurse, glistening in her rainbow aura, the world behind her, beside her, all around her, is a blur of grey tones, and the knee pain is gone.

Vashti explains that she is here to help him. She believes that she can. That she has to get back and finish her shift but she will text him afterwards, so that he has her number and can contact her when he needs to.

'I've only got a couple of hours left then I'm off for three days. We could meet up tomorrow, if you like? I need to get some sleep after the things I've seen today.'

Her back itches.

She thinks about going home to an empty house but it doesn't make her sad.

'I can't imagine the things you must see day to day.'

Cancer. Broken bones. Sick children.

Stigmata.

Vashti has belief. A belief that she is changing into something more. Perhaps she is changing back to something. But she believes she can use her compassion to heal the sportsman's will-never-be-the-same-again leg.

One could ask why he, a white, privileged male, would deserve such a gift. There are children dying and people freezing to death on the streets. Surely they are more deserving. But that is not how this works. Just as it is not God's will to choose to heal one person over another. The nurse is nursing. She is taking on whatever is put in front of her.

If everybody did that, there would be no reason for a God to make decisions on who lives and who dies. That would be a weight off His shoulders.

The sportsman continues: 'Okay, so, drop me a message when you're done and we can sort out the whens and wheres.'

'Will do. Okay, I need to get back. See you tomorrow.' She smiles and grips one of his wrists in reassurance. The colours from her arm pulse through his and finish in his chest. He can feel her love.

'Thank you. See you tomorrow.' He waits, watching her as she turns and heads back to the ward, colours bouncing with each step. When Vashti rounds a corner, the sportsman sets off, hobbling towards the tube station. He noticed on the way in that holding his bodyweight up on those crutches was most painful on his hands. They had bruised from holding the plastic-covered handles.

He takes three steps and realises there is no pain. The bruises have gone.

21   THE CIRCLE LINE (TEMPLE)

Don't I know that man from somewhere? Why does it feel like I have been here before? They call that déjà vu, you know? It's just a case of the brain tricking itself, moving too quickly or slowly when recollecting a time or place, but what if it isn't? What if it means we are remembering an experience from a time when we were not the person we are today? What if it is precognitive and we can see ahead?

How would you explain that?

.   Did you know it is a common occurrence for people with epilepsy or those who experience seizures? Did you know that it can also be attributed to some psychiatric problems or physical damage to the brain caused by something like a tumour or encephalitis? Did you know that you are more prone to déjà vu if you watch a lot of films or travel a lot?

Does that include somebody who travels in circles, night and day, open until close?

Where do I sleep? Why don't I know? Is that how it works? If I erase myself it becomes easier to erase others? I can't really do this, can I?

Why do I feel like I have seen him before? He would stay in my memory, surely? It's the crutches and the broken leg, right? Have you ever seen someone so broken yet so content? How does one achieve such a perfect state of equilibrium? How can I get to that point?

Has he ever experienced déjà vu?

Have you heard of string theory? Have you ever sat down to fully consider the idea of chaos? What about this notion of alternate realities? Is there a version of this situation where that man over there has a broken leg but is utterly devastated and suicidal? Is there another version where the bones in his leg are entirely in tact?

What about me?

As I talk now, could I simply be your narrator, guiding you

through these seemingly unrelated stories until we reach an end that I have had in my mind all along? Would I feel better about that?

What if that is some other reality that has not yet been negotiated?

Perhaps I am God, as I have wondered all along? Could this be that reality and, at some point, the questions will cease and I will step up to the plate and take another swing at human existence?

Is there an option three where I blow everyone to pieces?

Are there a million more options?

Which one do you want to hear?

Is every move I make a micro decision that can flutter its wings and create another path towards a different outcome?

Or do all the choices lead down separate paths but culminate in a decision delta where everything turns black?

What if there is that final flash of light but, somehow, everybody's ending is different?

22   THE NURSE (AND THE MESSAGE)

Juned calls again.

It's been years. The only way he knows to get hold of his sister is through the hospital. He doesn't even know if she still works there.

'Looks like you've just missed her, I'm afraid. Can I help in any way?'

'Um … it's a … it's a personal matter.' Ned doesn't even know why he is calling or whether he has anything specific to say to his sister. He hasn't even missed her. He never thinks about his parents. There are a million other things on his mind.

'Could you just tell her…'

That you need help?

That you are sorry?

That you are in way over your head?

That you're back in London?

That it would be good to meet up?

'…Tell her that Juned called and … Sorry, tell her that Ned called and maybe it would be … You know what, don't worry, I'll try again tomorrow, maybe.' And he hangs up.

The nurse writes a note: *Vash! (Ju)Ned called. Will call you back.*

Then she places the note behind the nurses' station, where it will never be seen and she can forget it ever happened.

23   THE WIFE

Light and darkness are not separate entities; there is often a point where they cross over and bleed into one another. The same is true of endings and beginnings.

Margaret tells herself that she was awake all night with worry about Ash, but that is because she thinks that she should feel that way. Her sleep was disturbed, she woke up to see he still wasn't home at one point, but her reaction was one of anger and mistrust rather than caring for his safety.

She wakes up early, and the bed feels huge without Ash in it. Maybe he got in drunk, made himself something to eat, put the television on and fell asleep on the sofa. It wouldn't be the first time.

The kids are difficult to wake up in the morning but it would be just her luck that they get up early today. She tiptoes past their bedrooms and heads downstairs, knocking her hip against the bannister on the way and causing unnecessary noise. But Margaret wants to get downstairs as quickly and quietly as possible because the last thing she wants is for one of the kids to see their father in that state.

She is protecting them.

And herself, to a certain extent.

Ash isn't there. She should panic, that's how she feels, but she doesn't.

In some other reality, Margaret and Ash are deeply in love. They spend their nights drinking red wine and feeding each other strawberries. They are passionate about art and charity and making love. Their children are content and do not misbehave.

In another universe that looks exactly like this one, Margaret finds Ash on the sofa and is so relieved that he is safe, although hungover, that she climbs on to him, holds one hand over his mouth and one over her own and takes him for a ride before the boys wake up for their breakfast.

But here, in this place, Margaret wants to care that her husband never came home after disappearing through the door last night, but her motherly instincts kick in, telling her that she has to behave normally so as not to upset her children, so they have no idea that their parents exist in a passionless and loveless marriage where both have lost their identities and desires.

Routine kicks in. Margaret has to physically shake them all out of slumber. They wash and get themselves dressed while she prepares them breakfast and herself a mug of coffee. They descend, bleary-eyed still, and sit at the kitchen island, forking waffles and maple syrup into their mouths. They eat all of the blueberries, too, which Margaret thinks cancels out the unhealthy aspect of her children's most important meal of the day.

In some other realm, they are eating freshly cut melon and drinking almond milk.

In another, they smother cornflakes in sugar and drink orange juice.

In another, Margaret stayed out overnight and Ash is preparing breakfast for his two daughters.

She drops both boys at school and talks to some of the other parents in the playground about the topics they always seem to discuss. Then she's home and clearing up the morning's mess. She makes herself another coffee and sits, allowing herself to finally take stock of the situation.

She can't imagine that Ash is out with another woman because she can't think who would want him. But you can pay for that kind of thing. She knows he has been worried about his father and he wanted the spare key to his dad's place, but that could just be a ruse, something to throw her off the scent.

Margaret calls Saul. It rings and rings and the answering-machine message that has always made her feel sad for the old man doesn't kick in.

Now she worries. Something must be wrong with Saul. That's where Ash will be. He must be. He's been so worried recently. And she feels guilty for doubting him.

Such a mess.

Margaret has nothing planned for today. She picks up her house keys from the kitchen counter and checks the drawer for her father-in-law's spare key. It's not there. Ash definitely took it. Something is wrong. She can feel it. She needs to be there.

On another planet, just like this one, Saul and Ada are together.

24 NAUGHTY DAVE (AND THE ENVELOPE)

Saboteur Dave did well to cover up his betrayal of burning the note that explained the other Dave's very treatable condition. He spent the rest of the day trying to make it up to his housemate. He cooked bacon at breakfast then washed up the plates and the pan. He made cups of tea and tidied the flat as much as he could, even taking the vacuum to the lounge carpet, which was thirty percent wine stains and twenty percent food crumbs.

He felt guilty.

But he forgot about the envelope.

'Let me help you. Maybe we could move the mattress out of the way for a bit.' Deceived Dave picks up one side of the mattress and leans it against the wall. The carpet underneath is surprisingly clean, considering how many times dead Dave wet himself there. The plastic bag really did the trick.

'You can rest and read some of your book,' offers guilty Dave. 'I've got this.'

That's when in-the-dark Dave spots the folded white envelope with the NHS logo on the outside.

He unfolds and opens the flap to find nothing inside.

'What is this?'

'What? I don't know. An envelope?' He doesn't sound convincing.

'I know it's a fucking envelope, but where is the letter that was in this envelope and when did it come? I've checked the post box three times today.'

'Look, Dave, I...'

'Don't you "look, Dave" me. Where is my letter? What did it say? Why are you hiding it from me?'

There is no evidence of what that letter said. It's burnt into vapour. Duplicitous Dave could say it was about a dentist appointment. He could say that it was confirmation of another required hospital visit.

He could say that it was the results of the test and that Dave only has another few weeks to live because the mass on his brain has spread to a size that is causing too much pressure in his skull but that his lifestyle means that an operation would undoubtedly kill him, anyway, so it's best left until he strains too hard on the toilet one day and an embolism pops in his brain.

But he doesn't. He tells the truth.

'Encephalitis.'

'What?'

'The letter said that you have encephalitis.'

'How long do I have?'

Dave looks at Dave, solemnly.

'Oh, God. I'm going to die, aren't I? Soon. Why did you hide the letter? To protect me? There's no protecting me. I'm going to die. I'm going to die.'

'We're both going to die, Dave. You know that.' The other Dave starts to cry. 'If you hadn't have unplugged the phone, the hospital could have reached you. It could have been treated.'

'That wasn't me. That was bad Dave.' He cries.

'Come on, Dave. You know it's all you.'

'Stop it.' He's angry and hurt and upset and worried about death. 'Stop it. You're a liar.'

'Why would I lie to you, Dave? Whatever happens to you affects me. I don't want you to die but I don't want you to leave me, either.'

Crying Dave runs to the front door.

'I should take this screwdriver and stick it into your skull.'

'What good would that do you? There'd be another one just like me as soon as I was dead. The only way you're really getting rid of me is to stick that thing in your own head.'

'You're a psycho.' He unlocks the door. 'I'm not sticking around here with you any longer.'

'Dave, come o—'

'No,' he interrupts. 'I'm not listening to you any more. I'm going outside. I'm going to the hospital.'

The other Dave takes a step forwards.

'Don't you fucking come anywhere near me.'

The neighbour hears the commotion and walks to his front door to get a better look at things. He uses his wide-feet technique so his shadow can't be seen beneath the door, and he looks through the peep hole. And he listens carefully.

The door opens and Dave is standing there, dishevelled and obviously upset. His eyes are red and his cheeks are wet and he is shouting at someone inside.

'Don't even try to follow me. You're a liar. A goddamned liar.' And he slams the door behind him.

The neighbour feels as though he should help. He should open his door and ask if everything is okay. But he's not a doer. He's the kind of guy who would have sat on that train carriage and watched the woman in the hijab be spat at and cajoled. He's the kind of man who would have frozen at the sight of the stigmatic on Vashti's ward. In another existence, he may have superpowers, but in this one, he is a bystander. A coward. A voyeur.

Dave runs down the stairs to get some air on his face.

25 THE FATHER AND THE SON (AND THE OPEN DOOR)

Saul gets out.

He's not stupid. He knows not to take the pill on his bedside cabinet. That's what makes him feel like he's about to have a seizure. It's the stupid thing that makes him feel dizzy and see those yellow dots in the corners of his vision.

He knows it. They're not angels and he's not dead.

But he is thirsty, so he drinks the water.

He looks down at himself. He feels dirty and soiled. He knows that he must smell. This is the most lucid he has felt since popping the handful of pills he thought would send him straight to Ada.

The lying angels are separate, for once. Both still naked, the male one looks bruised. Saul wants to look at the female one because she is beautiful and waiflike, and her skin is like porcelain. But he doesn't want to look, also. Because of Ada.

He creeps past them with ease. Saul isn't a heavy man but he has definitely withered since his suicide attempt. He is lighter on his filthy feet.

Down the stairs. Avoiding the ones that creak. There's no screwdriver in the door frame and the cold air is still rushing in through the splintered wood. He gets to the bottom and the bolt that has been broken for years. The latch isn't even down. It's just the chain. The flimsy links of metal that add almost no protection.

It's like they want him to leave.

But Saul can't help himself. Intrigue can get the better of people. We like to know things. We like to know the things that other people do not know. And the old man, as much as he needs to get out of that house, needs to know what the hell is making the blanket move in the corner.

He blinks twice. Dizziness. He should just leave. Get some air to his skin, into his lungs.

The old man looks over his shoulder and up the stairs. Nothing there. They are still asleep. Naked and asleep and not together.

He moves over to the blanket and lifts the corner gently.

Real angels don't die. They may get cast out. They may forget who they are for a while. They may want to experience a little more of what it is like to be human. But they go on forever. Just as God does. And religion does. And suffering. And heartache. And pain and selfishness.

And hope.

And passion. And caring. And life. And death.

Light. And dark.

Saul pulls up the corner of the blanket. His eyes widen and he noisily sucks in air. It's Ash. It's his son. He looks hurt. He looks fat. It has been a while since the old man has seen his boy but there is definitely more weight on him. Saul is both worried and repulsed.

He looks over his shoulder. The fake angels are still asleep. It's difficult to focus but he can at least make out that their shapes are not present. Saul shakes his head in an attempt to dislodge the fuzz.

'Ash?' he whispers. 'Ash. What happened? Ash. Can you hear me?'

Nothing.

The old man is confused. He doesn't want to be confused.

'Ash.' A louder whisper. He prods at the fat frame of the wounded beast in his hallway.

An eye opens.

'Dad?' He tries to open his other eye.

'Oh, Ash, you're okay. Thank God.'

Our thoughts and prayers go out to all the people who have been stabbed in the back and left to rot.

'Dad.'

Saul moves in closer because Ash is speaking so quietly.

'Get out of here, Dad. You have to run. Now.'

'I can't leave you here. Who did this to you? Was it the angels?'

'Angels? Dad, what are you talking about? Just go.' Saul shakes his head. 'I'm right behind you,' Ash lies.

Saul hesitates. They gaze into each other's eyes for a moment. A message passing between them but no words. The old man turns away from his son, yellow dots appearing in the corners of his eyes, he takes the chain off the door and opens it. The air hits his face, first, then strokes at it. He takes one last look back at his son.

'Hey. Old man.' A voice at the top of the stairs.

The fake male angel. Nathaniel.

Saul blinks his eyes to try to focus them.

Nathaniel smiles.

'Drank all your water, did you?'

The old man realises that the drugs were also in his drink. The pill was an extra to knock him out. He will feel the full effect of whatever it is they have been giving him, this time.

He looks out the open door.

'Don't even think about it.'

Too late.

The old man goes. He wants to get as far away as he can before his brain is totally compromised by the drugs. He can't move fast so he just goes straight. He half expects the bad angel to catch up with him and take him down but he doesn't look back.

Bad angel runs down the stairs but, at the bottom, is greeted by the man he left in the corner with a blanket over his head. The man hits him squarely on the nose with his fist and the wiry idiot drops to the floor, tears in his eye, blood in the back of his throat. Before he can get to his feet, the large weight of Ash is bearing down upon him and pressing his thumbs into the sides of Nathaniel's windpipe. He can't risk it this time. He will protect his father.

Saul keeps going. He is out on the street. There are cars and parents pushing buggies and people walking their dogs. He can smell Indian food being prepared by a local restaurant and, through the shapes that dance across his vision, he pulls out the image of fruit stacked outside the Polish supermarket.

His forearms start to itch but he doesn't stop. Saul has walked this road for half a century. He knows exactly where he is going.

Ash doesn't know where his strength came from. He hasn't been able to move for a day. At one point, he assumed that the screwdriver was in a part of his spine that meant he could no longer walk. He couldn't feel his legs.

Then, his father bolted out the door and whoever this psycho was that was holding him prisoner in his own home wasn't going to let him. Ash felt light and strong and protective.

The body beneath his starts to go limp. The thrashing of the legs begins to wane, but Ash holds his thumbs in place. As the not-real angel stops moving, the surge of adrenaline that caused Ash to attack dissipates. He releases his grip, and he looks down at Nathaniel.

He has no idea if he has just killed somebody.

He wonders how far his father has managed to move in that time.

He hopes Saul has made it to somewhere safe.

And then everything stops.

Lailah has come downstairs. She could see Ash choking the life out of Nathaniel and she watched as it happened. Waiting. He was screwing it up and Ash had given her a way out. A way to move on to another town to start over. Again.

As soon as it was done, she saw only one choice. The fat man was weakened, hunched over his victim. She can see the screwdriver she had thrust deep into his back once already.

And, then, that voice inside of her.

Lailah listens. Her hands as strong as her instincts, she pulls the screwdriver from Ash's back, lifts it high into the air with both hands on the handle and brings it down, suddenly, into the back of Ash's skull.

She holds it in there, moving it around in circles to open up the wound. The blood pours out and down the side of Ash's face and onto the face below.

All is silent.

Still and silent.

Whoever guards his mouth and his tongue keeps himself out of trouble.

Lailah takes a seat on the third step and breathes. She breathes and stares at the pile of flesh and bones in the downstairs hallway of her sweet, old neighbour.

It was too much action for one day.

Action will get you killed.

And it kills quickly.

Not even time for a life unlived to flash before your eyes.

Ash is dead.

It is the best thing he has ever done with his life.

INTELLIGENCE AND SECURITY COMMITTEE
35 Great Smith Street, London SW1P 3BQ

9th May 2023

Did MI5 make a mistake in not categorising some of the bombers as 'essential' targets?

In order for an individual to be placed on the 'essentials' list, they must be acting in a manner that suggests an involvement in potentially life-threatening activity.

Two of the eventual bombers had been monitored for overseas training but priority is always given to known threats within the UK.

Of course, in hindsight, many more connections can and have been made. However, during surveillance, decisions must be made quickly about the validity of the information available at that time. An individual can appear to be on the periphery of an extremist network, or may be entirely innocent. It is possible to be mobilised within a short time to a more radical ideology, resulting in attacks against the UK.

Given the number of people involved in the 22nd July attacks, MI5 would not have the capacity to have surveilled them for long enough to have picked up the conversations and wording needed to suggest an attack was imminent.

The intelligence services are still governed by laws that protect an individual's right to privacy. MI5 would require adequate reasoning to investigate an individual.

'Essential' targets are prioritised. Many of the 21st July bombers were not even categorised as 'desirable', for reasons outlined in their individual profiles. This fact alone suggests a larger organisation or the possibility of sleeper cells, which is not the focus of this investigation.

26   THE CIRCLE LINE (ALDGATE)

I see the dog collar then I smell the cinnamon from his vape, then his eyes meet mine, but I look away at the station sign and pretend to count the stops until the end of my journey but really I'm thinking, 'A priest, that has to be a sign, right?'

Is preaching the wrong way to go? Does it cause extremism because we are not allowing people to think for themselves? What are the effects of this? What is the impact on society?

It didn't end well for Jesus, did it?

What about Martin Luther King? Or Malcolm X? Or Kennedy? Was there a point where they should have stopped? Is it better to raise awareness and then let people think for themselves? If we try to show both sides of an argument, when it comes to politics, do we really end up showing no sides of an argument?

Does the press now have too much freedom?

Why do I care about these things? Is there a way to make more people care? Is it too late? Am I extreme? Is that why I am here? No God, no narrator, not even a petty thief, so am I simply here as a martyr to a cause that I have now forgotten?

How long have I been travelling on this line? It's only been a couple of days, hasn't it? Or a fortnight in Hell? An eternity in Paradise? Why didn't I just travel here today? Is there a reason I went off plan? Is routine the death of invention or does it breed efficiency?

Do you celebrate religious holidays without celebrating the reasons behind their existence? Do you give your loved ones gifts at Christmas and never think about Jesus? Do you set off fireworks because they are pretty without ever contemplating the victory of light over darkness, good over evil and knowledge over ignorance?

Can one truly believe with everything that their death, in the name of their Lord, will verily bring a bountiful provision in the afterlife? Is martyrdom easier if you are devout or if you are entirely lost?

There are people who travel the same circle each day until their death, and they have no faith, but they possess no malice, and they have no requirement for foresight and they don't look back in anger, and they do not ruffle feathers, nor do they inspire anything in others, but surely we should not look down on these as lesser people? Are they not a requirement? We cannot all make a mark, can we? Some of us have to be soldiers?

Who just stepped onto my carriage? What is that in their hand? An umbrella? Is it raining outside? Does that mean there will be fewer people on the streets above? Does it mean that there will be more on the trains?

How high is up? How long is enough?

So many questions but how do I find the answer that I am looking for?

Should I be more decisive?

Shall I say that 'this is it', today is my last day on this train?

Is it time to find out who I really am?

27 THE NURSE

She is anxious. Her change has been sudden. She has witnessed things that cannot be explained scientifically or medically. Vashti feels different. Care and concern consumes her. She wants to help.

She has to help.

The nurse wakes up alone in her bed. No man in her life, now. She could not give him what he wanted. She would never bear a child. When she wakes, Thomas Davant is in her mind. Something about him. His knowing looks. His advice. His support. That quiet, understated way he has about him. Like he knows exactly what is going on, what will happen and how to encourage others to leap forwards with courage. She had seen it before but it was rare. And she just couldn't place it.

There is a message on her phone from the sportsman about their meeting today. She can tell he is attempting to sound nonchalant but knows that he is desperate to see her.

As she is to see him.

Vashti wants to help.

She wants to heal.

Making herself forget what had happened did not help. She had lost herself. Blocking painful memories with alcohol or drugs or by working too hard, never stopping to take a breath, never having time to pause and reflect for fear of addressing the pain you feel, does not get rid of that pain. It sits there. Hunkered down deep.

Vashti had forced things inside. How those other boys *tricked* her brother into bringing a knife to school. How it got him expelled. How the next school reported his bad behaviour. He was always late. He was socially awkward, didn't get on with anyone in his classes. They said he was 'on the spectrum'. Attention deficit or learning difficulties. An easy diagnosis, she thought. Teachers, ignoring the problem and hoping it goes away. Burying him in a class with others like him, where he did not belong. He was smart. He used to do well at school. There was nothing wrong with him, he just stopped caring.

But she remembers everything now. His truancy. The people he hung around with. She recalls trying to support him, help him. Dr Edelstein thought it was an issue with his identity and how he saw himself. She can see Juned's face that last time she tried and how he looked right through her before he left. It wasn't him any more.

He had been told, consistently, that he did not belong, all it took was someone to say that he had a new family, a place to call home, and he left everything behind. Including a well-meaning sister who was now telling herself that she failed because she could not help.

The sportsman made her stop.

He could see her colours.

Stop.

Breathe.

Confrontation gave her strength.

Vashti lifts her hands and stares at them for a while. There is a power there. It's not electrical. She is not buzzing with an energy, it's more of a warm throbbing that pulsates with the beat of her heart. They are linked. Her hands and her heart. By laying them on another person, she can *push* her love into them.

Perhaps it is not love but empathy. Compassion. And with it, she can heal.

She believes it, wholeheartedly.

Last week, she was a zombie in scrubs, mindlessly floating from patient to patient, bed to bed, problem to problem, disease to incurable disease, without a care.

No throbbing of the hands.

No itching of the shoulder blades.

No tears in her eyes.

Today, she feels ready to explode.

28 THE CIRCLE LINE (BARBICAN)

Is it wrong of me to laugh at that? Because I know that today is the day that I detonate the box strapped to my chest? But, if I am to blow Vashti to pieces, if I am to commit this act of terror, if I am to admit that it is who I am, do I consider myself a terrorist or do I stick with the idea of being a martyr?

If I know that I am causing extreme fear, am I not a demon? Or do I not know? Do I not care?

Have I forgotten the point of this exercise?

Has the message been muddled?

Has it become more important for the revolution to be televised?

When will Vashti take a seat on this carriage so that we can get this finished?

29 THE NURSE (AND THE LOOP)

Vashti texts the sportsman back, agreeing to meet him at Paddington Station. She says that she will be there at nine. He opts for 'nine-ish' because he has a history of turning up late and he's still a little unsure on his crutches.

She smiles at his response and swings her legs out of bed. She feels lighter. More awake. Vashti looks at her face in the mirror. She runs her fingertips over her forehead, around her eyes, then down her cheeks towards her chin.

No wrinkles. No dark bags beneath her tired eyes. A natural rouge to her cheeks. She has never appeared so healthy. She looks ten years younger than she did when she went to bed the night before.

Is this what being good can do for you?

Is this what happens when you accept your own station in life and choose to dedicate yourself to giving something back?

Vashti feels free and energised.

She looks at the time. There is a large part of her that wants to get outside into the morning air and soak up her surroundings. She wants to walk. But, even though it is early, she would never make it to Paddington by nine-ish. She showers quickly and throws on a pair of jeans and a top that is lying over the arm of a chair in the bedroom.

There is a little time. If she leaves now, she can wander along the river for half an hour then jump on the tube when she reaches Embankment. She can take the Bakerloo line all the way to Paddington.

Vashti leaves her flat for the last time. She won't need to go back. The entire world is her home. She has been stuck in a loop of working and fucking, working and sleeping, dying and forgetting. No longer will she finish a shift, smoke her way back home and spread her legs. It is time to open out her wings.

30 THE CIRCLE LINE (BETWEEN BARBICAN AND FARRINGDON)

He's breathing heavily and just managed to make this train, but will he regret running for this carriage?

Have you ever run for such a long distance that your body, although aching, could go on much further but something in your mind trips and prevents you from continuing? How difficult is it to switch off your mind from this and keep running? And is it mental toughness that makes a champion and forges the greatest success?

When you switch on the news and see that children are being kept in cages or women are being stoned to death or animals are being skinned alive, how long does that horror last?

How do you then turn your minds off from what you have witnessed?

If you have lived through war and seen death and struggle and gassing and burning, if soldiers from another country have occupied your village and raped your women because they are fuelled by anger and music and drugs and misunderstanding, how do you digest such an atrocity?

Is this the gift that God gave mankind?

How do so many religious people turn their minds off from that?

Does God move in mysterious ways or is that an excuse? Is that the cop out? Was religion once used for good? Has it now been commandeered by the rich and the powerful for their own self-interest? Is there still good? Has it been lost? Can it be reversed?

How do we switch our minds back on when those who promote thought and change are taken away so easily? When great thinkers and orators are assassinated, should we be surprised that nobody wants to step into their place?

Shouting the most – or the loudest – doesn't always get the point across, does it? Is quiet the new loud? Will another explosion even tickle the effects of the imploding world? Am I just thinking this because the doors have opened on the platform at Westminster?

Who have you shut off from your mind? Saul? The neighbour? What about that female fake angel? Will she be allowed to leave the front door open and get away with the things she has done? Does it matter that she never gets on this train?

Who will show up first?

Are you hoping the runner gets off before Edgware Road?

31   DAVE (AND HIS FOLLOWER)

Dave is freaking out.

He knows the other Dave won't follow him because he doesn't like to go outside, but everywhere he looks, he thinks he can see him. His grey, matted hair poking over the top of a bush or his red, bulbous nose peeking around the trunk of a tree. The other Dave is showing up in shop-window reflections and passenger seats of taxis.

Encephalitis Dave is trying to look as normal as possible, though the pain in his brain is splitting him down the middle. It feels as though one side of his face is falling away, like the person he once was, who he no longer remembers fully, has been pulled in two.

The other Dave's eyes glow yellow in a roadside drain. As Dave walks across a bridge to the other side of the river, that evil version of himself flits between the crowd of commuters.

It's not right. This isn't why he likes to get outside. He is supposed to feel the wind against his cheeks. It is supposed to set him free.

But it's difficult when you know for sure that you are going to die. It was better when he was in Purgatory. When he was waiting for the letter to come through from the hospital that would either confirm or deny his brain tumour. But his mind played tricks on him. It shut him away. It unplugged his phone. It put a screwdriver through the door frame. It created Dave after Dave so he had someone else to blame for throwing his life away.

It could have all been fixed.

Maybe it still could.

In a moment of lucidity and hope, Dave tells his stupid brain that he had to get to St Mary's Hospital. He remembers that the imaging took place there. He knows it is near Paddington Station. And, above all, he knows that he has to get out of the air and away from the other Dave, get somewhere that he can't be followed.

It feels wrong somehow to think it but he has to get back inside, out of the light.

Across the bridge and through the crowd, Dave tries to only look straight ahead. He sees Parliament Square and the architecture that surrounds it. Something that would take his mind away from being followed. But he ducks underneath a walkway and down some stairs until he finds himself next to the barrier. He has his wallet, which contains his bank card and two credit cards. He holds it up against the yellow circle and payment is taken from one of his cards. He doesn't care which one. He is through.

He heads down. Deeper down. Holding the railing of the escalator with one hand and rubbing his forehead with the other. It hurts. He still stinks like urine. He hasn't brushed his teeth. His clothes are creased. His hair is greasy. He is a mess.

Dave blinks ferociously, trying to make the sign in front of him come into focus. He can't read it. He knows he needs the Circle or the District Line – that will get him where he needs to go.

He turns right and follows the corridor to the platform.

If he'd have turned left, his next stop would have been St James's Park, on the way to Paddington. Instead, he is taking the longer way around the track. It would still, eventually, end up at Paddington but his next stop will now be Embankment.

Dave manages to get a seat. He rests his elbows on his knees and clasps his head in both hands. And he massages his fingertips into that oily grey nest on his head, trying to find the right pressure point to relieve some pain.

Dave feels his broken brain swelling inside his skull, expanding his bones as it tries to escape somehow.

He, too, feels ready to explode.

Does anyone else smell that? A mixture of blood and urine? I see where it's coming from, and he looks as though he is ready to collapse on the floor but he's going to take the empty seat next to me, isn't he?

When people get drunk and have sex with somebody who is not their partner and say that they can't remember doing it, that always has to be a lie, doesn't it? How could you function, sexually, if you were that intoxicated? Is it more the fact that your inhibitions evaporate and your brain is not your own and you make terrible choices?

Have you ever heard the saying, 'Don't do drunk what you wouldn't do sober'? What about, 'Don't drink to feel better, drink to feel EVEN better'? Who comes up with these things?

What's wrong with his eyes? Are they rolling back in his head? Is he having a seizure?

Can he see me?

Now that Dave is sitting next to me, is his scent drawing more attention in my direction?

Have you ever had ten drinks and still felt sober? Have you ever had two drinks and felt entirely inebriated? Do you cover your glass when you go out so that nobody can slip a pill into your drink while you are not looking? Remember that story about some guy injecting his tainted blood into other people at clubs?

I know that one of the Daves is here on the carriage, does that mean more will follow? Am I complicit in their lie? Is today the day that I make my decision? If it turns out that I am God, how will this all end? If this was Hollywood or some piece of commercial fiction, you would expect that order would be regained from this chaos, wouldn't you? You would think that I would pull through and find my hunger for a peaceful humanity once more?

What's the difference between a twist and a reveal?

But, if I am to blow this train car to pieces, if the explosion that rips through my chest and kills other passengers, or maims them, or embeds the coins from their purse into the bones of their legs, or shatters the glass that blinds them, then what is the message? Is there a solution in that scenario?

What would be the point that I am making?

Do all the questions have to be answered?

Is that woman over there looking at Dave or me? Should I be worried? Am I sweating now? Is there an obvious bulge in my jacket? What is Dave looking at? Is he avoiding his own reflection?

What happens if he tries to talk to me?

Is this why farmers do not name the animals they know will eventually be slaughtered?

33 THE SPORTSMAN

It's not easy. The sportsman takes a plastic shopping bag from the cupboard beneath the sink and makes a slit across the bottom. He turns it upside down, places it over the foot of his broken leg and pulls it up to his waist, tucking the bag into his cast. The rest of the bag hangs down his thigh. It's not perfect but it should stop the thing getting wet.

He wants to look his best for Vashti. He wants to smell his best too – not that it will matter, if he is getting on the same carriage as the Daves – which is why the top ten inches of his cast are now wrapped in plastic. He wants a bath.

Vashti has responded to his message. He explained that he is heading out of town on the train to visit his coach around lunchtime and they agreed to meet at Paddington to keep things efficient.

The sportsman runs a shallow bath and pours in some muscle-relaxing salts. He is still working out as much as he can – hopping up and down his stairs and performing straight-leg sit-ups and single-leg squats – and adds the salts out of habit.

He lowers himself into the water, resting the heel of his broken leg on the side of the tub until he can lie flat on his back with his foot high against the wall and the top of the plastic kissing the hot water.

The blind on the window is a bright teal colour, he knows this, because he bought it for that reason; it's the same as his team's colour. But it looks grey. His mind tricks him, telling him it is a grey that is obviously blue, but he knows it is washed out.

The mind can so easily be tricked.

In the same way, he knows that the mango shower gel he always buys is yellow. It's a lighter grey than the blind, and he wants to say that it is a yellowy grey but it's not. It's another shade of faded black. The only colour he can see is the nurse who has agreed to meet him later.

And that's fine. For now.

He doesn't know why he is doing it. The sportsman hasn't stopped thinking about the nurse since he left the hospital. Is he expecting to sleep with her? Does he not possess the vocabulary to thank her as much as he would like? He has no idea what will happen when they get together but there is something within him that says it is the right thing to do.

This is supposed to happen.

In a world exactly like this one but somewhere else entirely, the sportsman is sitting in a deep bath, devoid of hope, the casted leg sits under the water and his wrists have been slit because he has been told that he will never run again.

He just wants to see her. He wants to see colour. He wants it to be private and unobstructed, so that he has the time to take it in. Drink her in. Perhaps she knows the reason. Maybe she has some answers. The sportsman knows that she calms him. He recalls, vividly, how her touch in the ward took away the pain in his leg for a moment.

She did it again when he pretended he was visiting Thomas Davant.

But he has no idea what power hides behind her colour and her care. He doesn't know what this meeting is or why he would ever agree to it.

The sportsman scrubs vigorously between his legs with the mango shower gel, he wants to be fresh in case things do turn sexual. He can't see the colour but he still loves the smell.

The cast survives. He dries himself with a towel whose true colour he can't remember, and gets dressed. All his clothes are black, white and grey, so he assumes they match even if they don't. And he leaves his house for the last time as a broken man.

Maybe it's the natural competitor in him but he seems to be getting faster and more confident on his crutches. The sportsman decides to take the tube from King's Cross because they have better disabled facilities – though the idea of having a disability fills him with fear and melancholy. He throws up into his mouth and swallows it back down. Not a lot, but it burns as it goes past his throat.

It's only fourteen minutes to Paddington on the Circle Line. There are four stations between. The app on his phone says that he will stop at Edgware Road at 8:51, sometimes passengers have to change there to go on to the next station, which is Paddington, so he should arrive just before the agreed time.

A woman with an expensive-looking, leather, monogrammed laptop bag stands up and offers the sportsman her seat.

'I only have a few stops,' he tells her. 'I'm sure I can manage.'

'Absolutely not. Please.' She gestures towards the seat and then scowls at the men who would not vacate theirs for somebody less fortunate than themselves.

'Thank you. That's very kind.'

He slumps. He doesn't want to show it but he is exhausted by his journey already. The sportsman takes a look around the carriage at some of the men that have been scowled at. Most of them are staring at phone screens. One has his face hidden behind what looks like a script. Another man, with bright-white hair, looks to be homeless. There's a stain on the front of his trousers and he is looking in any direction he can to avoid eye contact with a single other person.

And there's a man next to him, he's sweating the kind of sweat nervous flyers sweat on planes. He catches the sportsman's eye and seems shocked that he has even been seen. The sportsman nods a good morning in his direction in an attempt to disarm the situation. The man nods back, takes a deep breath, puts a hand to his chest and looks away.

Opposite him is a man who looks like a university professor. He has three bags by his side as though he is travelling somewhere or has returned from travelling.

Another man stands a few feet from the sweating passenger. He has the frame of a manual labourer. He will be lucky to survive a blast at that distance.

In another reality, he would only lose his legs.

34   THE CIRCLE LINE (KING'S CROSS)

Isn't this where I arrived two days ago? But where from? Why is my brain so frazzled? Isn't it supposed to be clean and washed and pure and ready? Could I cry, right now?

Did he just look at me? That man with the broken leg and the crutches, did he nod his head in my direction as some kind of morning salutation? Do you think he could see that I'm nervous? I would know that if I was your narrator, wouldn't I, because I'd have just told you his side of the story?

But I know it is the sportsman and I know he is on his way to meet the nurse, but how can he see me when nobody else has bothered to notice? Do I want to be seen because my life changed so drastically when I felt like I was being listened to?

There are no children on this carriage, I assume because it is early morning and it's predominantly commuters, but if I am doing this for a cause, would I worry about hurting a child? Am I even worried or is it just another question? Am I stalling?

Am I panicking because it's close? Do I know if there are more like me at this station? Is there something I should live for? Who persuaded me otherwise?

Who convinced the world that chocolate and orange is a flavour combination that works? I said that before, right? If I'm repeating, I must be running short on time? What's the funniest joke you've ever heard? Are you afraid of death? Were you told, as a child, that swallowing gum was bad because it stays in your stomach for seven years? When did you stop believing everything that your parents told you? What about your teachers? Do people still trust the church or doctors or politicians? Is there anything left to believe in?

What happens if I go through with this and there is nothing?

Maybe this is all in my head? Or worse, maybe it's in that guy's head? Or worse still, Dave's head?

If I have one of the Daves and the sportsman and the professor and the contractor and that woman who gave up her seat and the others past the doors, do I really need to wait for the nurse and the old man? How can I be sure that they will come? How many are on here now? Thirty? Thirty-two?

We can't let the fake angel get away with murder, can we?

Can killing be justified if the cause is much bigger than ourselves?

Am I a hypocrite? Aren't we all? Am I more paranoid than ever? Is that how they get you?

35 MARGARET (AND THE DEAD, FAKE ANGEL)

The splintered door has been left ajar and Margaret is greeted by the sight of her dead husband lying on top of a half-naked androgynous male with half his clothes missing, and the image in front of Ash's wife is not as disturbing to her as the one in her imagination.

A thousand questions race through her mind. A seed has been planted. She thinks back to the times when he would come home late from work and she worried that he was being a walking cliché and fucking his secretary or he was paying women to do things to him that she would not. Margaret was by no means a prude in the bedroom but perhaps her husband was into some kinky stuff.

Maybe Margaret couldn't give him what he wanted even if she tried.

Maybe he was more into men.

The half-naked man beneath her dead husband is beautiful. And he doesn't look exactly like a man, there is a feminine quality to him that she understands as attractive.

Margaret could have been checking her husband's pulse but she resigns herself to the loss quicker than one would expect and her attention is now focussed on her elderly father-in-law.

'Saul,' she calls out, cautiously, pushing the broken door open and stepping past the heap of possibly gay bodies at the bottom of the stairs. 'Saul, are you here? Are you okay?'

Margaret stops halfway up the stairs. What was she doing? Two (probably) dead people, an open front door, the upstairs is dark and the flesh on her arms has goosed. She doesn't need to be here.

She's a widow now. A single mother. She can't be putting herself into dangerous situations. She's all those kids have.

Margaret backtracks. She's so annoyed with Ash about this. If he wasn't so dead, she would be laying into him, verbally, about his irresponsibility. Why now? Why had he suddenly decided to give a damn about his father? Saul is a good man, Margaret has always liked him. He should have been an inspiration to Ash when it came to love. The way that man felt about Ada was written across his face and the same went for his utter despair at her leaving him behind.

She craved this for herself but has let it slide, it's easier to not want. To be comfortable. To have a house with a fireplace and heavy curtains and a £150 corkscrew that opens wine bottles perfectly every time and marble worktops in the kitchen and Farrow and Ball on every wall.

Live.

Laugh.

Love.

Paper wife with her paper kids.

She wants to feel sad about the man she had married but can't muster the emotion. Perhaps she is already so sad that she can't be brought down any further. Her emotions washed out like the colour in the sportsman's eyes.

'Saul? I'm going to call the police, okay?' She waits for some movement from upstairs. If there's anybody else there, that should make them move. But there's nothing.

At this exact time, in another place, Ash wakes up and the couple reconcile. Somewhere else, he does the same but Margaret sticks the screwdriver in deeper.

Here, she dials 999.

A friendly female voice answers and asks what her emergency is.

'My husband is dead. He looks to have been stabbed. There's another man with him that I have never seen before. He's dead, too.'

Margaret is asked whether she has checked for a pulse or whether either of the men are breathing. She gets angry and tells the friendly voice that they are not breathing and that she is not going to touch a dead body.

The police are apparently on their way.

After answering a few more insensitive questions about her involvement in the crime, Margaret is told that help has been dispatched, both police and ambulance. She hangs up the phone as the woman on the other end is explaining about staying on the line until aid arrives.

She walks up the stairs of Saul's place, less scared than before. It looks the same as it always did. Ada wasn't as much of a clean freak as Margaret, so it isn't like the flat could do with a feminine touch. It has never had one before.

Some of the furniture has moved around in the lounge. She goes into the kitchen and sees two glasses with red wine residue in the bottom. They belong to the fake angels but she assumes a bottle was shared between her husband and his male lover.

Then she opens the fridge. She doesn't know why but she does. An uncovered cheese sandwich is curling at the crusts. There's a bottle of ketchup in the door and a carrot on one shelf. And she discovers that there is still sadness within her when she begins to cry.

Margaret understood what it was like to feel lonely. It wasn't like Saul, she hadn't lost the great love of her life. Somewhere along the line, she had lost herself.

Now that the sportsman has seen me, does that mean that everybody can? Are they suspicious? Are they watching? Am I sweating? Oh, God, am I going to kill all of these people? Am I going to kill myself?

Do you ever get the feeling that somebody is looking at you? When you find that it's true and you realised without ever seeing them staring, how do you explain that? Have you been to Las Vegas? Have you stood around a roulette table and convinced yourself that the ball will land on a red, or an even, or number twenty? Can you quantify intuition?

How about luck?

Are there people you know who always come up smelling of roses? Do you hate them?

Did that woman with the bag just look at my bag? Does she know? Will the man who ran for the train get off at the next stop? If he does, will he realise how lucky he is?

Doesn't it come back to that question of destiny and whether everything is predetermined? Isn't that an awful way to live? Can we take advantage of it?

What about those idiots who say that everything happens for a reason? Another cop-out, right? Aren't you being told that it's lucky for a bird to crap on your head because it's a way of softening the fact that an animal chose to defaecate on you? Does this protect us in some way?

Have you ever been driving in your car and noticed that the same car has been behind you for a long time, turning when you turn, slowing when you slow?

Why would somebody follow you?

What did you do?

If I am the narrator of this mixed-up tale, why do I not talk about those fake angels more? Am I not supposed to make you care about every character?

Can you have someone in a story that is insignificant?

Do you find Lailah insignificant? Did you think her love for Nathaniel was too extreme? Can obsession be a good thing? Do you want her brought to justice? Or is it okay if she gets away?

What if I tell you that I can see her right now on this carriage? Would it be poetic for a pretend angel to come face to face with God?

As a human being, is it right to have no compassion about the death of another person, no matter how little we know them, no matter what they have done, no matter what has gone wrong? Even if a person does not inspire others, if they make no impact, if they achieve little, earn little, create little, do they not each have some significance? Do they not each have a place?

Can the butterfly who chooses not to beat its wings still cause a tidal wave?

Can I cause an impact by not going through with this?

37   LAILAH (AND THE DOUBLE-BACK)

Lailah is paranoid that she is being followed, she is being watched. She, too, is lost. Moving from town to town, city to city, a trail of emotional destruction in her wake. She didn't want to follow the old man, to make sure that he didn't talk, didn't describe her to the authorities. She would be long gone before they came after her.

She was fond of Saul. She never wanted to hurt him.

She didn't want to hurt anyone.

Lailah is searching for something, she just doesn't know what it is.

But Lailah wants to discover why she is here, what her purpose is. So she doesn't want to get caught. She's not a spy. She has no military training. But she has seen enough films and read enough books to know that she can't go home. The first place they look is the partner's house or the mother's home. She is not stupid. For now, she wants to keep moving.

She uses cash to buy a ticket for the Underground. She has no destination in mind. She stays on a few stops then switches lines. Stays on a few more stops then switches direction again. She tries not to make eye contact with anyone, which is difficult because men have always wanted to look at her. It sometimes makes her angry and it sometimes makes her feel wanted.

She's not going to Paddington. She doesn't even make it to Edgware Road. Lailah gets off the carriage before Vashti gets on. The sportsman notices her legs and she smells Dave's clothes.

Lailah leaves the train because Saul gets on.

She escapes their fate.

Cheats it, maybe.

Lailah changes trains once more then resurfaces into the polluted London air. She walks across the capital for three quarters of an hour before hopping on a bus that takes her through Tavistock Square and on to her final destination.

38   THE CIRCLE LINE (BETWEEN GREAT PORTLAND STREET – BAKER STREET)

Do you always sing that Gerry Rafferty song when you're heading towards this station? Was there more to him than Baker Street?

Am I deflecting again?

If I keep asking these things then I don't have to do it, do I?

I have to face up to this at some point, don't I? How soon?

Can you smell Dave's trousers even though you are not here? Is he really here or do I just know him? Is it that reality? What would you write on the sportsman's cast if he let you? Did you recognise any of the songs that the neighbour was singing in his apartment?

A priest, a psychopath and a prostitute walk into a bar; how many did you picture as a woman?

Has anybody ever drawn a perfect circle, freehand?

It's the stop after Baker Street, isn't it? Could I get off here? Can we forget all about this? Pretend it never happened?

Should I have made Lailah stay on for one extra stop? This will all be over soon, won't it? If there is such thing as another realm – and I am not talking about Heaven or Hell or Hades or anything like that, because I am sure of their existence; I am talking about the replica of this place – if there is another realm, another train car, another set of people just like this, another broken leg, another piss-drenched brain tumour, could there be one where I am good?

What is 'good', anyway?

If you come from nothing and make more money than you can ever spend, is it up to you to use that money you have earned to solve the world's problems? If, as one single person, your net worth is greater than that of the country of Denmark, are you supposed to feed the starving or stop trees from being cut down? What is the logic behind that? How does that teach the rest of the world? If you bail them out so easily, won't they just fuck it all up again?

Is it better to hand the world a metaphorical rod, rather than a metaphorical fish?

Did Lailah get off because she saw the old man get on? Or was this always her plan? Or is her plan to have a lack of plan? If she saw Saul, would she not want to avenge her fallen partner? Did she escape? Does anyone?

Am I only waiting for Vashti now? It seems that I have made up my mind, doesn't it?

Did you ever wonder what you would do in a situation where you are being forced to choose between a depressed God, a biographer and somebody willing to die for a cause they believe in? Do you think you lack empathy? Is there a part of you that thinks, 'the world isn't going to end in my lifetime, so why should I care about trees/animals/oceans/the ozone layer/my children's children?'

Why did the Daves and the fake angels both use a screwdriver in the door? Does the sportsman view the world differently now that he can only see in black and white? Do you think it makes things clearer somehow? Is somebody going to give up their seat for Saul? He looks frail and confused, and I can't see anybody moving to create some space for him, but that's probably more to do with the fact that he looks like he has taken a substance he can't handle, isn't it?

And the last thing I want to do is draw attention to myself in any way, when I'm still waiting for the nurse, but I also don't want a drugged-up pensioner ruining everything, and I find myself shifting forwards on my chair and I'm looking around to see if anyone is looking back and they're not because everyone hates everyone or they're scared or anxious or claustrophobic, and have you ever had a moment where your mind doesn't seem to be in control of your body and it moves unconsciously? Have you ever driven somewhere that you've been to a hundred times before and you can't remember how you got there?

Have you ever thought about saying something but the words somehow can't escape your mouth?

'Sir, would you like to take my seat?'

39 SAUL (AND THE KIND OFFER)

The old man has just enough clarity to hold his son's credit card against the sensor to open the barrier at Baker Street tube station. The escalators were not as much of a challenge as he had expected because he could hold on tightly and didn't have to move his feet.

He reaches the bottom and curses the spots on his vision. A part of him feels sick, another wants to giggle.

He misses Ada.

Where is she? This is worse than Purgatory.

He wants to cry. But he can't.

He wants to get away. But he doesn't know what he is getting away from. He has no idea where he is going. He just has to move.

The signs are blurred. A purple line. A grey line. A yellow line. Saul heads towards the yellow. He can still see colours. But doesn't know what they mean. Maybe, somewhere, sometime, he would take the purple and get the Hell out of there. But today, now, he takes the Circle Line. The one where God or our narrator or some confused individual that the news networks will say was 'quiet' and 'lonely', who has a bomb strapped to his chest, is watching.

The doors open on the carriage and he tries to step on before letting the passengers alight and is pushed back without a care. Weak and pale, Saul looks like he could die at any moment. The beating of that butterfly's wings could have blown the old man to the floor. A woman hit him in the shins with her buggy. A man swings his rucksack over his shoulder and hits our old man in the chest.

He laughs.

He feels sad. Tired.

Saul wants the train to carry him away.

The train begins to move towards Edgware Road. Saul has no idea, he is holding on to a pole to stop himself crashing to the floor. He's not expecting anybody to give up their seat for him. But he hears a voice. It sounds friendly. They call him 'sir'. They ask if he would like to take their seat.

Saul doesn't pay attention to the man with the bags or the one with the cast on his leg. He doesn't spot one of his fake angels at the other end of the carriage. She gets off, watches him through the window before disappearing into a tunnel.

He can't even make out the identity of the kind person who offered up their seat for an elderly traveller. To Saul, the compassionate commuter is masked, a ball of light. Much like Lailah and Nathaniel were when they discovered him.

The last time he was supposed to die.

In his head, he asks, *Am I dead?*

'Thank you. That's very kind.' Saul wobbles his way between the bent knees and feet and melts into the warmth of God's throne. He shuts his eyes. And he hopes that he won't have to ever open them again, and, if he does, Ada will be there.

The old man puts a hand in his pocket, feels the wallet, and it reminds him of Ash. His brave and selfless son.

His saviour.

His boy. His neglected, little boy.

Those tired, crepe-paper eyes stay shut until the shouting.

40 THE CIRCLE LINE (BETWEEN BAKER STREET – EDGWARE ROAD)

Could I be defined as an *unreliable* narrator? Has my credibility been compromised in some way? What have I told you so far that makes me untrustworthy? Haven't I only asked you questions?

Surely I am the one who knows how this all ends?

Do I have to be honest? Is that the rule?

What if none of the things I have said are true? What if three of them are true? What if I know exactly who I am, exactly why I am here and what I am to do?

Maybe I have been distracting you while the others get into place?

Have you ever noticed how neighbours react when they realise they have been living next to a serial killer or suicide bomber; they always say how 'normal' the killer seemed while a team of police work hard to piece the buried bones back together, they always say the terrorist was very quiet and kept himself to himself, isn't that odd? Is there a pattern? Can the police create a profile?

Do these people naturally fly in the face of societal norms or are they a product of this fucked-up society? Surely martyrs are not born but made?

Because we live in an increasingly secular society, I'm guessing that you have come to your own conclusion that I am not God, right? You think that there is no God so in any story where a person believes they are the big man upstairs or the second coming of Christ, they must be a cult leader or schizophrenic or something? When I first posed the question 'Am I God?' did you gloss over it because it was too early to determine what kind of a story this would be? Now you know me, you think you have me worked out, don't you?

I'm not God, am I? I'm not some regretful deity, deep in contemplation about the world I created and how I let the project run away with me, because wouldn't that make me no better than the cowboy entrepreneur who organised that Fyre Festival, trying desperately to dig my way out of a situation but only digging deeper?

That can't be right, can it? Would you not expect God, who can hear all the prayers of the world at once, to be better at planning?

Doesn't it show a surprising lack of multi-tasking ability that each day was dedicated to only one thing, during creation? Does this not go further in explaining why bad things happen to good people and children get shot in schools and buildings blow up?

And you don't think that I am the narrator because it's an odd concept to wrap your head around, isn't it? But can you deny that I have narrated a lot of this story?

You think I am a bomber? Does the questioning fit with that hypothesis? Am I quiet? Will my neighbours say that I keep myself to myself? Have you given any more thought to what I said earlier? Have I sown a seed? Are there more like me?

Would you believe me if I told you that I am still not sure?

I could still be the one who walks away?

Or are you now thinking about that unreliable narrator thing?

Have I made myself untrustworthy?

Do you think of me as a criminal?

Do you know how this ends?

41 THE LAST ONE

Vashti is the last member of the club to enter the train. Due to some maintenance issues on the Bakerloo Line, she is forced to exit her carriage and change at Edgware Road. She stands on the platform and checks her watch.

8:45. Thursday. July 21st. She's already walked 2,013 steps, apparently.

The next train will arrive in two minutes according to the board above the platform. Plenty of time to get to Paddington and meet with the sportsman.

After a shift like yesterday, she would normally turn off her alarms, pull down the blackout blind in her bedroom and emerge for breakfast in the early afternoon. But today is different. She doesn't even feel tired.

She is fresh. Renewed.

Born again.

There's a list of cult leaders and evangelical preachers who have spouted the words of disciples and prophets and laid their hands on the allegedly sick to heal them. They have done this not through altruism or to spread the word of their lord but for personal gain. For wealth, fame and notoriety. And many have done it for sex.

Not Vashti.

She looks up. One minute until the train arrives.

The nurse wants to help people. She has witnessed so much recently. The patient who had been stabbed, exhibiting marks that looked like stigmata – the wounds of Christ at the crucifixion. Thomas Davant: a prophet if ever there was one. And the sportsman. Damaged physically with his broken leg and mentally with his black-and-white vision. Perhaps, spiritually, too.

These were laid out before her to remind her of who she is and why she is here.

Vashti is good. She has always been good. She went through a phase when her faith had dwindled. She had fallen. But it could not be coincidence that she had seen the things she had seen, that she had done the things she had done. She had calmed the sick and injured with her touch.

She is not mad, she is remembering.

Vashti is a servant of God.

It's still coming back to her. She thinks about three days ago, ten years ago, a hundred years ago. That section of time where she was numb, she could not feel, she could not care, it was a blip. God was silent. But now she hears him with every cell of her body. Every vibration of the Earth.

There is a rumble beneath her feet as the train pulls in. A screech of brakes. A tingling sensation in her back. The doors open. She stays still as people step off.

She steps up and into the carriage. The smell of urine. The sound of mumbling and beeping as the doors shut behind her. A sense of unease. Disquiet.

And then joy as she spots the outstretched, casted leg of the sportsman she is supposed to be meeting at Paddington in twelve minutes.

She smiles at him warmly and clocks his reaction. Partly pleased to see that it is Vashti and partly, she knows, because he can see greens and blues and yellows and pinks.

'Well, look at this,' she says, enthusiastically. 'It seems that fate has dealt us a kind hand.' She leans in, hugs and kisses the air beside the sportsman's cheek.

'What a perfect surprise,' the broken man replies, love in his eyes, pain in his leg. 'The Lord does work in mysterious ways.'

42 THE OLD MAN AND DAVE AND THE SPORTSMAN AND THE NURSE. AND THE BOMBER (AND THE OTHERS)

The band's all here.

To our right, we have one of the Daves on keyboard. The wet patch on his crotch has dried but the stain is prominent. He taps his fingers on his legs, nervously, he swears that he can feel his brain expanding and pushing against his skull. The closer he gets to the hospital, the more his body reacts and fights against him. He keeps his eyes closed because he knows that his brain has been playing tricks on him. He's waiting for a voice to signal that he has reached his destination.

Next to that is old man Saul on the maracas. He fidgets in his seat. Nervous of everyone. He doesn't know who to trust. He is old and he is weak and misses being caught in the middle of the conversation that was the love affair with his wife.

The effect of the drugs are dissipating with the dots in the corners of the old man's eyes. But he keeps moving. Flitting his view from side to side. Seemingly looking at everything but, actually, taking in nothing.

On drums, to our left, is Vashti. The beating of her all-loving, all-knowing, all-believing heart provides the tempo for the soundtrack that is the lives of the people on that carriage. The thrum of the city. She keeps everyone in time. She is not flustered.

She is not scared.

She sits next the sportsman, our lead guitarist, and places a hand on his cast. She wants him to walk. She wants a miracle. For the broken man to stand up on that train, drop his crutches, tear at his cast and walk off into Paddington station.

But bands argue. They break up. Creative differences. Lovers. Losers. Different ideas and directions, and the lead singer has something he wants to say.

He starts shouting. Saying words that nobody can understand but the tone and intent is clear. It's another question. He is wondering who wants to die today.

Dave opens his eyes and takes notice.

Saul stops moving and stares at the man who kindly offered up his seat. Saul is not afraid.

The sportsman is frozen. His leg no longer aches. He wiggles the toes on his broken leg as he stares at the black-and-white lunatic. Grey innocents behind him, in front of him, all around him. And one red button.

The beating stops and Vashti stands up. Face to face with the crazed individual. She didn't notice him when she got on because she was so pleased to see the man she had come to meet.

She considers herself a healer and her immediate thought is to talk him down with her calming words.

She takes in his face. Dark eyes. Upset. Pretending to be brave while pissing his pants.

He looks her dead in the eyes.

She says, 'You.'

And she wants to stop what he is going to do.

She sees everyone on that carriage. The brain tumour, the heartache, the broken body, the traveller with three bags, the woman with the scowl and others in fear.

And the man with the bomb.

You.

Vashti takes a step forwards, hoping she can get closer and calm the bomber, like she calmed the sportsman. Like she calmed the stigmatic. But this is not a fairy tale. This is not how it is. The three acts do not move from order to chaos to regained order.

One step.

He says something quietly that nobody hears or understands.

One step.

He will not allow her to take another.

He knows who he is.

No question.

PART THREE

THE **GREY**

1   THE PRAYERS (AND THE THOUGHTS)

Our thoughts and prayers are with those people caught in an explosion on a Circle Line train at Edgware Road.

We send out waves of hope to those families still waiting to hear from loved ones.

A nation mourns at the tragedy inflicted by a confused fanatic, whose neighbours say he was quiet and always kept himself to himself.

This is what will happen.

Social media will become a breeding ground for both hatred and self-righteousness. News channels will go to war. Cue a solemn but sympathetic comment from a world leader. Watch as a pop star with a faint grasp of current affairs offers some guidance. Give it a second, maybe less, because everyone will have an opinion and almost everyone will voice it in some way, and the noise will become confusing and deafening, and somewhere, someone is being overwhelmed by the flapping of all these butterfly wings and will repeat the cycle of terror.

Another earthquake. Another tidal wave.

You have to search harder to find the true compassion.

Insert the words 'Just Be Kind' onto a neutral background, written in a noteworthy font with a pastel colour. Witness as the disparate community known as humankind collectively rolls its eyes at the insincerity of the platitude.

The concept is too simple

Get ready for stories of hardship and courage.

Truths and embellishments.

Facts and spin.

It is 8:51 and the dust has far from settled.

Things ended differently for everyone on that carriage but they all began in the same way. With a flash of white light.

The same flash was also seen on the Central Line at Bond Street. And the Bakerloo Line at Embankment.

And Aldgate East. And St John's Wood. Tottenham Court Road. And Russell Square.

Same time. Different place.

Attack after attack. Brutal and orchestrated.

An hour later came the buses. And the vans driving into crowds on bridges.

Once people were pushed inside and off the roads, the buildings would blow.

The ways of His working are yet more mysterious.

The problem with the conclusion of any story is that it is not the same for everyone. They may have all been in the same location, they may have all seen the light, but the way they saw it can vary significantly. And while that moment of purity marked the end for many, it sparked a rebirth in others.

We are a species unified by tragedy, disconnected through apathy. We cannot think beyond ourselves.

In another time and place, the train pulls in to Paddington Station. Vashti heals the sportsman's leg and he finds a new lease of life and faith. Dave makes it to the hospital and they start him on a course of medication, which sees improvement in his condition. Margaret takes care of Saul and eventually remarries a man who appreciates her for a while before getting caught with his dick in the mouth of another exploited secretary.

But that is not this story.

There were many vantage points on that train carriage. Everybody saw what happened, how it unfolded. Some saw a brainwashed kid, others saw horror. They saw a terrorist. And one may have even seen God.

All of their stories are different.

All of them happened.

And all are true.

Not one thought or prayer can make the slightest difference.

2   THE OLD MAN (AND THE END)

Saul was ripped apart.

A flash of light and the force of being that close to the explosion tore through his withered body and brittle bones and fragile heart.

That heart. That beautiful, endlessly loving heart, longing to meet with the great love of his life once again. A heart that decided it was so difficult to live without his Ada that he would take a couple of handfuls of pills to be with her once more.

A heart that was so blinded by his undying devotion, he saw the blur of two people holding him hostage as his guardian angels, delivering him slowly through Purgatory to be with his wife.

Saul was torn in half.

The flash of white light extinguished those yellow dots in the corners of his vision before his head was separated from the rest of his body.

He saw the man who had so kindly given up his seat, standing in the aisle. At first he was shouting. Saul was confused. It didn't seem like the same person. Then there was an attractive woman talking at him. He remembers her face. Kind. Colourful. True.

Saul looked back at the angry man. He didn't notice the bomb on his chest or the trigger in his hand. Saul noticed his eyes. Filled with fear and certainty. The old man didn't have time to wonder how such contrasting emotions could exist simultaneously.

He heard the man say something under his breath. To Saul, it sounded like, 'And so now I take them.' But that wasn't right.

First the flash.

Then the tearing.

An already-broken heart blasting into a splintered ribcage. Shredded.

And now he could ask the same question he asked of those fake angels.

'Am I dead?'

And the answer would be the same. And, if he was in his own personal Purgatory, it would look just like the flat he had shared with Ada and the fake angels. The one where his son came to his rescue and paid the greatest price.

Saul is dead. Parts of his body can be found on either side of his seat. Things that were solid are now liquid and would coat the window behind him if it hadn't been shattered by the blast. He is not in Heaven, nor is he in Hell. But he is dead. And he is not being guided through Purgatory to meet his soulmate because Ada is not waiting for him.

They lived long, and Saul loved for a couple of years longer.

They are not together.

They are not looking down on their grandchildren.

They have not been reunited with their hero son.

Ada had cancer and then she was nothing. Saul had heartache and then he was blown up.

Love was not enough to keep them for eternity. But that does not matter. Saul understood the magic of the moment. He did nothing spectacular with his life. He changed very little. He offered the world no great solutions. His flat was small. His food was unadventurous. But his heart was full and his gift was that he knew it.

If you want to see genuine laughter, show Saul the picture in your lounge that says, *Live. Laugh. Love.* Because he did that. And he didn't shout about it.

And his flat was small and his hobbies uninteresting, but his heart was full and he knew it. And he showed it.

And his flat was small and the fridge barely stocked and the ceiling yellow with age and the kiss of a thousand cigarettes.

And his flat was small and the doorway was splintered and the furniture was modest but well made and had lasted decades because *things* didn't matter to the old man. Possessions were not love. And love is what he had.

And he knew it.

For Saul, life had been a wondrous adventure because Ada had been a part of it. A blessing. Just as his death has been.

He is not with Ada. But he doesn't know that. He doesn't know why he was taken in such an aggressive fashion. He doesn't understand the motivation behind such an event. He doesn't need to.

Saul is dead. A pair of navy-blue slacks hang over the trouser press in his flat.

And he no longer hurts.

3 THE MAN WITH THE BAGS (AND THE SHRAPNEL)

He isn't integral to the story but it is important that he is mentioned and not forgotten. Because he was there and he was innocent.

And his injuries would have been much worse if the harder suitcase hadn't been in front of his legs.

It's typical bystander behaviour. He sees a man arguing with a woman and his self-preservation instincts kick straight in. He feels that he should try to protect her but his feet refuse to move. He keeps his gaze downwards. No book to read or mobile phone to scroll through meaninglessly, he opts for a twirling of thumbs and a rubbing of hands.

And even though he isn't looking directly at either of the two people in heated discussion, there comes a moment where everything turns white.

But he does not die.

Both eardrums are perforated. He loses his right eye, and several pieces of shrapnel have to be removed from his arms, shoulder and chest. Half a fifty-pence coin remains embedded in his thigh.

But he is not dead.

He has been away from his family for a week or so on business. He was returning to them that morning. His wife has been calling and going through to voicemail and she cries at the scenes on the news.

One bomb at Edgware Road. Another nearby at Swiss Cottage. Five more dotted around the capital. She can't think straight. Could he have been on any of those trains?

The man with the bags will eventually put his family's mind at ease. He is safe. He was on one of the carriages. He remembers a bright light. And now his vision is different, he is physically less than he once was and, though he survived, though this is not the end for him, though everyone around him will try to be optimistic and say that this is the beginning, 'A new beginning', for the man with the bags, who did not perish in the attack, the remainder of his life on Earth will be Hell.

It doesn't have to be.

Like Saul, the man with the bags could choose to recognise the things that he does have. His life. His wife. His children. Sight in his remaining eye. The constant reminder of how close he came to eternal blackness after that white blast.

Or he could find a new faith and purpose. He could become an inspiration to those around him. A survivor. A trier. A doer. A campaigner. He could decide to be one of the few who can make a difference. He could turn an atrocity into an opportunity.

But he doesn't.

The old man made very little impact on the world but his small corner was filled with love and the recognition and appreciation of that love. His time on Earth was not in vain. His time in the dark will be peaceful.

The man with the bags will do worse than Saul. He will do less than the nothing that made Saul's life so rich.

And it wasn't his fault. It wasn't his fight. He was in the wrong place at the wrong time. He was minding his own business, looking forward with a happiness he would never feel again.

And what kind of a God, a present, all-seeing God would allow that to happen. Because, even though the bomb on that train did not take the life of the man with the bags, it absolutely did prevent him from ever living again.

4   THE TERRORIST (AND THE END?)

So, this is it? The end? You've heard what happened so now you think you know me, know who I am and what I did? Is there a chance that even a flash of bright, white light can have some grey areas?

Do you think it is better to live with a disability and the memory of what happened on the train or to wipe the slate clean with death?

If you were told that you could live forever if you gave up something you loved, do you think you would be able to do it? Would you want to?

What if it was cheese? Or alcohol? Or music? Or sex?

What is the point of living forever if you can't have the things that make you want to live forever?

What if you are told, convincingly, that if you give up your own life you will go to a much better place and exist like a king? What if you are so disillusioned by the way you have been treated and have become so lonely and insecure and susceptible to suggestion that you start to believe the things you are being told?

What if you think these people are your friends, that they care?

How long before they ask you to do something for them? How do you say no when they strap one of these things to your chest? When do you start to believe it is the right thing to do? Why do believe them? What happened to you?

If I can be convinced to end my own life and that of many others, is it not possible to convince a suicidal geriatric that he has died?

If I was a terrorist, if one man was ripped open while another lost his eye and another left his legs behind, wouldn't I be dead? Wouldn't there be molecules of me sprayed around the carriage? And if I am dead, how am I recounting my version of events to you? Should I not be basking in Paradise, a martyr to the cause? Would I not be surrounded by virgins right now?

Where am I?

Am I dead?
Could I still be God?
Did I blow up this train?

She said 'you' though, didn't she? It wasn't a question, though, like all of my questions? Was it just me or did Vashti recognise me? Does she know who I am?

5   THE DAVES (AND THE END)

From his waist to his knees, Dave was encrusted with his own urine. Not drenched. He wasn't wet. But he had been. Over and over again. He needed a wash. The trousers needed a wash, or better, to be incinerated. That would have made him more tolerable to be around. That would have made him more presentable. That would have solved the problem.

Instead, he sits on a train that's three weeks too late for a hospital appointment. The damage to his brain is irreversible. He's been hallucinating and imagining things that have not happened. Calls that never occurred. Letters that refused to appear. He created versions of himself to live with so that he was less lonely. Versions of himself that he hated. Versions he wanted to get to know and understand.

This tormented individual, whose brain is slowly dying away, somehow, finds himself on a voyage of self-discovery. He wants to know who he really is before he loses himself entirely. And the disease in his head lets him understand that this is happening but also that he is powerless to prevent it. It has taken hold.

Dave is his own bomb. Waiting to get onto that train and detonate.

He sees the two people talking and, to him, it doesn't look peaceful. It seems manic. The man is so full of energy, he is almost vibrating. And the woman trying to talk him off the ledge seems mad but ethereal.

And he wonders about the Dave he left in the flat and whether all of this might be in that guy's head. Dave on the train is confused. Maybe Dave at the flat needs to wake up and it will all be over.

Wake up, Dave.

He watches how quickly the man standing in the aisle moves his hand towards his side and he says in his brain, *Wake up, Dave.*

Then the light.

The white.

And eventually grey.

Dave's trousers problem was solved because he lost both legs. He was blown out of the train window and onto his back. A passenger further down the carriage, who was not injured, tried to tie a tourniquet around each chewed, fleshy stump. One was tightened with his belt, the other with his T-shirt, which was less effective.

He lost a lot of blood. And he was in and out of consciousness on the platform as the brave passenger who came so instinctively to Dave's aid continued to apply pressure to the wounds. And he talked and talked, even when Dave blacked out, trying to keep Dave and his brain in this realm until help arrived.

When the transport police eventually got to the platform, Dave's would have been just another dead body to haul out of the station, where the air would hit his face and not be felt, not be appreciated, not make a difference. But he was kept alive long enough to get him to the hospital. The one he was heading for all along.

Somewhere across the universe, there's a version of Dave that is healthy and happy because he never unplugged his telephone. He never triple-locked his door. He didn't wedge a screwdriver into the frame. He never slept in a wardrobe or checked his post box six times each day. He never invented housemates to talk to, or slept in a puddle of his own urine, or tried too late to get the help he needed.

But here, in this reality, instead of taking a dose of antibiotics, Dave lost his mind, his legs, his spleen and his life.

Maybe it's for the best.

6 THE WOMAN WITH THE BAG (AND THE MISSING SHOES)

She gave up her seat and it saved her life.

Injuries to her arms and thigh. Scratches. Bruises.

She remembers the white light but no sound. For the woman with the bag, there was no explosion. It was a flood. The news would talk of catastrophe and terrorism but she did not see it that way.

It was a wash. A cleansing. For the woman who gave up her seat, this was a moment where she saw Heaven.

The man and the woman were arguing, or at least in deep discussion. They were the focus of the carriage, either way. And she was watching them. She looked away from her phone screen to examine something in real life. An altercation, as it was, but it was so real it was somehow beautiful. And then, the light. And the woman in the quarrel seemed to rise from the floor and envelope the man who would forever be blamed and immortalised as nefarious and disturbed.

It seemed she was protecting everyone.

Yet the windows smashed and heads rolled and the legs detached, but for the woman who gave up her seat for Dave, there were scratches and bruises and dents.

And shock.

She walked away from the scene. She got out. She walked up the escalator that had stopped moving. She went through the barrier and found a supermarket where the staff were tending to the wounded.

She spoke to them. She took on some water. There were police and paramedics. It was chaos.

'Were you on the train carriage? Did you see what happened? Are you hurt?'

Questions. So many questions.

'I'm Detective Sergeant Pace. Are you injured? What happened down there? I think she's in shock. Paramedic.'

Voices. So many voices.

In the confusion and the dust and the lack of phone reception, the woman with the bag managed to slip away. She just continued to walk away from the scene. She got back to the safety of her home. and she didn't even realise she had been walking the entire way without any shoes. Her feet were cut. She couldn't feel them.

The front door closed behind her, she curled into a ball on the floor, and that is where she stayed until the bright white of the next morning hit her fortunate face.

7 VASHTI (AND THE ITCH IN HER SHOULDERS)

That terrible couple who exploited the heartache of an old man whose wife had died and obliterated his outlook on life: how dare they? How dare they presume to know the difficulty of being an angel. Of being an angel in an increasingly secular society. In a world where religion is still a bigger killer than malaria.

Being an angel is difficult.

An existence of questioning and doubt.

Constant questioning.

And doubt.

'You,' she said.

This was not a question. She knew him. She knew the man who wanted to tell the world that his thoughts and ideals should be heard. That he was willing to die for what he believed in. Or, he wanted to say, 'I am God. And I have made a mistake. And I am back. And I will fix this.'

Vashti, the nurse with the healing hands and the itch in her shoulders, knew the man's eyes. Whether he was reaching for the trigger or she saw that he was ready to wipe everything out and start again, give the idea of humanity another go, Vashti reacted.

She spent years, decades, eons, examining humans, understanding their frailties and their strengths and their mistakes. And, yes, she was lost along the way and she found it more and more difficult to care, but she regained her faith and she felt that, deep down, beneath the insecurities and the fat-shaming and gay-bashing and plethora of words for those whose skin was a different colour, that humanity had worth. That it had lost its way to sins of greed and misrepresentation and self-interest of the few and misinformation and the utter abuse of our global connectivity.

Vashti saw the man in front of her. She saw his eyes. And her heels raised without her thinking as the itch on her shoulders intensified.

As the eyes on the man enlarged. As this world turned. As the sportsman behind her wanted to walk. As Saul thought of Ada. As Dave's brain scrambled. As the traveller longed for home and his family. As the woman who gave up her seat looked on intently. As the scars on her shoulders split open. Vashti's wings sprouted from her back and opened out with the light.

She was saying no to terror and apathy and giving up on people.

Her hands could heal but her wings could provide enough shield to protect.

When she looked into his eyes she knew. She knew that she was staring into the eyes of God. And she was saddened. Or she found someone she thought she had lost. And that made her sadder still.

But Vashti was reborn. She was here to make an impact.

And nobody would ever know.

Angels do not guide you through Purgatory.

They save you from Hell.

8 GOD? (AND HIS END)

Have you ever been driving in your car, and a song has come on the radio and you've thought to yourself, *If I lose control now and skid into that tree at this speed, I would probably die, and this would be the last song I ever heard*? Did you contemplate how sad that would make you? Have you ever had the urge to just turn into that tree and end it all? If that is the case, would you choose a song beforehand or do it in silence? Would you sing something in your head?

Do you like listening to music on vinyl? Do you know what I mean when I use the term 'analogue warmth'? Do you remember how eight-tracks used to fade out in the middle? Is nostalgia healthy? Isn't it a shame that books and films and music are all digital now and people rarely collect things that are physical? What is real?

If you were responsible for creating the entire world, would you only allow the music that you liked? Would you make sure that everybody listened to *The Hissing of Summer Lawns* and *Goodbye Yellow Brick Road* and *After the Goldrush* or would you give them the free will to listen to whatever music they desired?

What if you realised that you'd screwed this up? What if giving humans their own minds to thrive and fail and learn from that failure didn't work? What if they failed, then failed again and again, and again? Could you wipe the slate clean? What about sending an asteroid or a disease to clear things up a little? Perhaps a giant flood? Could you save two of everything that has worked and place them on a boat to ride things out?

Would you save two humans?

If you could create light in one day, would it not be easier to simply create complete darkness? Why would you inflict and endure the suffering?

On that seventh day, when it was time for a rest, could you not foresee the disaster ahead?

Was this not a time for reflection? Why is television so bad on a Sunday?

If you created men and women and gave them a brain and ambitions and time for reflection and the power to grieve with grace and love without prejudice, if you allow them to procreate and read and educate themselves, if you sit back as they create beauty and then destroy it, if you make them fear you and love you, are you not the one to blame for war and guns and pain and suffering?

Is it not God's fault that somebody would strap a bomb to themselves and detonate it in a nightclub or train carriage or taxi parked outside a hospital maternity ward?

Is it my fault?

As I stand on this train, surrounded by such disparate lives and existences, people who should not be connected in any way, should I love them all as my children? Should I forgive them? Does the woman ahead of me really see who I am more than I can see myself?

Am I her God?

Am I her brother?

Will I blow up this world?

When that glorious angel steps towards me on the train as everybody watches, as her voice soothes, as she says, 'You,' like she knows who I am, as I have a choice, do I reach inside my jacket for the trigger or do I cease? Do I answer my own questions?

In that final moment, do I press the button, killing innocent people and myself, booking a one-way trip to Paradise, or does that woman envelope the carriage in her light? Does she spread out her wings and show me what she is, show me who I am?

What is the truth? What happens now?

Am I dead?

Is she God?

Have I blown up this train?

Did everybody see the bright white light?

I see Heaven.

Is this how you create your darkness?
Would you like to start again?
Can you not do it quicker?
I have answered the questions, do I now get your prayers?

9 THE SPORTSMAN (AND THE COLOURS)

He saw it all. The sportsman. He had the greatest vantage point. And the greatest protection. Where the man with the bags was covered by his hard case, the sportsman was kept safe by Vashti. He was screened by her outstretched wings.

The noise he heard was not an explosion but the ferocity of a celestial voice, screaming. Beating down the evil in front of her. Saving people. Saving him. Again.

And, where everyone else saw a bright white light before they died or their head was separated from their body or their limbs were blown off or shrapnel was embedded into their bones and flesh, the sportsman saw colour. Every colour. Every kind of shade and texture, including ones he never knew existed.

The pain in his leg was gone and he, too, believed he was witnessing heaven.

To see is to believe.

But when he tells people what he saw that day, nobody will.

If God has given up, then why shouldn't His people?

Somewhere across the universe, the sportsman has become an evangelical speaker. He talks about healing through faith and he preaches about the existence of angels. He has seen one and she was magnificent, he says. She protected him so that he might go on and spread the word of their work. These unsung heroes who walk freely among us. He has his followers and he has those who ridicule.

He tours and he speaks. Huge crowds who have already listened to a man who claims he spent twenty-three minutes in Hell. A pastor and his wife lead the congregation in song before making a woman step out of her wheelchair and walk up three steps.

On the other side of space, the sportsman sells his story. Somebody else writes it down in a book but it is his name that is slapped across the front. It sells well. He tours and he speaks. Huge crowds assemble to hear him read from the book he could not write himself. Eventually, his name appears on the front of several successful children's novels.

Here, he remains a sportsman. His leg heals. His vision wavers, but he scores and he wins and he succeeds. In some beliefs, this is the Lord's work, in others it is hard work. For the sportsman, it doesn't feel like work at all. He is grateful.

10   THE COMMUTER (AND HIS BOOK)

Thomas Davant was on the train that day. He had inspired Vashti from her coma of apathy. He had pushed the sportsman into action, to take control of his future, to rediscover his passion. He had been spotted by the man on the train and he had lain in the hospital bed that had been meant for Saul.

For I am doing a work in your days that you would not believe if I told.

At exactly 8:46, Davant steps up and onto the carriage. He takes out his orange book. It's a play that he is particularly fond of. *The Visit.*

And that's what this is. A flying visit. He is here to make sure that everybody is where they are supposed to be.

Sportsman: check.

Angel: check.

Bomber: check.

Kind woman who gave up her seat: check.

Man with bags: check.

Helpful bystander: check.

One of the Daves: check.

Though it wasn't told how Davant may have featured in Dave's life or the life of the others, the look on his face was one of recognition. He knew them all. He had seen them all before. He had seen everyone, been everywhere. He was a commuter. He travelled. And he looked at each person on that doomed carriage, one by one, and he ticked them off in the margins of his favourite play.

Truly, you are a God who hides himself.

None of them saw him. They were focussed on the smell of the man with the stain on his trousers. Then, at 8:50, when a voice came over the tannoy and the doors began to close, Thomas Davant took a step backwards from the train and he turned, and left.

Everything was as it should be.

For I consider that the sufferings of this present time are not worth comparing to the glory that is to be revealed to us.

In some other realm, almost identical to this, Thomas Davant doesn't even exist.

11 THE FAKE ANGEL (AND HER DESTINY)

An unlucky/lucky woman is eventually evacuated from Aldgate East Station with injuries to her arms and leg. Her ribs are bruised, below her left eye is a too-close cut, but she is alive. Shocked, of course, but with enough lucidity to haul herself onto a bus to get the hell away from the carnage.

It has been almost an hour since the seven bombs went off on the London Underground, and the police have cordoned off areas close to the incidents and shut down roads. The bus driver announces that he has been instructed to take a different route.

He apologises for the inconvenience and opens the doors for anyone who would like to get off and try another route. Almost fifty people disembark. Many angry with how their morning was panning out and how inconvenienced they have been by the disruption caused by the unmitigated terror. The same kind of people who snarl at the 'jumper' who has delayed their train home.

There are still people left on the bus with the unlucky/lucky woman. They're not all heartless or in a rush to get to nowhere that's important. There's the woman with the laptop case, the man with the satchel and the elderly couple. There are the two chatty women on their way to a conference, apparently, and there's the pale waif of a woman on her own, ignoring the commotion, staring out the window as though everything outside is a new possibility.

Her name is Lailah.

She pretended to be an angel.

This is what she does.

She has her own story, and it deserves to be told in full, some day. Her appearance is deceiving. She was not under the control of Nathaniel, she loves with all her heart, she enters into a relationship and gives what she has. This is how she lives her life. Roaming from place to place, city to city, country to country, loving men and women, leaving when things go wrong. She has no idea where she is heading next but she has been doubling back on herself for the last hour and now she plans to stay on the bus until it reaches its final destination.

Of course, she is linked to Saul and the explosion at Edgware Road but, even after a tidal wave hits, the water continues to flow.

The seven men who caused death and destruction by taking their own lives each had a mobile phone. The same man has been trying to contact all seven for the last half an hour. Maybe he wants to make sure they have gone through with it. Maybe he is scared. Maybe he is having second thoughts. He has been picked up by cameras in and around King's Cross Station. He is in a rush.

Lailah's bus changes direction and heads towards Great Tower Street. The fake angel continues to gaze out the window, wondering what her future holds. The unlucky/lucky woman rolls her eyes as the chatty ladies moan about their bitter cup of coffee like it's the end of the world. They don't even see that she is scratched and hurt. The elderly couple smile and the woman kisses her husband on the cheek. He whispers something in her ear.

The man with the satchel looks at his watch. 09:47. Almost an hour since Saul was ripped in half and Dave lost his legs. Almost an hour since the unlucky/lucky woman saw her first flash of white light that morning.

Somehow, she would survive this explosion, too. As would one of the chatty women, who will be forced to crawl through dead bodies, including that of her work colleague. As would the woman with the laptop bag who chose not to sit next to the bomber because there wasn't enough room due to her baggage. As would the people who jumped ship when the detour was announced.

For the rest of the souls on that bus, whose lives are so unjustly whipped away, all that is left are the thoughts and prayers of insincere strangers and the absence of a God who refuses to flip the light switch.

12   THE NEIGHBOUR (AND REALITY)

It's difficult to know what is real any more. People can show a beautiful slice of their life online for all to see but keep hidden their truths. That inside, they are dying.

There's fake news and spin and the art of misdirection. And doesn't it feel like everyone is now an influencer? So does that mean that we are constantly being influenced? Does anybody have an opinion that wasn't given to them by somebody else?

The neighbour comes home. He's late but he's grateful to be alive and well. He has been watching the news all day. Seven Underground trains and three buses. Explosions. Death. Maiming. Innocent people walking to work or visiting the capital, mown down as they crossed the river. Workers picking up their morning coffee. He feels the terror that was intended by the people behind this act and he shares that fear with millions of others who will forever be fearful of public transport. Who will always take a coffee from home in the morning from now on.

That's the legacy.

The names of the bombers will be forgotten by most, but that feeling you get on a crowded tube, ten years later, when you don't want to think, *God, if one of these people is attached to a bomb, so many will die* – that's how they win.

It's not tangible but it is incredibly real.

You can't see it but it is there.

It is real.

And, for many, this is like God.

For the neighbour, this is fear. Yet, from nowhere, from an atrocity like this, there is also compassion.

He enters his block of flats and thinks about the Daves. And he wonders who else is thinking of them. Where were they today? They don't go out much but what if they did? What if they were on one of those tubes? Who would care? Who would know?

The neighbour still has the mobile-phone number of the daughter who came knocking that time. Surely, she will be worried for her father. And there is a part of him that is stuck. He doesn't want to stand by but it's not his place to interfere.

Love thy neighbour.

In a world where everyone is so connected through technology, we seem more emotionally disconnected than ever.

It would be easy to knock on the Daves' door and check in. Talk about the news and the weather. Ask about his health. They do it all the time in passing.

He reaches the top floor where only his and the Daves' flats are located. He opens the door that leads to their shared vestibule and somebody is standing outside.

'Jesus Christ, you scared me.'

'Sorry. Sorry.'

'What are you doing out here?'

'I didn't want to be alone tonight with everything that has happened, you know?'

'How did you…?'

'The door downstairs was unlocked.'

The neighbour's heart is beating fast, he wasn't expecting to see anyone. Of course his girlfriend is frightened to be alone. He wraps his arms around her and kisses the side of her head.

'Come on.'

He unlocks the front door and holds it open for her. And he forgets about the Daves. He has his own things going on. Dave does have family. They'll check on him.

The neighbour and his girlfriend eat a late dinner. They share a bottle and a half of red wine. They go to bed and make love. Not in the way they usually do. It's not even about the sex. It's just the chance to be close to another person that is real. And they sleep. Her, soundly. Him, turning constantly. Then, just after six, thirty minutes before his alarm, he remembers the Daves.

The neighbour knows that they always check their post box early in the morning because it's the slam of their door that usually wakes him before his alarm has a chance to sound.

He stands at the front door. He's naked. His feet are wide so as not to cast a shadow that one of the Daves might notice. And he waits. And he asks God to have one of them appear. To have either of them creep out and run down to check the post box even though their regular postman arrives after nine each day.

He waits.

There's nothing.

He can't hear the muttering. There's no coughing or cursing. Yet, the neighbour keeps his eye straining through that peephole.

Eventually, the alarm goes off in the bedroom. He has been standing there for almost half an hour. He's worried and he doesn't know why.

Surely the world is too large. The possibility that a Dave was on one of those carriages is minute. That couldn't really be the case.

Could it be real that a nurse had developed the ability to heal ailments with her hands and her compassion? Could it be real she was an angel and protected that carriage with her outstretched wings? Could it be real that she knew the man she argued with? Could it be real that he was her misunderstood God? Could it be real that her brother had returned home with a brain so washed he would terminate himself?

Could it be real that Dave perished at Edgware Road?

Could it be real that he never went there and his brain was so unwashed that it was continually playing tricks on him? It's another of his invented stories, like the exploding tongue or the brain tumour or the cheque in the post?

Somewhere, in the vast infinity of the universe, all of these possibilities are real. A god, so out of touch with his people, rode around on a train, asking endless questions of a humanity He could no longer control. He was met by one of His angels. Somewhere, everything began to make sense again to Him. Somewhere else, He turned the lights off and started over again.

But here, in this reality, a confused young man took two days to think. About everything. The largest and the smallest subjects. He considered everything and nothing, and he looked his sister in the eyes as he pressed a red button that would engulf that train carriage in a moment of bright, white purity, before the chaos.

Vashti knew it was the end. That her next meeting would be with her God. And, whether she opened out her wings or not, the sportsman and the woman with the bag saw her as their angel. That was their reality.

So that makes it true.

Somewhere else, this incident was subverted by the authorities and never reported on.

The neighbour continues with his daily routine, with one change: he calls a cab to take him to the office. He can't face the tube today, if they are even running.

Dave isn't at the post box when he gets home from work. They don't pass on the stairs. He can't hear his voice through the walls, either. Then the neighbour reminds himself that Dave had said he might be away for a couple of weeks at the hospital. At the time, he thought it could be another of Dave's embellishments, but that would make more sense than being blown up on a train carriage.

Three days go by and there is still nothing. The news coverage is already starting to die down with the announcement of another celebrity affair and a controversial sporting decision. Pretence, once again, taking over from reality.

The neighbour returns to his flat, ready for the weekend. He takes the keys from his pocket and searches for the one that will unlock his door. But he can't shake the feeling. He looks back at the door opposite his and he walks over. The neighbour doesn't know what he is going to do, what he is going to say if he knocks, he just knows that he needs to do something different.

He stands outside for a few moments. He breathes and lifts his hand to knock.

Then he hears it.

'Oh, there you are. And where the Hell have you been?'

The neighbour lowers his hand and smiles.

Another argument about to start between the Daves.

Our thoughts and prayers go out to both of them.

ACKNOWLEDGEMENTS

Thanks, as always, to my fearless champion, Karen Sullivan. In an industry where most can only see in black and white, you have a gift for finding the colour.

West. Brilliant. We smashed this edit. I wasn't sure we'd agree on things with this one but you absolutely got what I was trying to do.

Cole's trailer, Anne's blog tour, Mark's jacket design and the support of a stable of writers all doing things their own way. That's Team Orenda.

And the squad at Blake Friedmann – Kate, Julian and Sian – who are fighting every day to grow the Carver cult. (I don't make it easy with these books.)

Bolinda Publishing, who are producing consistently brilliant audio versions of my stories.

Writing is a collaborative process but a lonely business, yet there are writers who are always generous with their time, advice, support and a place to vent frustrations. Sarah Pinborough, Tom Wood, Steve Watson, Ian Rankin, Stephen Golds, Helen Fitzgerald, Matt Wesolowski and Victoria Selman, to name but a few.

My two favourite indie bookshops, Fourbears Books and Bert's Books, who fly the flag for all indie authors, but have done particularly well for me over the last year. Please don't stop.

Kel. My very own piece of magic. Forget all of the wonderful things you do that enable me to keep writing these things, I had a book that was missing a character and you made a joke about my strange neighbour being two people. *The Daves* were born. So this book is your fault.